BN

# KISSING SYBILLA

"Miss Smethwick, how is that George came to be scampering his way to the stables?"

"He tricked me. Shaming, I know, but that is what happened. At least he has displayed both wit and efficiency." Sybilla opened the book and started leafing through its pages.

"How could you let him do it? What folly is this, with his attempted murder so nearly accomplished not once but thrice!"

"Do you think I did not realize that? How do you think I felt when I found the room empty? And yet we cannot tell him the real reason for his incarceration."

"Not for much longer. The end is in sight, if Lindsay and I can just secure some evidence. And yet you jeopardize all this with your carelessness."

"Stop this hullabaloo. You blame yourself, and for once you have the right of it."

Ampthill came over to Sybilla and plucked the book from her fingers, tossing it aside before grasping her by the shoulders. "There is but one way to silence you. You may have the last word. But I shall have the final pleasure."

Then he took her head in both hands and, holding her still, kissed her. . . .

# BOOK YOUR PLACE ON OUR WEBSITE AND MAKE THE READING CONNECTION!

We've created a customized website just for our very special readers, where you can get the inside scoop on everything that's going on with Zebra, Pinnacle and Kensington books.

When you come online, you'll have the exciting opportunity to:

- View covers of upcoming books
- Read sample chapters
- Learn about our future publishing schedule (listed by publication month *and author*)
- Find out when your favorite authors will be visiting a city near you
- Search for and order backlist books from our online catalog
- Check out author bios and background information
- Send e-mail to your favorite authors
- Meet the Kensington staff online
- Join us in weekly chats with authors, readers and other guests
- Get writing guidelines
- AND MUCH MORE!

**Visit our website at
http://www.kensingtonbooks.com**

# SEDUCING SYBILLA

## MADELEINE CONWAY

**ZEBRA BOOKS**
Kensington Publishing Corp.
http://www.kensingtonbooks.com

ZEBRA BOOKS are published by

Kensington Publishing Corp.
850 Third Avenue
New York, NY 10022

All Kensington titles, imprints and distributed lines are available at special quantity discounts for bulk purchases for sales promotion, premiums, fund-raising, educational or institutional use.

Special book excerpts or customized printings can also be created to fit specific needs. For details, write or phone the office of the Kensington Special Sales Manager: Kensington Publishing Corp., 850 Third Avenue, New York, NY 10022. Attn. Special Sales Department. Phone: 1-800-221-2647.

Zebra and the Z logo Reg. U.S. Pat. & TM Off.

First Printing: September 2003
10 9 8 7 6 5 4 3 2 1

Printed in the United States of America

# PROLOGUE

The door creaked open. A surreptitious figure peered out, then emerged, shivering slightly, closing the door firmly behind him. He walked steadily away from the great house. He carried a shotgun and a burlap bag slung over one shoulder. The October sky was still dark and the air, fresh and cold, promised a fine day. With a firm pace, the walker crossed the formal lawns, heading up a hillside toward the northern end of the Park surrounding the great house. Soon, he entered woodland. He strode through bracken and bramble bushes purposefully, silencing the birds as he swished past their nests, sending small creatures scuttling back to their burrows. His breath came in short pants, the air now crystallized into puffs of steam by the chill of the dawn. The bag was heavy and the shotgun cumbersome.

He followed a path curving round another heavily forested hillside, the land dropping sharply away to one side, the slopes thick with undergrowth, beech and birch saplings. Suddenly, he dropped down the hillside, grasping at the trees for balance, the gun balanced cruelly on one shoulder. He crossed the dell and clambered up a shallower incline. At its crest, he stopped and sat, catching his breath. Then he opened the bag. Out came several muffled objects and small bags. He unwrapped the largest parcel with precise, gentle motions.

Soon lying on the ground before him were a pair of dueling pistols, their barrels glinting, the wooden stocks polished, a bag of powder, another of bullets and fuses, a tinder box and matches, and finally a kerchief wrapping bread and meat. He loaded the dueling pistols and the shotgun. Then he ate.

The sun was up now, filtering through the golden leaves, which were almost ready to drop. The ground was carpeted with the freshly fallen russet, brown, and yellow leaves brought down by the wind the previous day, damp with rainfall and dew. It was not comfortable, but the man settled himself against the trunk of an oak.

First he heard crackling and swishing sounds as the beaters swung their switches through the bracken, then voices. He lay full-length on the ground, only his head above the lip concealing the dell from the rest of the hillside. He raised one dueling pistol up and balanced it on his forearm for aim. In this position, he could survey all comers headed up or down the hillside and rise to his knees as soon as his target was in range.

Three louts from the village came first. He let them pass. Then he heard the unmistakable sound of young boys, their voices higher than usual with the excitement of being part of the shoot, even if it was in the menial role of beating the brush. First one lad appeared over the brow of the hillside, perhaps nine years old, his suit still tidy, the silver buttons glinting in the sunlight. The slighter figure of a boy of seven followed, jacket unbuttoned, shirt straying from the confinement of pantaloons, hair standing on end, clearly combed through by small fingers.

"Old Jessup said we should wait here for him," said the younger.

"Well, we shall, Harry. He won't be long." The boys sat near the top of the bank, swinging their switches idly over the grass.

"Why don't Cousin Carey like shooting, Gus?"

"It's the noise, perhaps, or the animals being dead. Mama says he is sensitive."

"Papa don't think he's up to much, do he?"

"Whatever Papa thinks, Harry, it isn't polite to say such things about our cousin and our guest. Besides, I'm not sure I think Papa is up to much," said the older boy, jaws clenched.

"He let us come on the shoot."

"He only allowed it because Mama did not wish us to come."

The man in the copse took aim. Insolent cubs! He would pick off the younger first. The shirt made an easier target. His finger squeezed on the trigger. A "Halloo" came from over the brow of the hill and the boys jumped up and ran towards the shouting. There had not been time to get off even one shot.

"Damnation!"

"What you doin' 'ere?" came a gruff voice from the other side of the pond.

The marksman turned abruptly. He stood up, the gun pointing towards the soil.

"I might ask the same of you. Been poaching, I believe. There appears to be a hare under that coat, no?"

"What if it is? What's that to you, when you're aimin' your shooter at them chillun?"

"Who will they believe, do you think? Me, when I say I was snug in my bed, my man to back up my word, or you, the poacher? A known renegade?"

"'Ere's a pickle."

"Indeed, a fine pickle." The man knelt and started wrapping the pistols. When he had replaced them in the burlap bag, he stood again and shouldered the shotgun. Then he walked round the pond towards the poacher.

"So, what do you say?"

"I says nothing, sir."

"A guinea or two will help you say nothing, will it not?"

"Might."

The elegant marksman reached into a pocket and withdrew several coins. He counted them, then handed them to the poacher, holding the shotgun by the barrel. The poacher bent his head first to count the coins, then to bite them. The man took the gun barrel by both hands and swung hard. The wooden stock made a wet thunking sound, as it fractured the side of the poacher's head. The coins tinkled to the ground as he fell forward into the pond. His assailant carefully set down the shotgun, waded in after the poacher, and held the body under the water. Then, quite coolly, he collected the coins and examined the vicinity of the pond before making his way through the undergrowth and back to the big house.

No one was likely to miss the poacher. Even if his disappearance was noticed, the body would surely not be found before next summer, by which time it would be impossible to tell just how it came to be in the pond in the dell.

Undetected, the killer slipped back to his room where his man was waiting for him with a steaming pitcher of chocolate.

"Good hunting, sir?"

"Distinctly inferior, Mortley." He lay back on his bed and stretched. "But there'll be other opportunities, I'm sure of it."

# ONE

In the house at Fitzroy Square, the gloomy weather made even the west-facing second floor back room somber at four o'clock. Although it must have been intended for sleeping, the room was in fact furnished with two large and one smaller draftsman's tables, two of which were occupied. At one of the larger tables sat a young woman dressed in a smock, frowning deeply at a sheet of calculations, checking these with her slide rule against the measurements marked on the large piece of drawing paper pinned to the table. From time to time she flicked an unruly blonde curl from her face. At the smaller table was a young lad of some seven years, equally intent on his work. He had a large gazetteer open at the pages concerning France and appeared to be noting distances between cities, writing them down, and adding them up as he hummed "Lilliburlero" under his breath as he worked.

"Aunt Sybilla," he complained, "I can barely see. Could we not light the lamps?"

"Or perhaps we should call it a day, Georgie? Shall we go downstairs and try to persuade your mama that we who have been working deserve some refreshment?"

A door slammed below. "That sounds like Mrs. Gurney back from the Exchange," said the boy, as he dashed to the door.

"George," said his aunt sternly, "come back. Before you run off helter-skelter downstairs, hang up your smock and tidy up your table properly."

Pens were wiped, pencils and rulers retrieved from under papers, papers covered with calculations were ordered, smocks hung on hooks beside the door, and finally the two emerged from their workroom and made their way down the stairs hand in hand.

"Help me jump," cried the boy, and his aunt Sybilla obediently stepped down an extra step and waited as George jumped two steps, then she moved down two extra steps so that he could jump three, and in this hobbledy-thump way they eventually reached the ground floor front room, where George's mother, Honoria, widow of Lord Henry Swaffham, was busy lighting the lamps.

"These east-facing rooms are so dark and cold in this weather that we are already obliged to light up. I have asked Mrs. Gurney to take tea with us while she tells us her news."

The room bustled with activity as Sally, the young maid-of-all-work, brought in the tea things; Mrs. Gurney, still shaking her petticoats from the damp outside, made her way to the fireside. The fire was lit and eventually four people settled themselves as comfortably as people might who are seated in rented rooms rather than in the ease of their own home. Closest to the fire sat Mrs. Gurney, a somewhat stout and handsome woman in her late fifties. She had been housekeeper to Mr. and Mrs. Smethwick, had helped raise Honoria and Sybilla, and since their parents' deaths was the sisters' main confidante and adviser.

Opposite sat George's mother, Honoria, a slight woman just turned thirty, distinguished by her delicate features, her large dark eyes, and above all by her heavy auburn hair which gleamed in the firelight. George and his aunt, in charge of the tea tray, sat on a couch opposite the fire.

"What news, Mrs. Gurney?" piped George, between mouthfuls of flapjack.

"Very little, I'm afraid to say. Today was no better than yesterday. I interviewed three stalwart young men, any of whom would have consented to escort a party of two ladies and a young gentleman through France; one even had a smattering of German and had already visited Prussia, but all refused point-blank to have anything to do with traveling in Spain. It seems, m'lady, that your scheme to start your travels with a visit to Badajoz is a major stumbling block."

"But if we don't start with Spain, I fear we shall never get there," said Lady Honoria. "Once we go to Paris and make contact with dear Professor Tournus, he is sure to give us so many introductions to engineers and mathematicians in France and Germany that we shall never have time to get to Spain at all. And besides, once we pay our respects to the professor, our tour becomes professional; our steps will be dictated by our need to make as many useful connections as possible with our colleagues on the Continent to ensure that our work here is recognized abroad as was dear Papa's."

"And have I no right to see where my brave father died?" queried George.

"Indeed you have, my dear," said his mother, "but it seems that Spain is a somewhat wilder place than we had imagined, with rather poor communications, and infested with bandits and desperadoes."

"But we shall be taking Papa's pistols," said George, "so we can shoot the bandits and desperadoes!"

"George," said his mother, "it is one thing to talk of shooting desperadoes, quite another to be called upon to defend oneself in such a way. We are endeavoring to arrange a peaceful excursion to pay our respects to your father's memory, without being called upon to shoot at anything or anybody at all."

"But we cannot be the only people who wish to visit the scenes where so many British lives were lost," interposed Sybilla. "Why, I have heard that five thousand of our men fell in the taking of Badajoz alone. Have you heard nothing from Harry's old regiment? Is there no hope of some kind of connection through the army?"

"None, I am afraid. I received a note from the Engineers just this afternoon," replied the widow. "Colonel Fletcher has been posted to India, and while the Regimental headquarters were most polite, they were very firm in saying that they could offer us no help. Indeed their advice was to give up that part of our projected itinerary altogether. There is no British army presence at all left in Spain, and while there are consulates and vice consuls at many of the major cities, they say that none of them is near Badajoz."

"And we want to go to Spain. I want to see Mireda, no, that's not it, Mérida. *Emeritum Augustum*. Reverend Hardisty had me learn all about it in our Latin class, and he said it is the Rome of Spain on account of its 'stupendous and well-preserved monuments.' It was founded in 23 B.C. and . . ."

"Yes, George dear, we all want to go to Spain," said his mother firmly, "it is just proving to be a more complicated matter than we had thought simply from looking at the atlas."

The striking of the clock interrupted them and Mrs. Gurney rose immediately.

"It's time for your bath, Master George." No one within the family circle could bring themselves to give the boy his formal title. "Let us go off and find whether Sally has got it ready."

"But just a minute, Mrs. Gurney, I have to tell Mama

about the new places I discovered today that we might visit in France!"

"After your bath, George. You may tell me all about them when I come to wish you goodnight."

The two sisters were silent for a while after Mrs. Gurney had finally managed to coax the reluctant George from the parlor. Sybilla spoke first.

"So the Army has failed us. Still, we expected nothing else. It would have been a coincidence indeed if anyone from Harry's company had been within reach."

"To tell the truth, I have been less concerned this afternoon about the details of our tour than perhaps I should. I am still distracted by this morning's caller."

That morning they had received a visit from Mr. Lindsay, who had announced himself as a close friend and legal adviser to the Earl of Ampthill. Augustus Swaffham, ninth earl of Ampthill, the late Harry's elder brother and uncle to young George, had recently returned from India. Mercifully, Mr. Lindsay had arrived while George was out on errands with Mrs. Gurney, and as yet the boy knew nothing of their visitor and the news he had brought. The sisters had agreed to say nothing to George until they had had time to discuss it thoroughly themselves.

Although it had been made no real secret, Lord Harry Swaffham had not told his family of his marriage to Miss Honoria Smethwick until the eve of his ill-fated departure to join Wellington's army. The closest Honoria had come to her new relations was a few precious nights spent with her husband at Ampthill House in Mayfair, before he set out for Portugal. After his death, the Swaffhams had made no effort to communicate with their younger son's widow, even when Honoria had written formally to tell them of George's birth.

The absence of any inquiry, any condolence, any communication whatsoever from Harry's family had embittered the months of her pregnancy, as she carried within her the child who would never know its father. Her sorrow while studying the face of the newly born George, seeking in his tiny features some reminiscence of his father, had been acute. It was her mother who had brought her the most comfort, less than a week after the boy was born.

"Don't you worry, now, that we may not be able to raise George as his father would have wished," said her mother. "Do you not remember how he used to complain that you two girls had all the luck, tutored by the best engineer in the Midlands? If the boy has a mind to it, your father will teach him his figures and his exactitude. Remember how Harry and your father enjoyed their work together. Your father loved Harry. He'll make sure of George, the boy I was never able to give him. And he's often grieved with me, as you do, that Harry never knew for sure that you were expecting a child."

The realization that her son was her parents' grandchild, not just her own and Harry's child, had given her courage to accept the reality of the situation. The sorrow must be forgotten, and George must grow up to make his own way in the world. This had been easy to achieve in the busily cheerful Smethwick home at Stourbridge. George had shown the very earliest interest in the mathematical instruments in his grandfather's office and by the age of five already proved the most apt and enthusiastic of pupils.

Over the years, the Smethwicks had almost forgotten about Harry's grand relations. Honoria and Sybilla were both skilled draftswomen and helped their father in his work. They accompanied him on many of his visits to fellow engineers and inventors and shared in the conferences and meetings which took place within their own home. Theirs was a busy and professional life, and it had always been intended that they should carry on in this vein. But a year and a half ago, Mrs. Smethwick had died of pneumonia and Josiah, quite unmanned by the loss, fell into a sad decline and followed her within three months.

In the sorry days following their father's death, the two girls had come to rely entirely on Mrs. Gurney. Josiah Smethwick's funeral had been a populous affair, with scientists from as far afield as Edinburgh traveling to pay their respects. Mrs. Gurney had seen them well disposed in the various local hostelries and took note of those who urged her to encourage the girls to keep up their father's work. She had made sure that this intention was confirmed to Josiah Smethwick's friends and was not beneath seeking the support of his closer colleagues in aiding the bereft sisters to overcome their loss by throwing themselves back into their work.

Thus it was that within twelve months of their father's passing the two girls were tolerably well-established in the Midlands, contributing specialized drawings to complement the schemes of larger projects and executing a number of smaller works on their own behalf. The previous November they had been visited by Professor Tournus, who had long been engaged in researches into hydraulics, a topic of especial interest to Sybilla. He had suggested that they come to visit him in Paris, to see his experiments, and over the winter the projected trip had grown into what was by now approaching the scale of a grand tour.

Their plans had coincided with a growing curiosity from young George to learn more about the circumstances of his father's death. Honoria had resisted his inquiries for as long as she could, but had finally been prevailed upon to disinter the bleak note from the Army Office in Whitehall (accompanying her last unopened letters to Harry telling him of George's impending arrival), which informed her merely that Lord Harry Swaffham had been killed in action at Badajoz.

At the end of the Peninsular War, Harry's commanding officer had paid a visit and offered to tell her the details. Her first reaction had been to send him away. Was it not enough that she had lost Harry? But her mother felt that it would be wrong as well as discourteous not to hear what the colonel had to say. Sybilla, then just nineteen, had said, "Dear Honoria, we should know everything. Let Colonel Fletcher tell me, and I shall write it all down so that when George wants to know we can explain it to him. Papa will also want to know the details."

Honoria, feeling herself unequal to sitting through whatever the colonel might have to relate, had left the room together with her mother, leaving Sybilla with the colonel.

Colonel Fletcher told of Harry's supervising the digging of the trenches guarding the gun emplacements before Badajoz. He told of Harry's journey from Lisbon where he had landed, escorting the guns and an enormous load of picks and spades to Elvas, the Portuguese city just across the border from the mightiest fortress standing in Spain. He told of the resentment felt by exhausted men digging trenches and raising mud parapets through day after day of seemingly endless torrential rain.

At last, a sortie from one of the French forts surrounding the city had surprised the unarmed men working on the first parallel, and abandoning their shovels, the men had scrambled to safety through the mud to wait for the appearance of their armed escort. Harry had leapt into the body of retreating men, yelling at them not to abandon their tools for, if the French had carried off all the spades, how would they complete the remaining essential earthworks? The men had rallied and in the ensuing mêlée most of the valuable tools were saved.

But Harry had fallen almost immediately to a musket shot from the marauding French. His action had contributed to the success of the siege, for without basic elements such as communications trenches and protective parapets, Badajoz would have taken valuable weeks to fall, weeks which Wellington could not afford for fear of French reinforcements.

Sybilla had insisted on the greatest amount of detail and Colonel Fletcher had carefully explained the role of engineers in an army, setting targets and calculating angles for the artillery, supervising the construction and deployment of pontoon bridges for crossing rivers, as well as supervising gunners, sappers, and all the other technicians involved in reducing a fortress. Colonel Fletcher had worked closely with men on Wellington's staff and had a huge respect for the Iron Duke as he was later nicknamed. He had rapidly conceived a great liking for Harry and his ready appreciation of all that was required. Harry had told him of his marriage into the talented Midlands engineering family and while on leave Fletcher had taken the first opportunity to visit his junior officer's widow.

"How did he become acquainted with your sister?" Fletcher had asked.

"One of his instructors at Woolwich, the late Colonel Thompson, was an old classmate of our father's," explained Sybilla. "Harry had determined to spend his summer leave inspecting some of the new works going up around the country and Colonel Thompson directed him to us as the people best equipped to show him all that was new in these parts at the time. That would have been in 1810. He was intrigued by much of my father's work, and became a regular visitor when his army duties permitted. He and Honoria both became very interested in canal construction and soon they were engaged. Papa was very fond of Harry; he will be most upset to have missed your visit. I must confess that many of the notes

I have been taking are as much for his benefit as for George's."

"Does your father do any work for our Armed Forces?"

"Not really. He had suggested some ideas to Colonel Thompson, but was unwilling to enter into a professional relationship with the army; I am afraid you might find him something of a pacifist! He says he would rather that his thoughts and energies be directed toward the well-being of mankind than to its destruction."

Mrs. Gurney and Honoria then came in, followed shortly thereafter by the tea tray, and the remainder of the colonel's brief visit had passed in common civilities, though not without his making sure that Honoria and George were both receiving the pensions which were their due, no matter how meager these might be.

As the girls began to plan their Continental excursion, the idea of going to Spain had come from young George. On the seventh anniversary of Harry's death, Honoria had given him Sybilla's account of his father's last weeks to read, and the idea of visiting the site of his death became increasingly dear to George and his mother.

"George knows so little of his father, and he is so pre-occupied these days with castles and fortresses and siege machines, that perhaps to visit the site of so terrible and bloody an onslaught will help clear his mind of these bellicose fantasies," said Honoria to Sybilla one evening. "Besides, I feel the need myself to visit the site. Even after all these years, I cannot fully get it into my head that Harry will never come back. When I first heard the news of his death, I used sometimes to imagine that somehow there had been a mistake, that somehow he would miraculously have escaped. And since the deaths of Mama and Papa, I sometimes find those old feelings coming back.

It would help I think, to go there, perhaps, finally to lay the ghosts of the past."

Honoria had sighed deeply as she spoke, and Sybilla had immediately embraced the plan. The sisters soon organized their business as to allow themselves up to a year's leave of absence from their work. There was nothing else to keep them. George was still being taught at home; Sybilla and Honoria divided most of the various schoolroom subjects between them; Josiah had taught them modern languages from an early age as essential for proper communications with French and German scientists. Before his death, their father had prevailed upon the Vicar of Stourbridge to provide his assistance in Latin, Greek, and Divinity, and although an enthusiastic teacher, Reverend Hardisty had announced that George was sufficiently advanced in these subjects to be allowed to let them drop for the months of their projected tour.

"Besides, the occasion of seeing ancient monuments and historic buildings in their rightful places will so broaden his mind that any loss of skill in Latin and Greek for his age will be compensated by a greater understanding of how history and geography overlap."

Accordingly, they had agreed with Mrs. Gurney to shut up the house in Stourbridge, and set off on the first step of their journey, namely to go to London in search of suitable escorts for their journey to Spain and France. Once arrangements with appropriate staff could be made, the sisters and George were to set off, and Mrs. Gurney would return to Stourbridge to look after the house, and attend to any correspondence that might arrive in their absence. Professor Tournus had assured them of relatively easy travel between France and the various German states he had recommended visiting, but they were experiencing the greatest difficulty in engaging suitable staff for the Spanish part of the journey on which all had set their hearts.

"And now this further interruption from George's uncle," thought Sybilla as she tidied up the parlor after their tea. "As if things were not complicated enough already. What can he want with George? Why should he come poking his nose into our business after his whole family has always ignored us? By what right should he even think we are in any way interested in receiving overbred ignoramuses with more money than feelings or sense?"

Despite her furious indignation, she recognized that Honoria must decide what was to be done, for Harry had been her husband, and George was her son. Reluctantly she admitted to herself that there might be advantages in the new connection. Sybilla thus waited impatiently for her sister to say more. But Honoria remained immersed in her thoughts. "That Mr. Lindsay seemed civil enough," prompted Sybilla.

"Yes, indeed. And I suppose his explanation of Lord Ampthill's prolonged silence is just about acceptable. Certainly, if the earl had arrived back in the country only in August, he has wasted little time in hunting us out. But he had very little specific to say about what his lordship intends for us." There was a hint of contempt in her expression as she continued, repeating Lindsay's words of the morning: " 'He believes that, provided there is no overwhelming objection, George should take his rightful place as Lord George Swaffham, and be recognized as the current heir to the titles and estate.' I wonder what all that might mean. I suppose we shall just have to wait and see."

"I suppose it means they will want to turn George into a stuck-up aristocrat with no mind for anything beyond hunting and gaming."

"I doubt it, Sybilla. Let us be careful not to let our prejudices color our judgment. After all, Harry was far from being a mindless aristocrat. And Lindsay struck me as a kind, intelligent man."

"I suppose so," said her sister, "and, after all, he did 'presume' to describe himself as Ampthill's closest friend, which suggests that Ampthill may be more than a wealthy stuck-up nabob. He reminded me of someone, Hono, not in his appearance, but in his manner. Who does he remind me of?"

"I think it might have been John Rennie. Lindsay is a Scots name. Although he does not have Rennie's accent, there certainly was something of that Edinburgh manner in his way of expressing himself."

"That's who it is, of course." Sybilla smiled inwardly. Three years ago Honoria and young John Rennie had been involved in exploring aspects of tidal drainage. Sybilla and her mother had nourished secret hopes that the comradeship of resolving scientific problems might develop into a more personal and lasting intimacy, but this had not happened, and in fact, early that spring they had received news of Rennie having married the Edinburgh born and bred daughter of one William Murdock. Even so, the resemblance, which Sybilla immediately acknowledged, was reassuring. If Lindsay came from that sort of background, perhaps he would turn out to be someone they could trust; someone from a background more closely resembling their own rather than that of the landed aristocracy for which they felt nothing but distrust and even contempt. The landed gentry understood little about industry and less about science. If Ampthill had a friend like Lindsay, then perhaps he might belong to that rare species, the enlightened aristocrat. But Sybilla was inclined, nonetheless, to pessimism.

"What I do not understand," she said, "is why Lord Ampthill need take any sort of interest at all in Georgie. From what Lindsay said, he must be one of the most eligible bachelors in the country. He has brought back immense wealth from India, quite enough to restore the family fortunes, and according to Lindsay, has a three- or four-hundred-year-old estate in Hampshire, and a title going back nine generations. He's bound to get married in a year or two to some equally eligible young aristocrat who will provide him with a son and heir within the twelvemonth. What can be the point in establishing Georgie as a temporary heir? It can only be for a year or two at most. And once he has his own son, then he will simply drop poor George, who by then will have acquired all sorts of tastes beyond his real expectations. Why could he not just leave us alone like his mother and father did? They never thought of Georgie as an heir presumptive or anything silly like that!"

"Sybilla, you are pre-judging him and his motives. While I admit I welcome the interruptions of our plans as little as you do, I am afraid I owe it to George at least to find out what his uncle is like. Who knows, he might turn out to be quite liberal and progressed in his views. He may, as Lindsay said, have been genuinely fond of Harry and really wish to do something for his nephew."

"I hope you may be right," said Sybilla, "for all our sakes. But if you are inclined to be favorable, I shall reserve for myself the role of a doubtful and distrustful aunt. We know so little of this kind of society. You may choose to play the charming widow but I shall remain cynical. For all we know, this Lord Augustus may have sinister intentions. He may find our way of life, and indeed that which we propose for George, too inappropriate for him to countenance." Sybilla felt a sudden fear. Would the Ampthill family really be prepared to tolerate the kind of lives they themselves led? Might the relative freedom they enjoyed, their working relationships with other scientists—almost exclusively male—the level of their emancipation, the fact that they were paid for their contributions to important engineering projects, that while they rejoiced in their professionalism it was also their means of making a living, might all this not prove too embarrassing to a family that had lived from the income derived from privileges gained nine generations ago without lifting a finger? Sybilla did not dare voice her real fear to her elder sister, but she was deeply alarmed that Ampthill might consider their way of life unsuitable for his precious nephew and try to take George from them.

"Very well," replied Honoria, laughing at Sybilla's intently suspicious expression, "but having settled our own behavior in the face of these developments, what are we to tell George?"

After further conference, the sisters agreed that it was their duty to make sure that the boy should approach his new relations in the most open and frank way possible. Whatever their own doubts and suspicions, they felt that the safest policy for George was to be himself. "Little hope of him being anything else, in any case," remarked his aunt drily.

"We have no right to prejudice him against his new relations," said his mother. "He must know nothing of our distrust, whatever doubts we feel ourselves."

Sybilla was glad then that she had not mentioned her fears that the Swaffham family might attempt to take over George's life; Honoria, she could see, shared this worry, which would only become greater if they fretted over it openly. They resolved accordingly to go upstairs together and tell George the momentous news, that with his uncle's return from India, his father's family were at last prepared to take notice of them.

In his room upstairs, they found George finishing his supper under the kind but firm control of Mrs. Gurney.

"Mrs. Gurney," said Honoria, "how glad I am that you are here, because while you and George were out this morning, Sybilla and I received a most interesting visitor. Now we can tell both you and George all about him."

Sybilla was impressed yet again at her sister's ability to make things seem easy, natural, and simple. Here was the most momentous event possible since their parents' death, and yet Honoria was presenting it to the small boy simply as a more than usually exciting variation on his regular goodnight story.

"George, what do you know of your father's family?" said Honoria. George looked disappointed. For all the sisters' egalitarian views, they had schooled him to know exactly who he was. Why did they look so excited when all they came to do was to invite him to make the usual recitation?

"That my father was killed at Badajoz before I was born, that his family seat is in Hampshire, that my Uncle Ampthill lives in India, and that my grandfather, the eighth earl, died last year."

"There is more now," said his mother. "Your uncle is returned from India, and he has sought us out. This morning we received a visit from his trusted friend and gentleman of business and furthermore your uncle proposes to visit us himself tomorrow afternoon."

"My uncle, my very own uncle," reflected the boy. Mr. and Mrs. Smethwick had both been only children, Sybilla was George's only aunt; the idea of new relations obviously intrigued him. "And from India!" he sighed expressively. "Do you think he will come dressed in a tiger skin? Will his skin be very dark?"

"Don't expect too much, George," cautioned Sybilla. "He is your father's elder brother. I daresay his skin will be exactly like ours, and that he will appear simply as an English gentleman. After all, if you had lived in India, you would not expect to change very much."

"Perhaps not," agreed George, "but I hope I should

know that what my nephew wanted above all would be to see a tiger skin."

"I fear you may be disappointed, dumpling!" said his mother, kissing him and laughing. "While he may have brought a tiger skin back with him from India for his own use, I doubt if he will bring it with him on his first formal visit to us tomorrow afternoon. Do you think you can forgive him such a grave oversight?"

"If he is my uncle, I shall forgive him a great deal," said George, "and no doubt you are right, Mama. He may well have a tiger skin hidden somewhere and I had better be nice to him so that he becomes convinced of the need to show it to me at the earliest opportunity."

Somewhat reassured by George's innocent curiosity and infectious excitement at the prospect of meeting the person who was indeed the boy's one and only "very own uncle," Sybilla kissed her nephew goodnight and left her sister to perform the final little ceremonies of putting the lad to bed.

Later that night, however, she tossed and turned in bed, fretting about what changes to their lives this new connection with Harry's family might bring. No matter how she turned the matter over in her mind, one thought remained uppermost, that Ampthill would surely find himself fully equipped with a wife and heir in eighteen months at the outside, thus any change in George's status must of necessity be only temporary.

Try as she might, she could only see unworthy motives behind Ampthill's sudden interest in Honoria and George. After all, if he had been so interested in George's welfare, he could easily have sent Lindsay to look them up in Stourbridge at any time in the last seven years. Even allowing for the months needed for news to reach India, he must have been aware of George's existence for at least five years. Why only now was he taking this sudden interest? Sybilla resolved to act out to the full her chosen role of the doubting, distrustful aunt. Honoria and George must be as charming as possible; that was without doubt necessary to avoid any excuse for rejection on the part of the new family, but she was determined that she would refuse all blandishments and maintain a judiciously watchful eye.

Next morning, however, she found that Honoria had also formed her own resolutions. George had also dreamed up more questions.

"Do you think my uncle may try to stop us from going to Spain?" had been his first question. "I think I should rather go to Spain than see his tiger skin."

"Since he has only just returned from India, I expect he will be very busy for the next few months," replied his mother. "I hope that we may agree that we should continue with our travels as planned, and leave further acquaintance with your relations until we are returned. I think, George, that is the arrangement that would best suit us. But let us see what his lordship has to suggest. As long as he realizes that we have managed quite well until now without his protection, and are quite prepared to do so indefinitely, then we have nothing to worry about. Now what did you and Aunt Sybilla have on your agenda for today?"

The next few minutes were spent organizing everyone's activities for the day. Sybilla and George retired to the second floor room with the draftsman's tables, which during the mornings did duty as schoolroom; Mrs. Gurney promised a further visit to the "Exchange" in the hope of finding new applicants for the posts of escorting the family to Spain. Honoria promised to take over George's lessons at mid-morning and, with their immediate preoccupations settled, they all went about their business.

# TWO

The tall, lean figure slouched at the window, disconsolately staring out at the light but persistent April rain. "How much longer will this weather keep up?" he growled at Brockley, who was checking that the chafing dishes on the sideboard were properly filled and warm. "And where the deuce is Lindsay? He was due at ten o'clock and it's well past the half hour." At that moment, the doorbell sounded and Brockley, much relieved, said, "That must be him now, m'lord."

Augustus Swaffham, ninth earl of Ampthill, crossed to the table and poured himself a third cup of the choice blend of Assam and Darjeeling teas that he had brought back with him from Calcutta. He had been happy these last twelve years in India, restoring the family fortunes while opening up new trade opportunities. He missed the dry heat, the excitement of *shikhar,* the elegance of the Maharajahs' palaces, the comradeship of his fellow entrepreneurs and the army officers. The month since he had returned to England had been tedious. Although the money from India had been kept firmly out of his dissolute father's hands, there had still been a number of gambling debts to settle, as well as wine merchants', tailors', and other tradesmen's bills, not to speak of some indiscreet accounts to be closed at insalubrious *maisons de passe* in Kensington and Bayswater. Swaffham Park, the family seat in Hampshire, was run-down, except for the shooting, and the house in Mount Street also needed redecorating after his father's tenure, which seemed to have been devoted to rumbustious gentleman's parties and little else.

Augustus had spent a month in the country, getting to grips with affairs there, and was now up in London for the start of the Season, hoping to wind up the last untidy remnants of his father's affairs. *At least there are no trees to drip in Mount Street, not like the oaks at home,* he thought morosely. *Why can't it even rain properly in England?* The monsoons in India had been dramatic, vast sheets of rain that thundered down remorselessly. Although eagerly awaited for the relief they brought from the summer heat, the rains were also powerful, threatening floods and destroyed crops. Not this insipid all-prevailing damp. And he was not at all looking forward to Lindsay's call or the news he might bring.

David Lindsay and Swaffham had been constant companions at Eton. Unlike many of their contemporaries, interested only in breaking bounds to follow women and horses, the two youngsters had shared a desire to do something useful with their lives. Augustus, sickened from an early age by his father's dissolute carryings on, had watched his mother's stoic endurance of her husband's prolonged absences, punctuated with rowdy visits for hunting parties, with growing distaste as he became aware of what their married life must be.

Lindsay was of Scots descent and had been brought up in the tradition of the great humanists and utilitarians. Augustus had been fascinated by his serious-mindedness and whereas their classmates had joshed Lindsay for his scholarly habits, the young lord had learned to emulate them. Lindsay was destined for the law. Augustus had had no idea of any specific occupation, so long as it would take him far away from his father's disorderly habits.

It was up in Scotland for the grouse with Lindsay that he had met Elphinstone, who had enthralled the company with his tales of tiger hunting from the backs of elephants, of wars against the native tribesmen, of the jewel-bedecked maharajas. Almost twenty, Augustus was well aware that his father was in the process of gambling away the family wealth. The combination of distance, adventure, and the possibility of accruing sufficient funds to withstand the depredations of his father were irresistible. Just over a year later, Augustus celebrated his coming of age, not with the grand parties that his father's tenants had hoped for, but in Calcutta, as a new recruit to the East India Company. Although he had soon chosen to leave the Company to make his own way, it had provided him with an invaluable apprenticeship in the convolutions of the India trade.

Brockley announced Lindsay and hovered helpfully as the successful lawyer helped himself to deviled kidneys and crisp bacon. Unlike Augustus, Lindsay took coffee. Augustus, sitting peevishly at the head of the table, watched his friend morosely. Lindsay clearly had news. He was obviously not going to say a word until his plate was filled. At last, he was seated.

"Deuce take it, man!" exclaimed Augustus. "Out with it!"

Lindsay glanced in the direction of the ever-helpful Brockley.

"Brockley's presence need not deter you from unloosing whatever dire tale you may have to relate," said Augustus. "He has been with us for years and is the soul of discretion. Besides, if your news refers to the whereabouts of the Smethwick woman, then he is the only one

who has ever clapped eyes on her and he will have to
vouch for her."

"I'll be happy to vouch for young master Harry's
widow."

"You were fond enough of my brother, weren't you
Brockley?"

"Indeed, sir, especially after you took off on your travels. . . ."

"Quite so, thank you, Brockley." Augustus cut off the
old man's reminiscences. The one thing he had regretted
about going to India had been abandoning his brother.
Harry had been a youngster of seventeen then, already
destined for the army. The last thing Augustus had managed to do for him before leaving was to help him into
the Engineering Corps. The eighth earl had been adamant
that his younger son should make a creditable showing in
the cavalry. But young Harry had always been fascinated
by the technical side of soldiering. He dreamed of bul-
warks and redoubts, catapults and siege machines.

To Augustus's amazement, Harry had shown early
promise as a scholar of mathematics, and even from their
earliest days in the schoolroom had far outshone his
brother in this abstruse art. Augustus had argued with his
father on Harry's behalf. The secretive Brockley had been
instrumental in Augustus's winning the argument, revealing all he felt able about the presence in the London
house of the succession of ladies of uncertain age and dubious character who the eighth earl had so frequently
entertained. Thus armed, Augustus had managed to put
his father sufficiently out of countenance that he reluctantly agreed to Harry's combining his talents and his
passion in the study of military engineering. Of course,
Augustus reflected gloomily, it was precisely this indul-
gence of Harry's passion that had killed him at Badajoz.

Before setting out to join Wellington's army in Spain,

Harry had, it seemed, somehow contrived to meet and marry the daughter of some Midlands engineer or inventor or some such. To Ampthill's way of thinking, the whole affair had been conducted in a mean and covert fashion. Harry had sent a letter to his mother, addressed from the London house, telling her that he was married, naming his bride as Honoria Smethwick, daughter of Josiah Smethwick, a renowned engineer residing in Stourbridge, near Birmingham. He confessed that he had not consulted the family at all about his intentions, secure in the knowledge that his father would disapprove, but on the eve of his departure and, given the possibility (remote as he felt it might be) that an accident would befall him while on campaign, he felt that the family should be appraised of the facts of the matter.

Harry's bride was reputed to be very pretty, and according to Brockley, who had abetted the pair when they stayed for Harry's last few nights in London before he set sail for Lisbon, she was nicely enough spoken. Augustus, however, paid no heed to the old butler's weakness for a bridal couple. As far as he was concerned, at best, she was a sentimental goose who had been beguiled by Harry's aristocratic name and looks, and at worst, an unprincipled adventuress. But seven years ago, already a widow, she had given birth to Harry's son. This much was certain. As soon as he recovered from his grief at Harry's untimely death, Augustus had written to Lindsay asking him to discover as much as he could. Thereafter, he had given the affair little thought, the more immediate concerns of his business in India relegating the issue of Harry's relict to the back of his mind.

Lindsay had ascertained that the marriage was entirely valid. Harry had wed the girl in her own parish, albeit quietly, with only her parents and young sister as witnesses. Augustus wondered indeed at the kind of people who would allow their daughter to get married in such a hugger-mugger way. The father, as described by Harry, was celebrated in his milieu, said to be good friends with like-minded folk such as Mr. Stephenson and members of the Wedgwood family. His two daughters were said to be well—if eccentrically—educated. Lindsay reported them to be more familiar with slide rules than embroidery frames.

On Harry's departure, Lady Harry had posted back to Stourbridge, at her own expense. Their son, George, had been born at her parents' house nine months later.

During the months of his voyage home, Augustus had taken to thinking of his nephew. Perhaps he might be a little like Harry? The lad would be all of seven by the time he reached England. In the midst of a storm off Muscat, the earl realized that if some mishap should occur, this boy was heir to Swaffham Park, not to mention the wealth he had accumulated during his twelve years in India; heir in fact, to all that Augustus held dear. Clearly something should be done. But what? As the remaining weeks at sea passed, Augustus found himself mulling over the existence of Lord George. This in turn brought home to him the realities of his own life. "I shall marry and have children of my own. This engineer lad need not inherit," reflected Ampthill. Still, the eighth earl's recent death, Harry's untimely demise, combined with the dangers he himself had experienced in India persuaded him of the risks of bidding on an uncertain future. For the time being, George was the heir apparent and so it was of prime importance that he should be investigated, inspected, and examined. If found presentable, he should take his rightful place in the family. If found wanting, means and ways to distance him from the Swaffham name could be employed.

These reflections were depressing to the new earl of

Ampthill. Quite apart from his suspicions about his brother's relict, the obvious conclusion was that one of his first duties on arriving home would be to provide himself with a suitable wife and for her to provide him with a suitable heir. The whole idea appalled Augustus. He thought about his own parents: his father's lamentable behavior and the long-suffering patience of his mother. He thought about Lakshmi, her recitals of poetry, her lithe body, her cheerful acknowledgment that their relations would end when he left Lahore. He smiled wryly as the memory of her uncomplicated excitement on receiving from him a small fortune just before his departure. She had revealed a host of plans which also made him realize how small a part of her life he had been. He also wondered about the fact that although they had been together for three years, there had been no sign of children. Even if he did manage to find a pale English girl whose company was sufficiently tolerable to contemplate matrimony, might it be that no children would ensue? Such thoughts brought him back again to George. His heir. The heir to nine generations must be rescued from whatever his ignominious Midlands mother had to provide.

Despite his doubts, he hoped sincerely that Harry's wife and son would turn out to be presentable. His mother, who had long adopted a habit of supreme indifference to others as a defense against the neglect of her husband and the rumors reaching Swaffham of his London carryings on, had struck him as sadly out of spirits, despite various attempts to rally herself and celebrate her elder son's return. She had clearly taken Harry's death more deeply to heart than she had admitted in her letters. She had also hinted that her presence at Swaffham would be redundant once he found a new mistress for the house and seemed set to wish herself into a state of permanent debility. Augustus remembered her easy and affectionate manners to himself and his brother as children. George might, he felt, encourage her to a new lease of life.

Once home, Augustus had requested Lindsay to enter into relations with the Smethwick household in Stourbridge. But to their united dismay, the lawyer had drawn a blank. Both the worthy Josiah, friend of Rennie and Telford, and his wife had passed away. Of Harry's widow and her younger sister, thus orphaned, there was no trace. Apparently, just over a year after their parents' deaths, they had shut up the family home and set off for no one knew where, although London was rumored. Local people believed that the Vicar and his wife were informed about the intentions of the Smethwick girls (as they were still called in Stourbridge), but at the time of Lindsay's visit, the Vicar had been called away to Cornwall on pressing family business, and no one else was prepared to advance any information to a stranger, no matter how gently spoken. Lindsay had managed to obtain a forwarding address in Newquay for the Reverend Hardisty. Ampthill and he had long anticipated a reply to their letter of inquiry to this gentleman.

From the tone of Lindsay's note the previous evening, announcing his intention of meeting his friend for breakfast, from the intensity of his gaze and the tenor of his voice, Augustus was certain that the lawyer had succeeded in flushing out Lord George Swaffham and his mother.

"They are uncovered," said Lindsay. "They have taken lodgings in Fitzroy Square. They are expecting you to call on them at five o'clock this afternoon."

# THREE

Augustus's heart sank as he stood outside Number 7 Fitzroy Square at five o'clock. The persistent rain had rendered everything dank. The sad sycamores in the gardens dripped lugubriously and the wet soaked upward through the seams and soles of his boots. The location was as dingy a neighborhood as Brockley had warned, boding ill for the state of the Smethwicks and Harry's widow. He wondered how they had fetched up in so unfashionable a district, equally distant from the bustling worlds of the Changes in the City, where he had recently gone with Lindsay and his man of business, and the great houses of Mayfair and Belgravia, which he had known since boyhood.

He suffered a momentary glimpse of the disturbance that his visit might cause to the two sisters within, but closed his heart with the hope that he might at long last see little George, and that this unknown boy might restore to life his younger brother.

He realized, from her dress, that the person who opened the door was no servant. "So you are young George's uncle then?" she said. "Mr. Lindsay warned us that you would be coming." And then she curtseyed. "Please come in, Lord Ampthill." Augustus was disturbed by her manner, which was barely welcoming.

Indeed there was a level of mockery in those shrewd gray eyes. He felt, suddenly, alone.

His steps on the stairs up to the first floor apartment were heavy. He was ushered into a sort of small drawing room, stiff with un-sat-upon chairs of dubious origin, comfort, and upholstery; and there he was requested to sit.

As he sat, smoothing the damp out of his gloves and trying to remember that he was the person in charge here, before he had time to remind himself that he was about to make these women happier than they had any right to deserve, the door burst open and a small child in nankeen erupted into the room, racing round, and waving a large sheet of brown paper and a pencil.

"Bring that back, you pestilential little hellhound!" rang a female voice, rapidly followed by the sound of footsteps. A tall girl with a tousled mop of blonde curls appeared in the doorway. She was wearing a most un-flattering smock in what appeared to be brown sacking and had a smudge of ink on her cheek.

"Grandpapa always said we should get someone to check our work. You know he did. Over and over, he said it should be checked, and you know I'm miles better than you at quadratic equations." The boy was bouncing up and down on a sofa, waving the paper above his head as the girl tried to snatch it from him, her curls threatening to fall to her shoulders as various precariously placed pins scattered to the floor.

"Miles better! What rot! Anyway, only when you've finished the plan, you buffle-headed chump. Now give it to me, it isn't ready for checking."

"Why won't you let me see it?"

"Because it isn't ready. Give it back to me, George, or it's stewed apple for a week." The girl's voice was steely.

The boy calmed down and handed the paper back contritely. "All right, Sybilla. Here it is."

As the girl carefully checked the paper for damage, young George looked up, saw Ampthill and gasped. The girl looked up, then turned, one eyebrow quirked in inquiry, to meet the earl's gaze. He bowed deeply.

"Ampthill, at your service, ma'am. I believe you are expecting me."

"I am not. My sister is. If you'll wait here, I shall go and fetch her. In the meantime, this is your nephew, Lord George Swaffham. Go on George, show a leg for your uncle."

Ampthill was disconcerted to find himself abruptly alone with the child. "They say you've been in India. What did you do there? Did you shoot tigers? And ride on elephants? Do they really have magic carpets? Are there really bottles with genies in them? Sybilla says those are all stories, but she has never been anywhere, so how should she know?"

Lord George had come over to him and was surveying him expectantly, with exactly the air Ampthill remembered Harry displaying when excited. The boy was almost identical to the late Lord Harry at the same age.

Ampthill swallowed as memories of their childhood flooded back. "I did ride on elephants, but I never shot a tiger. They are very hard to catch, you know. I never saw a magic carpet, or a bottle with a genie in it, but that is not to say that there weren't any. Who was that lady?"

"That was my aunt, Sybilla. Isn't it odd, you are my uncle, and she is my aunt, but you are not related. She is glad, I think."

"Glad about what?"

"That you aren't related. She says my father's family are very stuck-up and probably dull, for most aristocrats are dull and dim, you see. My father was the-the ex-ex-exception that proved the rule. But Grandpapa used to say that exceptions didn't prove rules, they just meant you had got your rule wrong if there was an exception."

"Have you kept your Uncle Ampthill entertained, young man?" came a soft question from the door. Man and boy looked up to see a lovely creature standing there in a pale violet tea gown. She came towards Ampthill, stopping behind George, her hands upon her son's shoulders. He examined her thoroughly. Where her sister was tall and gangly, she was delicately made, her hair smooth and neat, but undeniably red, her eyes the color of a mature oloroso sherry, her skin translucent and mercifully free of freckles.

"Lady Harry." He made his bow. In came Miss Sybilla. She now wore a simple blue gown with a Kashmir shawl and her hair had been disciplined. Ampthill realized that she was in her twenties, not her teens as he had previously imagined. And she was quite stunning. The Misses Smethwicks must have had every male pulse racing in Stourbridge.

"How can we help you, my lord?"

"I came to offer my services to you, Lady Honoria."

"Well, that is very kind, but I do not know how we may need them. We are planning a tour of the Continent, my sister and I. We wish to consult with certain of our correspondents directly, we wish to see Badajoz, and young George is simply eager to see anything and everything. So we will not be long in London." Her tone was cool, almost dismissive. Augustus realized that the widow and her family were rather suspicious of him. He wondered why.

"Ah. I see. And how long are you planning to travel?"

"As long as ever we can, we want to see Paris and Rome and lots of German places like—"

"Thank you, George." Lady Honoria cut her son short. "We plan to travel for up to a year. We are in London only to hire attendants. A courier."

"What of the lady who admitted me?"

"Mrs. Gurney? Oh, she is our housekeeper from Stourbridge. No, she must go back and look after our affairs there. Besides, Mrs. Gurney is of the mind that to cross the Channel is to mix with heathens and ruffians of the worst sort."

"Do you need any assistance?"

"It is handsome of you to offer. We will accept with pleasure, won't we, Honoria?" Miss Sybilla's tone was not particularly warm, but it was definite. "It has proven exceptionally difficult to find suitable people who will be able to accompany us to Spain. We are keen to be on our way, but it seems unlikely that we shall progress unless we press some poor soul to attend us."

"In that case, perhaps I may offer the services of my butler, Brockley, or my man Carstairs. Both are well versed in selecting staff. But I must beg a favor in return."

The ladies looked at him warily. "Yes?" said Lady Honoria.

"I must entreat you both to attend a ball I am giving at Ampthill House. It would look very ill if my sisters-in-law were in London, but absent." Augustus was unaware of the faint look of surprise on his own face, as if the invitation had emerged without preparation.

"What about Papa and Mama?" Honoria addressed Sybilla.

"It has been over eighteen months. We are still in mourning, but if we attended without dancing, no one could complain. When is the ball?"

"A week this Thursday. I do hope you are free. There will be a supper for a smaller party of friends and family, followed by the ball. I will send a carriage for you."

"How kind." Lady Honoria did not sound as though she thought Ampthill at all kind.

"Why now?" demanded Sybilla. "After all this time?"

"I had not been able to leave my position in India."

"Not even for Harry?" The ladies sounded shocked.

"I heard too late. It was six months after he died that your letter reached me. What would have been the good of arriving then?" replied the earl defensively.

"Not even a letter." There was unmistakable bitterness in Lady Honoria's response. Ampthill thought it best to withdraw swiftly. He was aware that the ladies had not offered him tea. A little town polish would do them no harm.

"We will talk at a more convenient time. I shall expect you to supper next week then. In the meantime, I shall send Brockley to you without delay."

At first, the ladies were inclined to reject Ampthill's invitation to the ball.

"He has such an air of arrogance, Honoria. I cannot like being in any way beholden to him. If we were to allow him any quarter, he would be ordering our lives to the last ell."

"I fear you have the right of it there. But for Harry's sake, I feel I owe George the opportunity to know his father's people."

"I suppose you are, but I never expected the earl to be so hawkish in both his appearance and his disposition. He is so somber and his eyes—well, I found his glance most penetrating, as though he were always seeing more than one wished."

"The configuration of his features is an accident, Sybilla, and no real indication of character."

"I am not so sure. He looks intelligent, Hono. He also looks forbidding and as arrogant as he behaves. Unlike you, I do think one's features indicate more of one's character than one would necessarily wish to share with the world, but he has the trick of making it peculiarly hard to tell what he is thinking. He makes me decidedly uncomfortable and I hope we will not have to endure much of his company, and as for his offers of help where couriers and servants for our trip are concerned, well, I fear that even though I accepted, he is not the sort to approve of our travels and may well hinder us."

"In that regard, Sybilla, I feel you are right. Though I am puzzled as to why you encouraged him to offer us service in this case, since I still see no need for help."

"That was abundantly clear. I agreed because I feared that you were about to bite his head off. Rarely have I seen you look so ferocious. You know as well as I do that Mrs. Gurney has made three trips to the Exchange with no success."

"I do know," sighed Honoria. "But when I saw him, all I could think was of his neglect of Harry and our dear George."

When Brockley appeared, he was a familiar figure to Honoria at least, and they were persuaded that they did need assistance for their tour of Europe.

"I'll help, though what you want to go gallivanting round the Continent for when his lordship has a mind to take you under his wing is what I don't understand," said the blunt fellow. "You'd be doing right by Lord Harry if you was to stay, and so he'd tell you himself. Your romping round might wait until you're established in society. It'll make all that traveling a deal easier, I might say. Doors open for those connected with earls as stay firmly shut for rash young women."

This sour homily was followed by a heavily gilt embossed invitation to the ball which, Brockley assured them, would be the grandest start to the London Season for this year and indeed for some years since. A sneaking desire to see how the Upper Ten Thousand disported themselves made itself felt, and with Mrs. Gurney, they unpacked their smartest gowns and pondered the addition of furbelows and ribbons.

Only a day or two later, Ampthill sent round a curtly worded note recommending Mme La Vielle's dress-making service, much to the irritation of both sisters and Mrs. Gurney, all of whom prided themselves on their sense of style and ability with a needle. Steadfastly ignoring the recommendation, Sybilla and Honoria whipped organza and stitched taffeta and pinned and tacked, while George twiddled his thumbs and drew elaborate pictures of elephants surmounted by complicated platforms on which people carried on a range of daily activities from cooking to sleeping.

Ampthill, meanwhile, was intent on recruiting able scientists for a laboratory, to be established at Swaffham Park for the pursuit of research into electricity, gases, and pumping machinery. He had first formed this intention in India, where he had thrown himself into a new life first in Calcutta and then in the Punjab. He had mixed with maharajahs and mechanics, developing trade routes for goods within India as well as investing time and money in the lucrative textile and tea trades.

In the wake of the 1813 Charter Act, there were opportunities aplenty for trade thrown open following the removal of rights and privileges formerly monopolized by the East India Company. In the search for ever-swifter means of getting goods to markets, Ampthill understood that man's ingenuity must be harnessed. The textile trade suffered as British mill owners developed machines to accelerate spinning and weaving, undercutting the cost of transporting fine cotton from India. There was talk of chemists making dyes in England that might match the rich colorings achieved by the Indian weavers and dyers.

Although he had taken precautions to spread his investments, nonetheless, Ampthill was familiar with tales of fortunes lost with as much speed as they had been amassed. When he received the notification of his father's death and the necessity of returning to England could no longer be avoided, he was not overly sorry to turn his back on the East.

It was on the journey home, interspersed with thoughts of Harry and his unknown offspring, that he first hit on the notion of setting up a workshop of some sort at Swaffham, a research center where experiments might be undertaken, where he might be a party to the discoveries of the age.

After his time in India, Ampthill had no thought of sitting idle. He had no real interest in agriculture, and having recently employed a reliable steward, was relieved to be able to supervise the running of the estate at one remove. But neither had he any desire to participate in politics, the other sphere to which he might be expected to devote his hours. Then there was the consideration that he wished to stay relatively close to Swaffham Park. His mother had, he felt, spent too long alone, allowing herself to linger in melancholic starts. She must be brought out of herself and encouraged to take an interest in the world and its doings.

Of the options available to Ampthill, science seemed far more exciting to a man of his practical bent, and the scheme had drawn warm approbation from Lindsay who knew of numerous professional men currently in some want, lacking either means to support their researches or homes for their families and their work. Lindsay and his partners at law were keen supporters of such men, offering their services for the filing of patents and in chasing up promises of remuneration which had failed to materialize. Together, the earl and his friend had already drawn up a list of possible candidates who might be prepared to immure themselves in the country for months at a time in pursuit of their goals. Soon, he would interview these men.

As yet, the earl was unsure as to whether he wanted a laboratory focused on a single goal or a diversity of projects, a whole scientific community spreading its net as wide as feasible. There were so many possibilities, from road building to heat exchange, from the study of animals to the exploration of the skies and its stars. Then there were the improvements to be made at Swaffham itself: the gardens restored, the buildings repaired, the modernizing of the kitchens, the laundries, and the brewhouse, the introduction of new breeding strains for the sheep and the dairy herds, improvements at the mill house, efficiencies in the sowing and harvesting of the crops. Here too, there was room for men of learning and experience, perhaps an expert in steam engines or pumps. It did not occur to the earl that the two women he had just met were a part of the scientific community he wished to woo.

# FOUR

When Mr. Lindsay came to escort the ladies to Ampthill House on the evening of the ball, they were ready, wrapped in their pelisses. They were delighted to see him again, for he represented a world in which the sisters felt secure and at ease, unlike the London social whirl which they were about to encounter for the first time.

"How many are sitting down to supper?" asked Sybilla as they were handed into the carriage.

"Eighteen or twenty of us, I think," reported Lindsay. "The four of us are joined by at least one of the Lady Patronesses at Almack's, probably Lady Jersey, possibly Countess Lieven. I believe we may also be joined by sundry politicians of both Whig and Tory persuasion. They are all keenly petitioning Ampthill to sit on their side of the House. And, of course, there is your cousin, Mr. Carey Swaffham."

"Our cousin? Oh, you mean George's cousin," said Sybilla.

"The dowager countess does not attend?" queried Honoria.

"By no means. She is delicate, you know, and rarely leaves the Park. But I am sure Ampthill will wish to introduce you at the earliest possible point."

"Are you sure? He seems to think we are very green. Perhaps too rough for the countess."

Lindsay was taken aback by Honoria's sharp reply.

"Not at all. But you must speak with Ampthill yourself."

There was no time for private conversation after they arrived at Ampthill House. An imposing mansion in the heart of Mayfair, the doors were thrown wide and a line of carriages was already queuing to disgorge their passengers. The ladies were whisked upstairs to rearrange themselves, then ushered into a morning room bright with candles. Sybilla's attention was caught by a clock whose mechanism was clearly visible beneath a glass bell, but before she could go over and gaze at it, Ampthill was at Honoria's side, greeting first her and then Sybilla with a sweeping bow and a neat lifting of their gloved hands to his mouth. They each swept him a curtsey then opened their fans.

"You will set London tongues wagging. Everyone will wish to know the Fair Unknowns. You both look bang up to the mark. But I do not detect the handiwork of Madame La Vielle."

"It was kind in you to think of us, but we provincials had no desire to leave London with the impression that we are utterly ignorant of fashion's dictates," replied Sybilla.

"My apologies. I shall remember in future that where fashion is concerned, you are well able to fend for yourselves. But let me introduce you."

Ampthill whirled the girls about the room, until their heads were full of introductions and witticisms, some of which were almost brutally frank about their physical charms. But they found a kindly soul in Sally Jersey, who promised them vouchers for that Mecca of Society, Almack's Assembly Rooms.

"Nor must you think of sitting out the night. Ampthill mentioned that you did not intend to dance, but since it is well over a year since your parents died, you should no longer consider yourselves in mourning. Dear Countess Lieven and I are quite in agreement that a year's mourning is more than sufficient. Of course, one never stops grieving for the loss of our dear ones, but in public, a year is the maximum necessary. Now, you must tell me the name of your modiste, I have seen nothing so charming since I was back in London."

Before they needed to answer this query with the distinctly unfashionable revelation that the gowns were homesewn, Lady Jersey was called away and replaced by a figure of imposing bulk, cheery mien, and booming voice.

"You must call me cousin. Lindsay is saying that you will not want to call me cousin, but I must beg of you, both of you, to name me your cousin Swaffham. You will be the toast of town before the night is out, or my name is not Swaffham; but I'd stake my best waistcoat on it, you will be launched and I should be so miserable if everyone knew you had refused to call me cousin, it would quite set me down."

"Of course if you desire it so deeply, cousin, we could call you nothing else," replied Honoria. "But how are we cousins?"

"Why, my grandfather and Ampthill's grandfather were brothers. Or so I believe it went. But my grandfather was very much a younger son. Did well for himself though, married money, so we lesser Swaffhams are quite as warm as Ampthill. Mind, I don't envy Ampthill his position. I believe I am much better off, plenty of brass and no tiresome tenants to worry me."

Brockley came into the room and announced that supper was ready. Honoria was seated in the place of honor at Ampthill's right, and between Honoria and Sybilla sat Lindsay. Sybilla asked about the corpulent cousin.

"Who is he exactly?"

"Why, I thought I had mentioned him. That is Carey Swaffham. He cuts quite a figure in the town."

"A figure of fun?" queried Sybilla softly.

"Why, not at all, he is one of the finest of our bucks," responded Lindsay, equally softly, quirking an ironic eyebrow. "Both his grandmother and his mother were heiresses. He is much sought after as an arbiter of taste and a catch on the marriage mart."

"But he's old! Nearly fifty."

"Very finely preserved."

"Very finely corseted."

"So he does not take your fancy, then, Miss Sybilla?"

Honoria turned to Sybilla. "Did you hear, Syb, did you hear Ampthill? He is installing a marvel at Swaffham Park; he plans a cascade and he wants to try experiments, like that man in the colonies, Franklin, and like Mr. Faraday. He is going to set up a workshop to investigate gases and light."

"Is this really so? You are a scientist?"

"I would not go so far as to say that. I am a dabbler. But I have asked Sir Humphrey Davy to find me one or two men who wish to pursue investigations in a variety of fields. At Swaffham, there are always places for such people, and there they may also have the time to complete some useful research, and train me a little."

"And how do you propose to operate your cascade? By pump? Have you considered a steam engine? Mr. Watt has made such progress with them, and if you sited it carefully, it might not make too much noise. Perhaps you could place an engine room under the cascade. What a project!" Sybilla had come alive, her eyes alight with enthusiasm, her whole demeanor eager and sympathetic.

"Why, I had no notion that such a thing could interest a young lady."

"Why should it not? After all, our father surrounded us by such business. It was his life's work, and we all had to help. He assisted Mr. Watt, you know, and was in correspondence with Mr. Arkwright and Mr. Hargreave about their weaving and spinning machines. He said that all the things we need people to make now would one day be made by machines and that would free us all to think up even more new ideas."

"I believe he was correct in that assumption."

Sybilla smiled with approbation. It was the first time she had smiled at the earl, and he felt the effect to be as electrifying as success in any experiment. This perturbed him, but he concealed it by turning to the lady to his left as a footman came up, bearing yet another dish, this time of boiled capons, which the earl recommended heartily.

"Mr. Lindsay," said Honoria, "is Lord Augustus really determined on this course of action? Does he truly intend to become a sponsor of scientific endeavor?"

Sybilla only half heard her neighbor's reply as she found herself studying Ampthill himself. The man was mercurial, one minute proposing himself in all seriousness as Maecenas to needy scientists and the next exchanging trivial banter with Lady Jersey on his left. This was the first chance she had had of seeing George's uncle in his own social milieu. He certainly looked the part of the noble aristocrat; his thick dark hair swept back from the merest hint of a widow's peak, a firmly determined chin, and that slightly aquiline nose contributed to the hawk-like impression he had first made. Although there was a hint of sensuousness in the full lips, there was also something severe about the mouth in repose, even if in company, as now, his broad smile was amiable enough. His eyes were very striking, a deep gray-blue, so intense that under certain light, they appeared almost black. She observed his light-hearted expression as he chatted merrily with Lady Jersey and her neighbor. He was obviously at ease and seemed to be heartily enjoying his role as host. His manner contrasted markedly with the rather chilly and abrupt behavior of a week ago.

Carey's voice came booming up the table, praising some horse that had won him a packet at Newmarket. A frown of displeasure fleeted across the earl's face, his eyes suddenly cold and dark with suppressed annoyance, the social smile replaced with a hint of a sneer of contempt. Lady Jersey soon reclaimed his attention, however, and the easy manner and warm smile returned. Honoria caught Sybilla's eye and arched her brow in query: she had noted her younger sister's intent examination of the earl's face.

Talk flowed easily and by the time the party was partaking of sweetmeats, fruit, and cheese, there was a distant flurry as guests began to arrive for the ball proper, welcomed by a trio playing chamber music by various composers including Mozart and Haydn. The ladies were offered the opportunity to retire briefly before reentering the fray. Sybilla and Honoria came down the stairway together, a dazzling sight in their gauzy dresses of silver tulle with matching fans. Honoria wore the pearls Harry had given her at their wedding, and Sybilla wore a black and coral cameo on a silver ribbon left her by her mother.

Lindsay and Carey Swaffham were waiting at the foot of the staircase to escort them into the ballroom where Ampthill was opening the dancing with Lady Jersey in a quadrille. Carey Swaffham begged for the pleasure of Lady Honoria's hand, and Lindsay speedily followed with Sybilla onto the dance floor. The dance offered the opportunity for conversation, and Lindsay took the opportunity to warn Sybilla against waltzing.

"Lady Honoria may, for she is a widow, but in you, it would be considered fast until you have been to Almack's, where one of the patronesses may approve. I am sure Ampthill will get up a party, and there will be no difficulty in procuring vouchers."

"I do find it rather silly, but Honoria wants us to be a success, so I shall follow the rules as closely as possible."

"Does it matter very much to her?" Lindsay could not disguise his surprise.

"Not to her, but for George's sake, she feels we must never do anything that might put him out of countenance or make him in any way ashamed of us. We are well aware that having been so close to Papa and helping him in his office has set us apart, and it is clear that the Swaffhams think us of little account."

"You need fear nothing. Both Lady Honoria and you are well on the way to complete acceptance from the *ton*."

So indeed it seemed. Neither Sybilla nor Honoria had a chance to sit out a dance. Then Ampthill came up to Sybilla and begged the honor of escorting her around the room while the waltz was danced.

"You both dance very well."

"For bluestockings?"

"For ladies brought up in some seclusion."

"Well, both Mama and Papa loved a dance, and we were visited by families from the Continent. We could not be at our figures all the time, and in the evening, we would teach them our English country dances, and our visitors would reciprocate. Mama was a fine pianist and Papa played the fiddle, so we always had accompaniment. We were not as secluded as all that."

"Can you waltz?"

"I can, but Mr. Lindsay made it very clear that I should not."

"You find society a little constraining?"

"Well, I never expected to be in it, and of course, we shall not be for long, for as soon as your man Carstairs has assisted us, we shall be on our way. So I find it entertaining rather than constraining. Perhaps it is more so for you, after your time in India."

"You see more than I meant to say."

"Well, you have not put on your manners for us."

"My manners?" Ampthill was astounded. "What do you mean?"

"You are very different with company. With Honoria and me, you were ready to be overbearing and then you found we weren't to be overborne, which made you out of reason cross, and now I think you are simply relieved that we are presentable. But with people to whom you feel you owe no obligation, you seem very polite. Distant, but polite."

"I find you impertinent," responded Ampthill, teeth gritted.

"I daresay you do. There is little I can do about it."

"You might keep your opinion to yourself."

"I might, but then you would be in such a stew wondering what I was thinking that you wouldn't like it any better than my telling you what I do think."

"You are a deal too clever for your own good. Sharp misses need to curb their tongues if they are to find a decent match."

"Why should you think I want what you call 'a decent match'? I have no need to marry. Honoria and I have means sufficient to meet our needs, we have each other's company and more than enough work to keep ourselves fully occupied. Why should I concern myself with a husband?" Sybilla was genuinely baffled.

"What about love?" demanded Ampthill, outraged by

Sybilla's cool demeanor as she expressed her outrageous notions.

"What about it?"

"Well, what if you fall in love? Would you not wish to marry then? Or will you carry on like—like Mary Godwin or some other lunatic free thinker?"

"Honoria is the sort to fall in love. I never have myself, and I consider myself immune by now."

"By now? You are hardly in your dotage. What are you? Twenty-two? Twenty-three? You may not have been presented at sixteen, but for heaven's sake, people fall in love all the time. Look at Caroline Lamb, making a cake of herself over that squalid poet. Look at Harry and your sister."

"I have seen people fall in love, but I just don't think I will. In any case, what has it to do with you whether I believe in love or not?"

"Nothing. It has nothing whatever to do with me, but it is nonsense."

Sybilla was at once astonished and mortified by the earl's vehemence and his dismissive tone. A ripple of applause rang round the ballroom, and a young man approached to remind Sybilla that she had agreed to dance with him. She swept off, sparing the earl not even a glance. He stood, watching as the couple joined a set for the Lancers, his features rigid with disapproval. Never had he met so infuriating a wench. Determined to put her out of his mind, he turned abruptly and continued in his obligations as host by dancing with as many young ladies as he could, so long as none of them was the maddening Miss Smethwick.

The ball was an undoubted success, a thorough squeeze, and it was a simple matter to avoid Miss Sybilla, although he caught frequent glimpses of her on the dance floor and at the buffet tables sampling ices and lemonade.

The evening seemed to be going on forever, and it must
have been nearly two hours later that Lindsay came up to
him and whispered urgently, "Come, Augustus, come immediately." The two men pushed their way through the
throng to meet Sybilla, her cheeks flushed with fury as
she stood, listening to Sir Everard Venables's slurred
tones.

"Comin' here, foistin' your by-blow on one of the
finest families in the land! A pack of monstrous blue-
stockin's, puttin' on airs and pushin' their bastard under
our noses."

"You, sirrah, are drunk. At least, that is the only explanation for the monstrous lies you are spouting. It is
certainly no excuse. You are no gentleman." Whereupon
the irate Sybilla pulled back her arm and landed the
baronet an unerring uppercut with her apparently strong
right hand. He staggered back a pace or two, then surged
forward, yelling, "Well, if I am no gent, then you're no
demmed lady." Sybilla failed to avoid his flailing arms as
he lurched towards her. His hand caught her bodice and
there was a sickening rending of fine material and the
crowd around the couple gasped deeply. Ampthill struggled to the front of the crowd, whisked off his evening
jacket and draped it round Sybilla's stripped form. Holding the jacket firmly shut with one hand, he embraced her
with the other and propelled her through the crush of
gawpers assembled about them. As he neared the door, he
whispered hurriedly to two footmen, desperately attempting to appear impassive. They maneuvered their
way through the mêlée to seize Sir Everard Venables and
escort him away.

Sybilla and Ampthill were joined immediately by
Lindsay and Lady Honoria and withdrew first into a parlor and then into a small booklined study. Sybilla
appeared stiffly defiant.

"What on earth happened?" demanded Honoria.

"I would rather not say, Honoria. He uttered such filth, I do not wish to repeat it. Suffice to say both your honor and mine were impugned." The glitter of unshed tears lit her eyes.

"I am afraid, Miss Smethwick, that I must be in full possesion of the facts before I decide what is to be done with Sir Everard. I need to know what poison it is that has been spread if I am to administer an antidote." Ampthill's tone was measured, but his fists were clenched with rage.

"Perhaps you are right. Perhaps. But need Honoria hear it?"

"Don't be silly, Syb, you have heard it and it hasn't killed you. What is he saying about us?"

Sybilla swallowed and closed her eyes.

"First he tried to take liberties. When I wouldn't let him, he started. We are sly hussies. We have ensnared one Swaffham, and now we have our caps set at another. That . . . that your marriage to Harry was a sham and George is a by-blow. Everyone knows it, and is laughing at Ampthill and despising us."

"Syb, dearest, is that all? We shall scarcely be in London long enough for this to last. It is not as if we ever wanted to go into society. We are quite content with our own pursuits. The quicker we leave London, the better, for then it will be nothing but a ten days wonder and entirely forgot by the end of May."

"But what about George? You wanted him to be able to take his place in society. What chance has he now?"

"I only ever wished that he might be able to make his bow if he wanted when he was a young man. You know all he wants now is the chance to own a monkey and perfect that blasted dynamo of his. In eleven or twelve years, no one will remember this night at all."

"I fear you are too sanguine, Lady Honoria. I know it

is the fashion for ladies' gowns to mimic dishabille, but it is fortunately all too rare that they actually appear in public without their clothes." Ampthill was icily sardonic.

Sybilla was quick to spring to her sister's defense. "Honoria was only trying to cheer me up. It is all very well to suggest that I shouldn't have lost my temper. Of course I shouldn't. But if I had been a man, I could have challenged that vile dandified monstrosity to a duel and that would have been that."

"If you had been a man, the case would probably never have arisen," commented Lindsay drily.

"That is not a productive avenue of thought, dear David," responded Ampthill crisply. "I suggest you escort the ladies back to Fitzroy Square. In the morning, you will all go to Swaffham Park, where you will stay until we can ship you to the Continent. This will have the double merit of showing that you are under my mother's wing and removing you from the London scene."

"You are abominably high-handed. Why should we go to Swaffham Park? Why should we remove ourselves from London? We are planning to go to France as soon as we can in any case, and it seems ridiculous to hoick ourselves to some remote location to suit your notions of propriety." Sybilla's voice was even, but venomous. "Our house is taken for another three weeks, we have many preparations to see to, and the last thing we need to do is dawdle away the time in the country."

"Lady Honoria," continued Ampthill, pointedly ignoring Sybilla, "I am offering you shelter and the opportunity for your child to meet and be recognized by his grandmother, who may not, if she is to be believed, last beyond Christmas, by which time you will be galloping round who knows what part of Spain or France.

"There is also the slight consideration that if you are taken firmly under the Swaffham wing, this gossip will be once and for all quelled. If, on the other hand, you choose to remain in London, it can do nothing but bring unpleasantness to you. There is a further consideration, that in the places where attendants and servants congregate, stories travel swiftly, and this incident may—I do not say will, but it may—make it harder to secure the proper staff to accompany you on your travels. It does not seem to me that a delay of a few weeks will impair the pleasures of your tour in the longer term, and this delay, indeed may bring benefits.

"May I count on you to discuss this with your sister and on the morrow, Brockley will attend you, at the ready to escort you directly to Swaffham Park. As to the house and the contents, my people will know how to deal with this business, in conjunction with your own admirable Gurney, who I believe, will shortly be leaving you in any case to return to your home in Stourbridge."

The young women were silent as Ampthill left the room in stately dignity.

"I believe that he is right. It doesn't do to admit too frequently that he is in the right," said Lindsay in an attempt to soothe the sisters' jangled feelings. "But in this case, he has read the situation clearly. Of course, if you choose to remain in London, we shall both do our utmost to support you, but the wisest course is the one Ampthill has outlined, however disagreeable and inconvenient that may seem in the first instance."

The uncomfortable silence deepened as all three waited for the carriage to be summoned to return the ladies to Fitzroy Square.

# FIVE

At first, in the dark of the carriage, a solitary tear or two edged its way down Sybilla's cheek, but as the horses clattered through the streets, almost empty in the early hours of the morning, the tears began to course freely down her cheeks, and soon she could not contain the sobs which shook her. Nothing she had yet experienced could have prepared her for the public humiliation of this night.

Tucked close under a travel rug and held close by Honoria, it was as though all the misery of the past year and a half, their father and mother lost to them, had caught up with Sybilla. Every moment she had spent trying to be brave for George's sake, for Honoria, for herself, was laid waste by the malignant words and actions of a minor member of the aristocracy. David Lindsay wished himself far away, recognizing that there was no consolation he could provide for the sorrow wracking the girl in the seat opposite him. He escorted the ladies in to the ministrations of an expectant Mrs. Gurney, who immediately turned tiger when she saw the state of one of her precious nurslings.

"What have they done to her? Who has done this?" she exclaimed over and over, hustling Sybilla upstairs and away.

Lady Honoria turned to Mr. Lindsay.

"Thank you."

"It was nothing. The least a gentleman could do."

"What will Ampthill do?" She clutched his arm fiercely.

"I cannot say."

"But you can guess."

"He will make it uncomfortable for Venables."

"How?" Honoria looked him straight in the eye. He returned her gaze steadily.

"I do not yet know."

"A duel?"

"Lady Honoria, if I knew, I would tell you."

"If he fights a duel, won't that leave her reputation even further tarnished?"

"I think if he fails to challenge Venables, rumor will run even more rampant."

"A duel. It is everything that dear Mama and Papa despised. This whole business has been a foolish error on my part. And now my folly has led us to this."

"You are not to blame for the rantings of a drunken sot." Lindsay's emphatic rejoinder roused Honoria.

"Perhaps you are right. And I should keep you no longer. Thank you again. Shall we see you at Swaffham Park?"

"Naturally."

Having made his farewell to Lady Honoria, Lindsay returned to Ampthill House as swiftly as the horses would take him there. Brockley admitted him into the eerily silent building. It was a little over an hour since he had left the teeming ballroom.

"His lordship is in the library."

"The ball is over? Already?"

"His lordship had lost his taste for festivities. He chose to remind his guests that there are fireworks in Vauxhall Gardens just before dawn. A fitting end to the night's entertainments."

"Indeed, Brockley."

Ampthill was sipping some cognac as he sat in a low chair, a candle flickering on the adjacent table. He indicated the decanter.

"Here, David, have some. It is very fine. Smuggled, I am sure, but we must thank Brockley for the provisioning of the house."

"Am I to stand by as your second?"

Ampthill stood and his smile was warm.

"If you will."

"Naturally. Who has Venables nominated?"

"Edmund Fitch. He is with Venables in the music room. May I ask you to arrange the details now. For tomorrow—or I should say, today. I am at Venables's disposal."

"The choice of weapons?"

"I have no preference. Pistols or small sword, it is all one to me."

"Have you kept in practice?"

"There were some very competent masters in Calcutta. I have been under the tutelage of several."

"You could never be faulted at school. I wonder whether Venables realizes what he has taken upon himself. But you do know the consequences?"

"Exile if I manage to kill him. Removal from London if I pink him. It is no hardship, I shall go to Swaffham and attend to the disrepair there."

"You will, of course, have the lovely Smethwick sisters for company."

"And Mama. It is time in any case that I devoted myself more closely to her."

"As you say. Shall we take it to the first cut only?"

"By all means. I have no intention of finishing off Venables."

"Let us hope he has no intention of finishing you off."

It did not take Lindsay long to sort out the details of

the encounter which Ampthill was determined on. The earl's reputation had reached Venables, who had instructed his second, Fitch, to opt for the mildest possible form of engagement. Sobered by the prospect of facing an opponent known to be a notoriously competent fencer, the bibulous baron was in a cold sweat and eager to follow the thing through with all possible speed. A meeting at dawn was agreed upon, which would allow Ampthill, traveling in a speedy curricle, ample time to reach Swaffham Park ahead of the ladies. They would be using the heavy family landau and stopping frequently to rest and stretch their limbs. Ampthill also reckoned that where the ladies would need to spend the night at Farnham, he might safely tackle the journey in ten hours. This was duly arranged with Brockley, who engaged to travel with the ladies, since they knew and seemed to trust him.

The next morning, Brockley presented himself at Fitzroy Square. Although it took considerable effort, he managed not to reveal to Lady Honoria or Miss Smethwick that his lordship had fought a duel, packed up his curricle, and was by now well on the way to Swaffham Park. As Lindsay had foreseen, Ampthill had administered with surgical precision a flesh wound to the upper arm of Sir Everard, bowed, and absented himself from the scene. It was Lindsay's job to spread the news abroad in London, giving the earl a cast-iron reason to remain at Swaffham Park until the ladies could be safely dispatched to the Continent. However, Lindsay himself was still determined to encourage Augustus to make the most of the ladies' expertise in establishing his workshop at Swaffham Park. He hoped that Honoria might be persuaded to prolong her stay in England as long as possible—or at least until he could free himself of his current obligations in London so as to be able to accompany the sisters around Europe.

The tedium of leaving the heavy carriage traffic in and

out of London was somewhat relieved by passing first the home of Mr. Hogarth, the artist, particularly admired by Mr. Smethwick, and consequently an idol of his daughters, and then Kew Gardens, where they knew Sir Joseph Banks was working on His Majesty's instructions at botanical researches. They did not have the confidence of long acquaintance, nor, Brockley assured them, the time, to stop at Kew to explore the grounds, but he did assure them that, given time, Lord Ampthill was sure to be able to secure permission for them to visit there. This put a damper on the ladies, both considering their obligation to his lordship for spiriting them away from the scene of Sybilla's embarrassment, and neither realizing how their obligation had deepened still further.

The country through which they traveled was much softer than their native landscapes, but the horses were nonetheless stretched by numerous hills. They paused for lunch at Bushy Park, allowing George to stretch his legs and the ladies to rest a little. Ampthill's French cook had supplied a magnificent cold collation. Sybilla and George made significant inroads into the dishes provided, but Lady Honoria, who felt the motion of the carriage, lay in the shadow of a venerable chestnut, her eyes closed. She was not used to any malaise, but the old landau was not so well sprung as the stage coach that had carried them to London. She hoped that carriages on the Continent would prove more comfortable.

It was early evening when they arrived at Farnham, Honoria finding herself much improved, for the traffic lessened after Kingston, the speed of the landau increased to a steady pace, and there were no pauses while the coachman spent a full fifteen minutes hurling abuse at sundry passersby whom he considered to be blocking his way and instructing the post boy to blow his trumpet. George's exuberant enthusiasm also encouraged her, for the boy took well to travel, staying securely in his seat, but calling all manner of sights to her and Sybilla's attention.

Brockley found that his lordship had warned the landlord of his sister-in-law's arrival, so all had been made ready for the ladies, rooms aired and a parlor set aside, where they found madeira, porte, and a choice of other restoratives with ratafia biscuits and the promise of supper within the hour. George protested at the use of this hour for a wash, but was told firmly that he could look at the stables first thing on the morrow, but that he should not come down to supper looking like a savage.

The ladies were discommoded by one thing only. Halfway through their supper, a surly lout burst into their parlor. Propping himself in the doorway, he gazed on them, swinging his tankard and belching.

"Come here, Abel Mortley, that's no place for the likes of you," bellowed the landlady, catching at the fellow's arm and tugging ineffectually. "Come on, I say, don't disturb these Christian folk at their supper. Come now."

"Yer got gentry mort in your house now, Sairey. Our sort are too low for you, s'that it, Sairey."

"Don't you be talkin' your tomfoolery, Abel Mortley. That parlor 'as bin paid for, private like, an' I won't have them as pays good brass disturbed by those who haven't ha'penny to rub together. Be off with you now, back to the bar."

The man lurched away; the landlady popped her head through the door, apologized, and disappeared.

The next morning, George woke his mother and aunt promptly, importuning them to help him out of his nightshirt and into his suit so that he might inspect the horseflesh and watch as they were harnessed to the landau. "And you will come in for breakfast as soon as you are called, young man," stipulated his mother, familiar with her son's forgetfulness when absorbed in observing novelties.

"Indeed I will, of course I shall, for I am half-starved already," promised the squirming lad, wriggling away from the comb Sybilla was brandishing. The sisters dressed themselves in their merino traveling gowns and followed George downstairs at a considerably more sedate pace. They found that breakfast was not quite ready, so made their own way to the stables to collect the boy. He was teetering on a mounting block, engaged in running a currycomb over the shining flanks of a solid chestnut gelding.

"This is one of Uncle Augustus's horses, you know. He keeps them all along the road from here to London. Imagine that, three mounts all eating their heads off. Jem the groom, he says that he is allowed to exercise him."

Just then, Jem himself emerged from a stall. Briefly acknowledging the ladies, he asked George, "Would you like to lead him round a bit, warm him up before he goes between the shafts?"

"Would I?" replied George, his whole face lit up with excitement. He hopped off the block and came round to untether the beast from the hitching post.

"Don't fret, ladies, old Caesar is calm as a rabbit."

Sybilla and Honoria were perfectly happy to see George so occupied, scurrying to keep pace with the lengthy strides of the gelding. He led him round and round the yard until Jem asked for the horse to be brought over to the landau. They all watched as the groom buckled and knotted the leathers in place. As the groom took a step back to admire his handiwork, a groan erupted from one of the stalls. A shabby figure emerged from the gloom. It was Abel Mortley, the drunkard who had briefly interrupted their supper. He lurched over to the horse trough and plunged his head full in, then lifted it and shook it like a dog coming out of a pond, spraying the yard with water.

"Pardon me, yez leddyships, pardon me." He swiped his sleeve across his face then stretched. "Fine mornin', I'm sure."

"I hear something coming, something fast!" cried George, racing towards the archway leading into the yard. Abel Mortley followed, trailed by Honoria and Sybilla, both women calling after the boy in an attempt to curb his headlong rush into the path of the oncoming vehicle. He was on the verge, looking up the road, where, thundering through the mud, there was a curricle, driven by a heavily muffled figure. The horse seemed to check slightly as first George, then Abel Mortley appeared there, but the driver whipped the horse on and Honoria and Sybilla looked on in horror as he unmistakably twitched the reins, forcing the horse closer and closer to the verge where George stood, directly in the curricle's path.

Abel Mortley yelled, "No, Seth!" For a man with a hangover, he moved astonishingly fast, sweeping the boy round and out of the way of horse and carriage. And then they were round the curve of the road and the lane was silent once more, apart from Abel's heavy panting. George was white faced as he moved out of the man's arms and stood shakily in the archway.

"Thank you, Mr. Mortley. Thank you very much. Without you, who knows what injury may have befallen George!" Up came Honoria, sweeping her boy into her embrace, checking him carefully for injury. "If there is anything we can do for you, anything, please tell me. My sister and I will be at Swaffham Park. If you need money or work, you have only to call on me."

"Swaffham Park?" said the man. Leaning against a wall, he took a deep breath. "Swaffham Park. I'm headed that way myself. Might I beg a place by your coachman?"

"You might indeed," replied Sybilla. "Is that all?"

"My sister works in the laundry at Swaffham Park. It is

where all we Mortleys were born. If that bonehead won't take me on, I will call on you ladies for a word in my favor. But 'struth, anyone'd done what I done for yon lad."

"No, Mr. Mortley. You saved my boy's life, I am sure of it, and not many would have acted with such speed and such sense. We cannot thank you enough."

Escorting George as though he were more fragile than porcelain, the two women withdrew to the parlor for their breakfast, but neither they nor George could muster their customary appetites. As they were sitting over tea and toast, Brockley bustled in, agog with the tale of George's narrow escape.

"Mortley saving the boy, what an extraordinary turn! Why, he stormed off the estate more than four years ago, swearing he'd never be back. So he wants a position, does he? Well, I'm sure once his lordship has heard of this, he'll find something for the man. Two men less like brothers than Seth and Abel I've yet to meet. But you seem a bit shaken by this business. Don't dwell on it, I beg. A narrow squeak is best forgotten."

Brockley's cheerful banter galvanized Sybilla. "Come on, Hono, get George to eat a little more, while I make sure that girl has packed our bags." She left the parlor where Honoria did indeed encourage George to make his way through scrambled eggs and a slice of ham. Before long, they were pressing on in the carriage, that morning's narrow escape distanced by time as well as miles.

# SIX

There was no doubt that the approach to Swaffham Park was impressive. For a mile or two it had been apparent that the land on either side of the high road was in private hands. The rolling landscape was graced with carefully planted trees; ashes, oaks, and elms had all been positioned to add to the elegance of the gentle hills and vales; the occasional copse of conifers added a touch of darker green, almost black, contrasting strongly with the bright spring green of the fields. It was a brilliant day; the bright sunshine, occasionally veiled behind scudding clouds, helped show off the subtle differences of shape and coloring so skillfully contrived by man and nature, working, as it seemed, in perfect tandem.

Sybilla was impressed. "I cannot believe that these particular trees were planted here by accident," she said. "Somebody has plotted exactly where the trees should be in order to best set off the natural landscape. Do you remember how Papa used to talk of Capability Brown and other landscapers? How they would plant trees and shrubs to take best advantage of the lie of the land, to enhance its natural beauties? This is the first time I have ever appreciated what it was that he was trying to tell us. I had always thought that the country must be rather dull, hereabouts, with so little opportunity for bridges or other works. But it now occurs to me that as much science might go into the design of an agreeable prospect as into a bridge or a viaduct."

"Yes, the overall effect is lovely. The whole seems carefully crafted, as if someone has carefully studied the topography, and worked out exactly the shapes of the trees, their colors, how long they take to grow, and has contrived it all, yet managing to make it all look so natural."

"Are we nearly there yet? Is this it?" George, not a whit discomfited by the accident earlier in the day, interrupted his mother and aunt.

"I suppose we might be," said his mother. "I notice that the fences and hedgerows are not in the best repair and Harry used to complain bitterly that his father cared nothing for the Park, other than the hunting he could offer his debauched London friends on the few occasions they thought to refresh their jaundiced complexions with a little country air. I wonder if this is it."

Despite her high-minded feelings, she could not conceal from herself a thrill that, even if only temporarily, George was heir to all this. Her thoughts drifted off into fantasy. For so long now she had been accustomed to thinking of her own family as sole providers for George's future, that the idea of all this grandeur was, she admitted to herself, a little heady. Their whole care had been to make George think of himself as an engineer, a person whose reputation and importance would depend only on his own skills. How strange to think of him as a "gentleman of property," a person of importance, a swell who might inherit the responsibilities of title and estate, rather than having his mind stimulated by the need to prove himself as a scientist. Honoria suddenly recoiled at the idea of these foreign and unknown responsibilities being forced upon her son. It was not, after all, as if they were poor. Why should his peculiarly acute mind be distracted with these other claims upon his attention? Then she remembered the events of the previous day. Her strong feeling that there had been some purpose underlying the "accident" came increasingly to the fore.

As so often, George's insatiable need to quantify things interrupted her gloomier thoughts. They could feel the horses strain as they climbed. "What gradient do you suppose it is?" asked George. "I'm going to shut my eyes and guess, and then I shall look out and take another guess." In a trice his head was out of the window, and the shrill tones of "Mother, look! How pretty!" made both Sybilla and Honoria lean to the window as the coach topped the hill. What George had seen was a gatehouse, in pure renaissance style, set at the crest of the hill. And indeed, the coach slowed, and turned into these very gates, elegant structures of wrought iron.

"What curly geometry!" said George.

What came next was even more impressive, since the road now became completely straight. "Someone must have put the gate precisely there," thought Sybilla, "because it must be the only place from which there is a straight access to the house." And indeed, this proved to be the case. There were a few gentle ups and downs, as they generally proceeded downhill, but the road itself was as straight as a taut string, running through grassland dotted with venerable oak trees. Deer grazed on one side of the road and on the other, sheep, some in the shade, others exquisitely dappled by the fleeting sunlight.

After a mile or so, George spotted the house. By now his head was permanently stuck out of the window, but his excited descriptions of what he saw were lost on his mother and aunt as they realized that this was Swaffham Park. They each attempted to remedy somewhat the effect of the journey on their disordered hair and faces, and to prepare themselves for dealing with Ampthill.

From a distance it had become apparent that the overall character of the house was Tudor imposed on an earlier martial style. The coach passed through a narrow archway, obviously potentially fortifiable, and there drew to a halt.

"Here we are then," said Sybilla to her sister. And suddenly, "We don't have to stay, you know. This need not change us. Oh, we should have been thinking about how to make our escape instead of my running on about landscape gardening."

Honoria sighed as she silently reflected, *You, my dear sister, can always get away. I'm not sure that George can escape though. And if George has to stay, why, so must I.* Instead of saying a word, she simply gave her sister a quick, firm, warm grasp of the hand, and thus fortified, stepped out of the coach.

Lord Augustus was very plainly dressed in buff breeches, plain white shirt, and a handsome dark green leather waistcoat. "My mother is looking forward to meeting you," he said, "but I insisted you would need a minute or two to put yourselves to rights after the journey. Tabitha here will show you to your rooms and make sure you have everything you need."

A young country girl curtseyed in the background. "She will show you the way to my mother's drawing room in a quarter of an hour." Tabitha led the two sisters away.

They passed rapidly through a Grand Hall in the old style, and up a staircase to more modern rooms, two rooms side by side, looking out to the south, and with connecting doors. Tabitha left them for a moment as they smoothed down their frocks, only to reappear with a pair of young men bearing jugs of hot water, which were poured into the pretty porcelain bowls atop the washstands. "Master says y'are to have everything ye need," she said, in her homely Hampshire accent, "so if there's anything amiss, be sure to tell us. I'll be back in a moment to fetch you to the mistress."

As soon as the doors were closed behind Tabitha and her pair of young stalwarts, Sybilla hurried into her sister's room. So far, things were not too intimidating. As she crossed the threshold into Honoria's rooms, however, she suddenly realized the difference between them. She herself was only a visitor, while Honoria was on trial. Honoria was George's mother. George was, for the time being at least, heir to "all this." What would Harry's mother be like? Would she be unassuming and gently fun-loving like Harry? Would she be at all interested in the explorations of science? Or would she be a stiff, unbending old lady who assumed that all women must be ignorant in order to conserve their virtue? How would these people react to the kind of values Honoria, George, and herself had been brought up to respect?

Sybilla was determined to quell the deep sense of foreboding with an air of cheerfulness. But as she entered the room, her sister asked, "Is George with you?" The two girls looked quickly at each other. For an instant time stood still. And for the second time in their lives, they became wildly frightened about George. They burst out of the room and chased each other down the stairs in search of George.

Startled by the clatter on the stairway, Ampthill erupted from his study in time to intercept Sybilla. "What the deuce is going on?" he spluttered.

"George!" gasped Sybilla.

"Where's George?" Augustus was about to suggest that George might have gone on an exploration of his own, that given his own, albeit short, acquaintance with the young man in question he had perceived that his nephew was gifted with insatiable curiosity and skill enough to survive the effects, ill or otherwise of the same, but something in his sister-in-law's manner checked his thoughts. "Follow me," was all he said.

Mindless, Sybilla followed him as he strode rapidly across the courtyard where they had so recently alighted from their coach, through yet more narrow archways across a stable yard, open to orchards on one side, and into a huge barn from which, as they approached, came a persistent throbbing. "This is the brew house," said Ampthill, "where we make our cider and beer. I daresay the noise of the machinery attracted George, given his mechanical turn of mind. He's sure to be somewhere about here."

Honoria, who had dashed to the farther edge of the stable yard to scan the orchard, hurried up behind them, her features rigid with anxiety. Sybilla stared at the huge copper still in amazement, for she had not expected to find any such thing at a country house, and was sure that Ampthill was right about George having been unable to resist the temptation to explore. Ampthill moved into the adjoining room where there was a huge uncovered vat filled with an unsavory-smelling fermenting liquid being slowly stirred by a contraption suspended from the loft above. He looked slowly around the room and, following his gaze, Sybilla saw a rather rickety-looking ladder leading up to the loft where the machinery was lodged. Just at the top of the ladder, was George, obviously trying to work out how to move his weight from the ladder to the floor of the loft.

"What the devil!" exclaimed Ampthill. "The ladder has been moved. It should not be there at all. That part of the loft flooring is in a terrible state, repairs are to start next week. Who in God's name can have moved the ladder?" Honoria stood silently staring upward, her attitude one of frozen horror. Sybilla opened her mouth, but before she could call to her nephew, Ampthill clapped a hand over her mouth. "Be silent," he hissed at her. "If you disturb him now or make him look round, he might lose his balance."

Then as the three of them stood watching, the ladder started to sway gently but inexorably away from the wall falling backwards as George, looking now very small and vulnerable, clung on for dear life. For a moment the ladder hovered, and then with a crash fell, depositing George neatly into the huge vat below. Ampthill leapt to the side of the barn where a number of long paddle-like poles were stacked, and, clambering up the steps at the side of the vat, leaned over the edge.

"George, can you see the paddle? Grasp hold of it, George. That's right, well done. Now hold on tight." The two women watched anxiously as the earl slowly hauled George out of the foul-smelling brew. A young lad who, intrigued by their progress across the yard, had come to see what the excitement might be about and, unnoticed by Sybilla and Honoria, had witnessed George's accident, now reappeared with what looked like a horse blanket, and gave this to the earl.

"Good lad, Barnes," said Augustus, as he wrapped up the frightened little boy and handed him to his mother.

"Better get him into a hot bath," was all he said. Honoria was still speechless. Sybilla turned to Ampthill to thank him, but was startled into silence by his stern expression and the anger in his eyes.

"Go quickly," he said curtly, "your sister needs your help."

Tabitha was waiting for them at the door, accompanied by an older woman dressed in fustian with a huge ring of keys suspended from her waist.

"Tabitha, get a bath ready at once. Surely you can smell from here that the boy must have fallen into the brewing vat. Those fermenting hops are mortal cold."

She smiled at Honoria. "This way, m'lady. I can see the young lad takes after his father. He managed to fall into that vat at much the same age. Nearly drowned he did, for most of the men were attending to his late lordship's hunting party. Luckily, my Jonas was about, fetching some beer for the men against their return, and heard his cries. I am Mrs. Glover, by the way. My family and my husband's have lived and worked at Swaffham since our great grandparents' time. Tabitha is our only daughter. I started in service at the Great House when I was but a child. It was much harder then." Mrs. Glover's incessant talk succeeded in calming down the Smethwick family as she led them off.

It was thus some time before the sisters could make the acquaintance of George's grandmama. George quickly recovered after his bath, a beaker of warm spiced milk, and a piece of solidly restorative fruitcake. Ampthill had sent up glasses of Madeira wine for the girls, "to restore their spirits," said Mrs. Glover, standing over Sybilla to make sure she drank her master's offering. But once Honoria had changed, for her traveling dress was stained with hops, they were at last ready to meet the Dowager Lady Ampthill.

Tabitha led them down the stairs hung with ranks of portraits on all the walls, across the dark paneled hall, through a vast dining room, and a series of formal rooms until they came to a white paneled door. George, subdued for once, held tightly to his mother's hand. He was not at all sure how anyone living on such a scale could be a real grandmother. He had been much loved by those whom he considered his real grandparents and still missed them sorely on occasion. Dressed smartly in one of his newly acquired suits, the dark green velvet setting off his unruly auburn curls, he felt uncomfortable and unsure of himself. Tabitha knocked, opened the door and announced them.

"Lady Honoria, Miss Smethwick, and Lord George, m'lady."

She curtseyed and left. George wished he could do the same. Being a servant here looked as though it could be good fun, but he was not sure that he liked the idea of Swaffham Park as a home for himself.

The dowager's drawing room, for as such it was now known, was delightful. The walls were covered with yellow damask, against which gleamed mahogany bookshelves and a number of light paintings of Italian cities. The bow windows were prettily curtained and looked out over the rose garden to a lake beyond. In the distance, the hills rose softly and the afternoon sun made splendid patterns of light and shade. In one window stood an exquisite writing desk. The other contained a chaise longue where the room's owner was reclining, reading a slim leather-bound volume. The body of the room was elegantly furnished, with slender-legged tawny satinwood occasional tables, *bonheurs-du-jour,* and a small piano, as well as a number of small but comfortable armchairs covered in blue chintz. There were flowers everywhere.

Lady Ampthill herself was a slight figure, although somewhat thickened with age. Her toilette, in the softest of pale grays, was simple and elegant, her hair immaculately dressed. Her finely chiseled features and delicate skin suggested that she had been a beauty in her youth, and now, in her fifties, she was still undeniably handsome. Her expression, however, was languid in the extreme.

"Good afternoon," she said, extending a hand to Honoria. "Do be seated." There was barely a ghost of a welcome in her manner.

"Please bring George to me; I should like him to sit

with me here," and she pointed to a small upholstered stool beside her chaise. She examined the boy coolly through her lorgnette for what to George seemed an interminable age.

"Augustus is right, he is astonishingly like his father," she said at last. "What do you like to do best, young man?" she asked.

"Best of all I like drawing, ma'am," the boy replied solemnly.

The girls had only at the last moment thought about how George should address his new relative, and Honoria had decided on formality to begin with, but the dowager clearly had other ideas.

"You must not call me ma'am. Let us see, how did you address your late grandmother?"

"She was my beloved Grandma, but sometimes she let me call her Granny," confided George.

"Well it wouldn't do for me to have her name, but perhaps you could manage to call me Grandmama? We shall get to know each other quicker that way, I hope."

"Very well, Grandmama."

"And perhaps you might draw something for me one day soon?"

"Yes, Grandmama, that would be an honor, with all the lovely pictures you have in here. May I look at them more closely, if you please?"

Sybilla suppressed a smile. When George said drawing, he did not mean pictures of animals or people, but technical drawings for the construction of bridges or buildings. Although his hand was far from perfect, he could already produce creditable elevations for the castles and walled cities his fertile imagination dreamed up. The Italian pictures were beautifully detailed paintings of buildings, which was no doubt what had drawn George's attention.

"You may look at the pictures another day, George," replied his grandmother. "We shall examine them together. But not this afternoon. My eyes are weary with reading."

From George, she turned her attention to Honoria.

"And you, my dear, how do you prefer to amuse yourself? Do you embroider, or sketch, or sing or play?"

Despite the use of the term "my dear," there was no real interest in the dowager's inquiry. Sybilla was very pleased with her sister's reply:

"When indoors, madam, we all draw. It is a family failing, I fear. But out of doors, we tend to ride a great deal."

In fact, as well as being tolerable musicians, both sisters were accomplished horsewomen. Their father had insisted. With a sense of loss, Sybilla remembered his endless urging that they should be able to manage all sorts of mounts. "If ye want to build a bridge where no one has ever dreamed it possible to build before, you must be free to inspect and verify every inch of the terrain. And while it's always possible to walk up hill and down dale, it's a lot more comfortable to do so on the back of a four-legged beast than on shank's pony." So the two girls, and later George, had been trained to sit in comfortable control on every kind of beast that could be found in England. One of their father's few disappointments in Harry had been that he had never managed to ride a camel. "Mark my words," he used to say, "there will be call for roads and bridges and viaducts and aqueducts in places where up 'til now the only transport has been by camel. It is an engineer's duty to understand the needs of every kind of transport that might be using his roads."

"And you, miss?" To her horror, Sybilla found the dowager's attention, dilatory though it might be, had now passed to herself.

"Other than riding and drawing, madam, I have few accomplishments."

She hoped that her elder sister would refrain from mentioning her skills at the piano. Although she longed to turn her hand to the little satinwood instrument across the room, she had no wish to play for Harry's mother. And in fact she was spared further inquiry.

"I myself spend a good deal of time reading," said the dowager. "I am very fond of Pope and Dryden. Do any of you read poetry at all?"

Faced with the difficulty of admitting that they preferred the younger, less respectable poets such as Byron, the two girls preferred to claim fair ignorance of poetry. "We shall meet at dinner, no doubt," said their hostess abruptly. It was a dismissal. The interview was at an end.

They found Tabitha awaiting them outside the door.

"We keep London hours here at Swaffham," she told them. "The master wondered if you might care for me to show you into the gardens at all. Although he hopes to be allowed the privilege of showing you round the Park himself, tomorrow."

"His lordship is most kind," said Honoria, "but I think that just now my sister and I should best like to sit quietly in our rooms until dinner." And so the two women withdrew with George.

Sitting quietly was not altogether what they had in mind, however. They both needed the opportunity to discuss their situation at Swaffham Park, the two accidents that had befallen George in so short a time, and what they might do next. Both felt in need of some moments of shared privacy and each was wondering how they might be able to talk things over without George interfering and listening. They need not have worried. The boy's room opened onto his mother's on the far side from Sybilla's;

it was furnished with a large writing table and there George hurried.

"I am going to start on my drawing for Grandmama," he announced. "She was better than I had feared, and not so old. I shall do my best to like her."

He quickly settled to his drawing and his mother closed the connecting doors firmly as the two sisters retreated to Sybilla's room for their discussion.

"He's right, you know," observed Sybilla. "The dowager is not as old as I expected." They settled themselves in two chairs side by side looking out over the same prospect as the dowager's drawing room.

"She was married to the late earl when only nineteen," explained Honoria. "He was very much older than she was, and I believe she has led rather a retired life down here for many years. Harry did not speak much about his parents, we had so little time." She paused sadly, as she thought really how little she had discovered about Harry's short life. And of course, what with school and his army training he had been home relatively little.

"I gained the impression that she was not happy with her husband's style of life in London, and after the very early years, once Harry was born, she spent most of her time here. I think she tried to avoid rather than seek the company of her husband."

"But she must read something besides Dryden and Pope surely," said Sybilla. "I found her very cool toward us. I suppose she thinks we are beneath her."

"But she was pleasant enough to Georgie," pointed out Honoria. "I understand her life has been rather lonely and sad. I think we should wait until we know more of her before passing judgment."

"The light is so beautiful on the hills," said Sybilla. "I wish we could just relax and enjoy the scenery, without the strain of having to be among such strangers and . . ."

"And without George getting into trouble all the time. What do you think Ampthill meant? 'That someone must have moved the ladder?' Oh, Sybilla, the first accident looked like more than pure chance, and now this! Am I imagining things? I don't believe I am in the habit of being an anxious mother, but then nothing untoward has ever happened to George before, except the usual things like falling out of Papa's favorite apple tree."

This had happened the previous autumn, and both girls were for once relieved that their father was no longer with them, since George had managed to break off a branch of the very choicest pippins as he tried to break his fall. Their dear papa would have been more than somewhat exercised to maintain his usual tolerance of his beloved grandson's escapades.

"To be honest, I didn't want to alarm you, but I have been wondering too. I don't suppose you saw Lord Augustus's face in the barn this afternoon. You had just been given Georgie, and were busy with him, but when I tried to thank Ampthill, the words just died in my throat. I have never seen a man look so angry. My first thought was that he was angry with us or with George, but I've been thinking about it, and I cannot believe it. Everything he has said to us has been full of compliment about the little rascal's abilities, his openness, and above all about how like Harry he is. I suspect that he may turn into a very fond and indulgent uncle.

"Besides," continued Sybilla, "Mrs. Glover said that Harry had got himself into a similar pickle, so there was no real call to be so very angry with George. I cannot begin to describe how stern and furious he looked. I was quite frightened. I have noticed him look cold and arrogant or displeased, especially when Carey Swaffham says something indiscreet, but this was quite different. There was a look of anxiety as well as anger, and he was so stern. And we have yet to tell him of the earlier accident."

"We do not need to tell him ourselves," said Honoria. "While we were giving George his bath, Mrs. Glover told me that she had had already heard about it from Brockley almost as soon as we arrived. The earl had been questioning the poor fellow about the incident just as we felt the absence of young George and set off headlong to search for him." She paused fretfully. "From what you say about his strange expression, perhaps, like us, he also feels that two accidents coming so close are overly coincidental. Oh, Sybilla, what can it all mean? I do so hate to think that I might have to worry all the time about George. After all, he is only the heir for the time being. Ampthill is far too grand a prize to be left single for long. Doubtless within a year, some great heiress will ensnare him and between them they will secure the inheritance with a whole gaggle of children and George and I shall be returned to relative obscurity and left to pursue our own lives as before. At least, so I earnestly hope. George is no real threat to anyone; why should these horrid accidents suddenly start to befall him?"

The two sisters spent the next half hour reviewing the tiniest details of everything about the two accidents. No stone was left unturned in their anxiety to uncover and recall the precise sequence of events on each occasion. Eventually their thoughts turned to more trivial things such as the choice of gown for dinner, what George might be given for his supper. And indeed, as if by clockwork, as soon as his mother's thoughts turned to her son's supper, there he was, coming through the door.

"Here is a rough sketch, Mama. I thought I would draw the lady an impregnable castle, but what do you think of the keep? Do you not think it is a touch too high?"

Mother and son left Sybilla to change for dinner, and

as she opened her closet she could hear her nephew's piercing voice expounding the reasons for this particular castle's resistance to all manner of siege.

While she completed her toilette, Sybilla continued to ponder the situation. Presumably Ampthill would soon leave them for London, and she wondered how they would pass the time with the poetry-reading dowager. She hoped that they would be able to ride. For if they were to be cooped up indoors, Sybilla felt unable to trust to her own temper. First of all, of course, they needed reassurance about George's safety. Swaffham Park might be a source of great pleasure to him if he were allowed a certain amount of liberty, at least within the immediate precincts of the house and its many dependencies, but if it turned out that he was to be restricted in any way, then he too would become impatient and restive. Of course, he would need to have his lessons.

Once dressed and groomed to her satisfaction, Sybilla allowed herself the pleasure of contemplating the view in the delicate evening light. She had a better view of the lake than from the dowager's windows, and wondered about the source of the water. Little had been done to the acres spreading from the lake to the hills. Perhaps, if their stay here was to be prolonged, she might indulge in some attempts at improving the prospect and the landscape. The impertinence of the idea surprised her. After all, this was not her house, she had no rights here, and she resolved to keep any ideas she might have for improvements strictly to herself.

Thus determined, she crossed her sister's room to find Honoria sitting with George while he finished his supper of coddled eggs and yet more fruitcake.

"They brought me rice pudding at first," he told his aunt, "but then Mrs. Glover came in, and I told her how delicious the fruitcake had been, and it turns out that she has taught the cook to make it from a receipt of her own grandma's invention and she was so pleased that I like it that she took away the pudding and brought me this piece herself. Was that not kind?"

"Very kind, dumpling," said the boy's mother, "but you must to bed, and we must go down to dine. Shall I tell your grandmama that you have begun her drawing?"

"You may tell her it is begun, but don't tell her what it is. I wish to surprise her."

"I daresay you may be sure of that," laughed Sybilla.

And at that moment was a knock on the door, which opened to reveal Tabitha.

"Lord Augustus attends upon you in the library," she said, "and I am sent to bring you there and then I'm to come right back here to put Lord George to bed."

Goodnight kisses were administered to George, and promises exacted from him that he would do exactly as he was told by Tabitha in the matter of ablutions before going to bed and straight to sleep. But sufficient yawns had been interspersed with the consumption of Mrs. Glover's grandma's fruitcake to assure his mother that he would soon be fast and peacefully asleep.

"And, Tabitha, please leave the door to his room just the tiniest bit ajar, and that lamp by my bedside alight. It is his first night here after all, and I wish him to know that my first care is still of him."

# SEVEN

As the sisters entered the library, Ampthill was struck, yet again, by how lovely they looked together. The soft violets and blues of their dresses seemed chosen, like their different coloring, to set each other off. But what impressed him yet more was the sense of their togetherness as they entered the room. They were not two wholly separate individuals, but somehow deeply united. It reminded him, yet again, of his own closeness to Harry.

Never before had it occurred to him that sisterhood might confer that same special closeness that he had shared with his brother. He realized too, that it was Sybilla who was trying to protect her elder sister in the same way that he had been used to try to protect Harry when together they had faced uncomfortable interviews with their father in this very room.

"I apologize for asking you to come here before we go in to my mother," he said, "but I feel I must give some explanation to Miss Smethwick for my discourtesy after young George's mishap this afternoon. Just before you came downstairs, Brockley was telling me about the incident at the inn. I am afraid a second mishap occurring so fast upon the heels of the first caused me no little concern. It seems that you need some assistance in caring for the young man."

"Lord Ampthill," Sybilla's tone was outraged, "it is

only since he has been connected with you that any sort of mishap has occurred."

There was an uncomfortable silence. Sybilla cursed her impetuosity: this was precisely the sort of thing she had been determined not to say. Mercifully they were saved by a discreet tap at the door, and Carstairs appeared.

"Mr. Swaffham has just arrived, m'lord. He begs not to delay dinner and that he will come in after the soup."

This time it was Honoria who was surprised by the look of anger that crossed Ampthill's face. But his voice was totally controlled when he spoke.

"Be so good as to tell him to make haste, Carstairs. If he can be ready in twenty minutes, he need not miss the soup. I assume you have shown him to his usual rooms?"

As Carstairs left, Lord Augustus longed to take at least Sybilla into his confidence. His dislike of and contempt for his cousin was, he felt sure, more than apparent; how he longed to explain it. Carey had managed to ingratiate himself with his mother. He was an unprincipled hypocrite and while in London he had urged on the previous earl in all his excesses, whereas at Swaffham he never failed to deplore them. Indeed, much of this deploring had consisted in giving her ladyship quite needlessly detailed and distressing accounts of what went on in London.

Carey had no taste for the out of doors, and when the late earl's London friends had set out through the early morning mists to shoot their bag of pheasant or duck, Carey would sit "entertaining" Lady Evelyn with carefully amended tales of the late earl's London carryings on. In every story, Carey was the one who urged constraint and discretion upon his uncle. Additionally, Carey was well-read. He indulged Lady Evelyn's passion for poetry, and would sigh endlessly at her side as she read out her rather pallid imitations of Dryden and Pope. He knew exactly how best to insinuate the most tactful improvements "into your already impeccable lines." On his return from India, Augustus had been rather shocked at his mother's tolerance and affection for his disreputable cousin.

"But Augustus, I could not prevent you from going to India, any more than I could willingly have stopped Harry from pursuing his chosen career," his mother had said. "During all these years of neglect, Carey has been my one constant friend."

While Augustus could not help condemning his mother's lack of judgment in trusting the bounder, he could not find it in his heart to blame her.

Carey's mother had died in childbirth, and his father followed her to the grave not long after, although not as a result of his grief. While hunting in Northamptonshire, he fell from his horse into a half frozen stream, leading him to contract pneumonia. Carey, then aged two, had been brought to Swaffham Park. Augustus's father, nearly thirty when the boy arrived, developed considerable fondness for the orphan, made sure he was sent to the best schools (he was asked to leave first Eton and later Rugby), and in general brought him up to become his young soul mate. After Carey was dismissed from Rugby at the age of seventeen, he followed no further formal course of education but remained at Swaffham as the earl's companion.

His friendship with Countess Evelyn dated from his school days. As a young bride she had been kind to the orphaned lad who returned from the summer half at Eton. As a fifteen-year-old he had admired her extravagantly. By the time he was nineteen and she in her mid-twenties, she began to feel the sorrow of her husband's neglect. Carey was still romantic enough to decide that he was infatuated with her, and as the years passed he gradually came to realize that the romantic attachment of his youth had its usefulness. It was far more pleasant to sit warmly indoors flirting with his aunt than risk his neck out hunting or shooting, and her friendship ensured his welcome at Swaffham Park, rather than merely being one more of his uncle's tedious acquaintances. Indeed, it would be fair to say that what little there was in Carey's character that was refined had been placed there by the days spent in company with his aunt.

"Let us go in to my mother," said Ampthill. "She will be expecting us. But I think it might be wiser not to speak of George's two accidents in front of my cousin. My mother was amused to hear that he had replicated Harry's feat of falling into the vat of hops and may bring it up, but she knows nothing of what occurred yesterday. I should be grateful if you would make no mention of it. Carey has a careless tongue, and the two events occurring so closely upon one another are just the sort of matter he could easily turn into the subject of light-hearted gossip in London."

The seriousness of his tone surprised Sybilla. It was clear that Ampthill was worried about his nephew and temporary heir's well-being. She prayed that Honoria might not be further alarmed, and resolved to find some opportunity to pursue the matter on the morrow. If Ampthill thought that something might be amiss then here indeed was serious ground for concern.

Lady Evelyn was magnificently attired. She wore an exquisite emerald green silk gown, albeit not of the latest fashion, that set off perfectly her fair complexion and gently graying hair. Rather than reclining on her chaise lounge, she was sitting bolt upright in what was obviously the senior chair in her drawing room.

"Augustus, is it true? I understand that Carey, the

scamp, has just arrived. Does he propose that we wait dinner for him?"

"I believe that he will be among us in some fifteen minutes. Perhaps you would enjoy a glass of Madeira while we wait? I do not believe he will detain us for much beyond our usual time. I see that you are wearing your favorite costume."

"Indeed I am. I wondered how to celebrate George being recovered to us, and it seemed to me a fitting occasion to dig out this old thing, which your brother admired so."

What with glasses of wine being handed around, explanations about how Harry had loved to see his mother arrayed in this particular dress, and general chatter, the next fifteen minutes passed quickly enough, until Carey appeared. After greeting his aunt effusively, he next turned his attentions to Honoria.

"Good evening, dear Cousin Honoria. I trust young George is recovered from his accidents."

"You mean repeating his father's skill in locating the vat of hops?" asked the dowager.

There was an almost imperceptible silence. Was it possible that after only twenty minutes indoors Carey should have managed to inform himself of the accident at Farnham? Carey was also taken aback as he realized that Lady Evelyn might not have been apprised of the earlier incident.

"Why of course, my dear aunt, what else should I mean?"

"But you said accidents," said Lady Evelyn. "Has anything else happened?"

"Of course not, Mother," said Ampthill, glaring at Carey. "And I understand the lad was sufficiently recovered to have persuaded Mrs. Glover to have given him fruitcake instead of rice pudding for his supper."

"I should hope so too," boomed Carey. "Mrs. Glover's fruitcake is famous in London as the best to be had. If she had a mind to it she could retire from Swaffham and spend her days supervising its production for Mr. Fortnum who would dearly love to add such a delicacy to his wares."

"Carey, I hope you will not mention such an idea to her. We could not manage here without her and Jonas."

At this point Carstairs appeared to announce dinner, and somewhat to Honoria and Sybilla's relief they passed into a small dining parlor rather than the large formal dining room they had seen earlier in the day. The meal went on agreeably enough, with Carey booming on to his aunt about the poetry books he had brought her. To give him his due, he was honest enough about the selection: "Only what m'bookseller recommends, dear lady."

Augustus meanwhile, entertained Honoria and Sybilla with the business of the estate or, to be more particular, the improvements he wished to bring into effect. He described his desire to improve the prospect from the south-facing windows, and his progress so far in diverting the stream of the insignificant tributary of the River Arun that flowed through his property. The two girls were quite happy in hearing all this, and Sybilla especially so since she had herself felt the lack of some detail between the lake and the hills to make the view perfect. Their somewhat technical conversation was, however, rudely interrupted by Carey.

"Augustus, my dear fellow, when are we to expect you back in London? That evening at Ampthill House excited the whole town. All the heiresses of London are preening themselves in the expectation of your early return."

"I may yet disappoint them, then," laughed Ampthill. "I find there are many things here to amuse and entertain me. You Londoners forget that I have been away for twelve years. There will be plenty to occupy me at Swaffham for the foreseeable future. It was never my intention to spend the whole Season in town. Furthermore, I wish properly to renew my acquaintance with the person who above all should be dear." At these words he bowed gently toward his mother. "With such fair guests to entertain, I propose to omit the London Season entirely until next year at the very earliest."

Honoria and Sybilla exchanged a meaningful glance. Their previous understanding had been that Lord Augustus would accompany them to Swaffham Park, would make sure that they were sufficiently acquainted with its conventions, and then return to London in order to get on with his most pressing commitment, namely, to provide himself with a wife and thereby a means to a proper heir, rather than with the makeshift young scapegrace personified by little George. This was the first intelligence they had received that he might be their everyday companion for a number of weeks.

"In that case, my dear," interposed the countess, "we had better have a gathering here. If you have determined to accept these young people as our relations, then the sooner they are introduced the better. They appear very nice young ladies to me but we should leave the county in no doubt."

Sybilla was appalled by hearing herself and her sister discussed in such a condescending way, but Honoria caught her eye pleadingly and she held her tongue.

"I am sorry, my dears," continued Lady Evelyn, turning to Honoria, "but I think we have all taken to the two of you and to George. I am afraid we must display you to our neighbors."

"Lady Evelyn," said Honoria, "while I am deeply sensible of your regard and sincerely look forward to meeting your friends and acquaintance in the county, you will recall that until a few weeks ago we had had no word from any of your family. I have brought up my son knowing only that his father died honorably at Badajoz. Of course we are pleased that so far you like us, and honored that you might consider us relations, but until a fortnight ago, my sister and I were counting on an extended tour of the Continental countries. We therefore hope not to impose too long upon your hospitality and to resume our plans before the summer heat makes Spain unpleasant. We must be on our way early in the month if we are to reach Italy before the winter."

"Yes, Augustus did mention something of that sort, but it seems rather fatiguing. I was hoping that you would be here at least until my birthday, which falls on the twenty-ninth of May. It has been many years since we have had a family celebration. But I suppose that is too much presumption on such a short acquaintance."

As she spoke, her previously animated expression faded into one of complete resignation. Honoria found herself wondering how often the unfortunate wife of the late earl must have had to renounce similar occasions of straightforward family pleasure.

Sybilla's thoughts were rather less sympathetic. *They want to take Georgie over and make him one of their own,* she said to herself, *and Lady Evelyn will try to take advantage of every sentimental opportunity to try to have her own way.* Her thoughts were interrupted by Carey's reaction to the news of their tour.

"What? Set off gallivantin' to Spain, of all places, when you are all just admitted into one of the best families in this part of the country! Ha ha! That indeed will set the London tongues a-wagging! Especially if Augustus insists on moldering down here in the country when every heiress in London is longing to make an impression. It will be taken as an insult, m'dears, unless Augustus attends every party of the Season; if he fails to make his appearance, he will be thought to be sulking."

Sybilla remembered Ampthill's warning about Carey's tendency to gossip, and realized that it had probably been a mistake for Honoria to bring up the topic of their tour. For once in her life, she felt conciliatory.

"It is true that we had intended to travel, but today is a little too soon to decide what our future plans might be. The change in our fortunes has happened so suddenly. I am sure in the next week or so, as we begin to know Lady Evelyn better, as I most sincerely hope we shall, our plans will become clear."

"Besides," added Honoria, "Lady Evelyn must be given every chance to take her rightful place alongside my dear mama as one of George's doting grandmamas."

Honoria was rewarded for this pretty speech by a smile from Lady Evelyn.

Ampthill was somewhat surprised at the sisters' quickness in discovering for themselves that anything said before Carey was likely to be, at best, repeated or, more probably, maliciously distorted in London. It seemed that they had instantly decided, as one, that neither would utter anything that could not safely be gossiped about. Carey had started to press Sybilla about the cities and monuments they intended to visit. But she refused to be drawn.

"Why, cousin, since we shall certainly have to modify our proposed itinerary, the old one can have no significance. I have no idea where we shall go, and to say we intend to go to Florence and Pisa when we might in the end see only Rome and Venice would terribly mislead you."

To disguise the implied rebuke, she added, "Once our routes and destinations are known, we shall be sure to tell you all about our plans."

The remainder of the meal passed quietly. Carey regaled his aunt with all sorts of tidbits of London gossip, especially those relating to their various acquaintance in the county. Honoria observed that Lady Evelyn showed relatively little interest in his tales. Ampthill resumed the subject of his improvements, and begged the honor of the sisters accompanying him on a promenade round the nearer parts of the grounds in the morning, hoping they would be kind enough to indulge him by inspecting the site of his proposed works.

At the meal's conclusion, the two girls pleaded exhaustion and withdrew as soon as they decently could. But they agreed to meet again in Sybilla's room once in their night attire. As she tiptoed about her room (for the door between her room and George's was still ajar), Honoria feared that her sister might accuse her of capitulating to her mother-in-law's wiles, and indeed, this was the first subject that engaged them.

"You're going to agree to stay here until the end of May, I can tell," said Sybilla as her sister entered the room. "You're beginning to feel sorry for Harry's mother, despite how cold she is. And the condescension! 'Very nice young ladies,' indeed!"

"Oh, Sybilla. Did you not see the look on her face as I said we wanted to get off early in May? It was as if something had been opening up inside her, and when I said we wanted to keep as close as possible to our plans, why, if I had slammed a prison door in her face, she could not have looked more resigned."

"I wonder if you are right; that she really has had so little of normal family intercourse that she is to be pitied! It is so hard when one remembers the affectionate honesty of our parents' home to imagine what sorrows all this grandeur might bring. But we shall have weeks in which to study the dowager. Did you hear what Mr. Swaffham said when he came in?"

"Of course I did; after all, he said it to me. He asked

about George's accidents. I felt quite a chill. It is most natural for Lord Augustus to question his most trusted servant, whom he had sent to accompany us, about the circumstances and events of our journey, but since Brockley is very much Ampthill's man, I exceedingly doubt that he would have mentioned yesterday's incident to Mr. Swaffham. Also, you will recall Lord Augustus particularly required us to make no mention of the matter."

"Then how did he know about the curricle? He quickly realized that the dowager knew nothing about it and that we were determined to say nothing."

"Did you not see the look Ampthill gave him?" said Honoria, smiling at the memory.

"Oh, indeed, it was enough to silence the last trump!" Sybilla paused. "So he must have known from somebody else. Honoria, what exactly is Mr. Swaffham's relationship to your brother-in-law? Their grandfathers were brothers, were they not? Ampthill's father was an only son, so at the moment, George is Ampthill's heir. You and I have never given this much importance, since we have assumed that the eligible Ampthill will find himself a wife and heir of his own in a year or two. But, after the death of Harry, and while Ampthill was in India, Swaffham may well have come to think of himself as next in line."

"Oh, Sybbie, Carey Swaffham is just a professional bachelor and man about town. Surely you don't wish to imply . . ."

"Dear Honoria," Sybilla was quick to try to reassure her sister, "no, of course I do not wish to imply anything, but nonetheless, it is very odd that he should know that more than one accident had befallen George in the space of two days."

"Perhaps he did not know," said Honoria, trying to temporize. "Perhaps it was a slip of the tongue."

"I do not believe that the gentleman is so prone to slips of the tongue."

"No, you are right. He is a most disagreeable gossip. One can say nothing before him. If Lady Evelyn had not called us 'nice young ladies' I should have been more guarded and thought twice about mentioning our proposed tour."

"But his reaction served to remind us how dangerous a friend he might be."

"Indeed it did, and if he is so dangerous a friend, how much more dangerous might he be as an enemy." Honoria sighed. "But I sincerely hope he is not so ruthless an enemy as you imply."

"I'm not implying anything, Honoria, but it is very clear that we must be most strenuously on guard whenever Mr. Swaffham is near us."

"And even when, apparently, he is not, I suppose. After all, no one got a glimpse of the driver of the curricle, he was so completely muffled up. And no one at the inn recalled how long it had been there, nor anything else about it or its driver."

"Honoria," said Sybilla sternly, "either you are deliberately teasing me, or you are just as bad as I am. You cannot wish to imply that Carey himself was the driver of that vehicle."

"Not for the world," replied the elder of the two girls. "I cannot imagine Mr. Swaffham being half so energetic. But to be serious, my dear sister, we cannot pretend to believe that the gentle aristocracy of England is so violent. You'll have me convinced that we are walking characters from Mrs. Randolph and quite give me the vapors if we continue this late night discussion any longer. I agree with you entirely insofar as Carey Swaffham will always do his best to give trouble, but I cannot believe his frustrations are so great as to make him take active steps to do away with little George. And now I must to bed. George will no doubt be up with the sun, which rises earlier than I should like, and while you lie abed dreaming of Cousin Swaffham's villainy, I shall probably be called upon to express my views on impregnability before the cock has crowed twice, let alone three times."

The sisters embraced and said goodnight.

Sybilla tossed and turned for some time. At first she fretted that she might have alarmed her sister unduly, but reflecting on their conversation, decided that nothing that could have been said would have worsened any alarm she might feel. Indeed her laughing reference to the Gothic horrors so gruesomely purveyed by Mrs. Randolph and her colleagues, showed that Honoria's common sense would not allow her to worry overmuch about her son.

Sybilla's thoughts next turned to Ampthill himself, and she wondered about his many motives: first, in insisting that they attend his ball; second, rather than expediting their departure on tour after that *débâcle,* that he should have decided that their retiring to Swaffham Park was the best way of helping London forget the fuss; third, that apparently, after having inaugurated a London Season, he should have decided to renounce it. Her earlier instincts had been to reject him in body, person, and character as an unwanted intrusion into their lives. But, not entirely to her contentment, she had to admit that his behavior toward Honoria, George, and even herself had been gracious and magnanimous.

It occurred to her that he, no less than themselves, was encumbered with the need to find his way in a world utterly different from that in which he had been living for the last twelve years. Her life and Honoria's had been changed most dramatically in the last nine years. First,

Honoria's marriage to Harry, their friend and engineering companion, who had only owned up, almost apologetically, to his aristocratic lineage when he asked Mr. Smethwick for Honoria's hand in marriage. Then, their excited discovery of Honoria's state, so swiftly followed by the news of Harry's death. Then George's birth. And now their parents' death, so soon one upon the other.

Sybilla still found it difficult to come to terms with her father's death. Mothers die, as surely as they give birth. But she had always considered her father to be so special a person. Tears came to her eyes, as they always did when she thought of him, and she forced herself to think again of Ampthill, to try to imagine what he must have felt when his father died. In so doing she was suddenly aghast. Ampthill had fled his father while he was still alive. He had gone away to India to escape his father. This was such an entirely different way of life from her own.

Nonetheless, it struck Sybilla with a sudden flash of empathy that poor Ampthill, who had hitherto been living an independent life of business so far away from his family, must, surely, be finding his first months in England as disconcerting as Honoria and she had found the year and a half since their own beloved parents' deaths. Even Sybilla had to own that his desire to seek out his nephew, and moreover his consideration to her sister, and by extension to herself, were exemplary.

While she might tease her elder sister about her sympathy for Lady Evelyn, who after all was not entirely to be trusted, given her apparent friendship with Carey Swaffham, she appreciated that Honoria's main motive must be the interests of George. To be the Earl of Swaffham's acknowledged nephew would no doubt help him in his career. It was obvious that both mother and son had been most touchingly reminded of Harry when they first saw the little boy. But at last she forgot about the Swaffhams, and her last thoughts as she sank into sleep were keen anticipation at reviewing the site of "the improvements" the next day.

# EIGHT

Breakfast was not taken in the rather gloomy formal dining room at Swaffham, but in a charming parlor facing the east, overlooking the gardens and catching the best of the morning light. This morning, the French windows were thrown open onto the terrace and a parlor maid was in attendance. Sybilla came down late, to find Honoria and George well ensconced, Ampthill long in his study with his bailiff, and neither the countess nor Carey yet risen.

"You should have wakened me!" she exclaimed as she seated herself beside her nephew and reached for ham.

"We tried, but you were fast asleep and Mama said I shouldn't disturb you."

"What time was that?"

"A little after six, I believe. I allowed George to peer round the door into your chamber to prove that you would indeed be enjoying your rest. This scientific experiment established that you were not ready to assist in his drawing for Lady Evelyn. We practiced our Spanish instead."

"I can say 'Your money or your life' now, which I think will be very useful when we meet bandits. It will put the fear of G—"

"George! The wrath of someone far closer than the

Lord will be visited on you if you run on so," Honoria snapped.

Sybilla intervened. "You know you mustn't take the Lord's name in vain, Georgie, even if dear Grandpapa had no such hesitation. After breakfast, you shall show me your drawing and we shall see where it needs improvement. Mama will then have time to catch up with her own correspondence. Are we agreed?"

These plans were disrupted by the earl's arrival in the breakfast room. Although he was wearing nothing out of the way, Sybilla could not help noticing that his coat needed no padding to achieve the correct silhouette, and that his buckskin breeches appeared skin-tight. He also wore Hessian boots buffed to a high sheen. George was less reticent.

"You look much better in the country, Uncle Augustus!"

"Better than what, sprig?"

"Than you did in town. People look silly in London; they are able to do nothing, because they wear such foolish things. You looked quite starchy. But here you look bang up to the mark. I wish I had Hessian boots. May I have some, Mama, for traveling in? I should wear them every day so there would be no need to take any additional shoes for me. It would save space."

"George, quiet. Perhaps Lord Augustus has some urgent message for us."

"Nothing urgent at all, I assure you, but a request. Well, two. First, Lady Honoria, Miss Smethwick, could you bear to call me Augustus? Lord Augustus is a terrible mouthful. George may call me Uncle Gus. And secondly, I was wondering whether you would be up to taking a tour of the grounds. I could show you our planned site for the cascade. But perhaps you have other occupation in mind for the morning."

"We would be delighted," replied Sybilla, although to add "Augustus" was beyond her. It seemed the height of familiarity, a height she was not yet ready to scale, though Honoria might well be able to.

"I shall only call you Augustus if you stop calling me Lady Honoria. I have never used the title. It doesn't seem mine, somehow."

"Very well, Honoria. We are brother and sister after all. And so I must be brother to Miss Smethwick also."

"You are right, we should be on family terms. For George. So you must call me Sybilla."

Ampthill's conciliatory manner brought down any remaining barriers on the sisters' part towards their host. It was next to impossible to be formal with someone so intent on being charming. Once pelisses and stout shoes had been brought to the breakfast parlor and donned in haste, he escorted his nephew and fair guests onto the terrace and commenced the tour by a turn around the knot garden, where roses and box hedge neatly formed an intricate series of walkways.

"Here, I am planning to install a simple fountain. But I was wondering whether it would be better to connect all the waterworks in some way."

"Install a circuit of some sort?" queried Sybilla, immediately engaged.

"Yes, I suppose so, though I know little of such things."

"I believe there are such circuits at the Alhambra in Granada," mentioned Honoria. "Perhaps we should try to go there during our stay in Spain. Although I believe it is some way from Badajoz."

"With a competent courier, it may be possible to arrange matters so that you go to both places. But let me lead you into our park."

Ampthill set a brisk pace away from the house over a swath of lawn. The air was fresh and crisp, the sky a glo-

rious azure. To the east lay a series of hills, but the vista
to the west opened out over a substantial ornamental lake
and then onto the country beyond. The party proceeded
at high speed up the first hill toward a copse of horse
chestnuts although it was not sufficiently swift to prohibit
George or the ladies from bombarding the earl with questions, some of which he could answer, many of which
he had to admit he did not know the answers.

"I should have asked my steward to accompany us.
Causeley was raised here, and is the greatest authority on
the country roundabouts that I know. You must remember, I have only been back a few months. The boat
docked in January."

"But you were raised here," exclaimed Sybilla.
"Surely, as a boy you learnt all sorts of things about the
soil and the wildlife."

Ampthill's features shuttered over. "Both Harry and I
spent little time here. We were sent to school early."

"I don't want to go to school. Reverend Hardisty told
me all about it. He was beaten and had to learn strings
and strings of useless things. The only interesting thing
he ever learnt was about Hannibal and the Pumice Wars."

"Punic, I think you mean. But otherwise, you are quite
right. I have never worked out the value of memorizing
the speeches of Cicero to the Senate. Yet that is what we
had to know. And a caning followed if you could not re-
cite your lines promptly."

"It sounds utterly barbaric. And wasteful. Guaranteed
to inhibit an inquiring turn of mind. You need not fear any
such fate, George. It would be the last thing that Papa
would have wanted for you. Or Harry, come to that."

"I am glad to hear you say so, Honoria. But I hope that
I may be able to provide an alternative center of learning for our young charge."

"How so, Augustus?"

"Here," he continued, with a sweep of his arm, "is the site for my laboratory." The stretch of rough land was tucked behind a low ridge of hills, out of view of the house itself. Nearby was a pond with a stream trickling in from the hills above and draining out in the direction of the big lake at the rear of the main house. A substantial wall marked the limits of the grounds to the east, but it had several gates along it. Ampthill expanded on his plans.

"I want this to be a place of learning and advancement. There are cottages in the village where those with families can live, and I am planning to convert one of the stables into quarters for the single men. Then here, we shall have the working area. Each one shall have a study, and then there will be a vast workshop where experiments can be performed. Perhaps two. In the living quarters, there will be a dining room and a common room, where all can repair and discuss the day's work. I want it to be a real community, a place where everyone works together. With plenty of stimulating minds ready to encourage young George."

"This is a wonderful plan, Augustus. But how closely have you worked with scientific people?" queried Honoria.

"Several times in India. There were engineers, working on roads and bridges to open up the interior. Then there were dye masters, and the experts in tea and spices. All sorts of people."

"Did you see them working together?" asked Sybilla.

"Not together, no, for they were all working on different projects."

"Men of science are like men of any other stamp, you know, Augustus," she commented. "They are proud and possessive of their knowledge, reluctant to share, and prone to as many follies as the fine bucks that grace London's salons. I do not mean to drench your dreams in a shower of cold water, but you will need someone sensible in charge of the research. Someone who can soothe temperamental freaks and smooth ruffled feathers."

Honoria was distracted by George who had decided that all this adult talk was dull and it would be much better to see what velocity he could achieve if he rolled down the slope towards the pond. With a yell, he plummeted down the hillside, followed by his irate mother, despairing at the state his clothes would be in by the end of this experiment.

"You do not mince your words, my dear Miss Smethwick."

"I thought we were to be on family terms."

"Of course. Sybilla."

"It is not that we do not admire your project. We do. If only there were more like you, prepared to be benefactors in the most generous manner. But my father tried in a much smaller way to provide a similar environment and it brought him a great deal of botheration, in measure equal to, if not greater than, the rewards. He was forever arbitrating between unreasonable individuals and having to refuse further funds to those who could not admit that their researches would proceed nowhere. Sometimes it interfered with his own work quite intolerably."

"Ah, but that is where I have the advantage. I have no work of my own, and while I may be a layman, I have experience in organizing my fellow men. You must give my time in India some credit."

"You are quite right, and you must think me inexcusably rude for dousing your plans with the chill blast of my father's experience without taking into account your own."

"That is a handsome apology, indeed."

"It is only the first of the apologies I should be making to you. I sank us all into the most abominable of scrapes and I am bitterly ashamed." Sybilla swallowed before continuing. "Now, instead of not recognizing us as you had every right to do, you have taken us into your home. It is very generous in you."

Ampthill took her hand, and she looked up. Her eyes shimmered with unshed tears, and as she gazed into his warm, unwavering eyes, a tear slipped down her cheek.

"It is no crying matter. You were offered the most intolerable of insults, in part because we Swaffhams chose to pretend that your sister and her son did not exist. You are here as some small reparation for the neglect that my family has shown yours since Harry's departure for the Peninsula."

"Cousin! Cousin!" came a halloo from beyond the crest of the hill. "Or should I say cousins," panted Carey Swaffham, rounding the crest of the hill. "Am I too late to join your stroll? Do say I am not. But what a deuce of a way you have come. I nearly did not bother to follow, but then I thought, what a glorious morning, what a chance to see the Park utterly at its best." He finally stopped to lean heavily on his cane, which sank gently into the moist ground.

"Indeed, Mr. Swaffham, the blossom is quite wonderful, much more advanced than at our home in Stourbridge. Why, we have gone into May without such a show on the cherries."

"Oh, do you have trees in the Midlands? How unexpected. I thought it was only chimney stacks and manufactories. Of course, if Ampthill has his way, we shall see all these fine trees gone, removed in the name of progress so that he may bring such monstrosities here to this sylvan idyll."

"You exaggerate, Carey. There are two older trees that must be brought down in any case, for the one is near dead from age and the other from disease. If we are not to lose all the elms in the Park, the two must go."

"I'm sure since you have made such a study of the trees in the Park since your return from the East, that it must be so. But, do tell me, what is Lady Honoria doing? Is that Lord George with her? He was abed by the time I joined you."

Mother and son were crouched over something on the ground, examining it intently, some hundred yards or so away from Lord Augustus and his cousin.

"It looks as though George has found a skeleton."

"Ugh! Is he the sort of child who enjoys mud? Most seem to be. I do not remember this tendency from my own childhood. But do tell me, dear Miss Smethwick, do you not think my cousin's plans for some horrid laboratory are a desecration?"

"A desecration? How so?"

"He will mar this vista with machines and engines and piles of coal. He will take this little section of heaven and turn it into an inferno. There will be smoke billowing over the countryside from dawn to dusk and the thump of devices designed to carry out tasks more fitted to human hands. What an abomination! And all in the name of progress. I do not believe in progress. Progress is vulgar."

"You forget," responded Sybilla icily, "that my father was just such a vulgar scientist who would most have applauded his lordship's plans, eager to make progress so that the tedium of our workday world might be relieved a little by human ingenuity. Perhaps you also forget that I have lived amidst chimneys and machinery all my life and found such surroundings both stimulating and absorbing."

"Ah, Miss Smethwick, you must allow this rural idyll to work its magic a little longer and then you will appreciate the perfection of our land and understand why it must not be marred by ill-conceived notions of advancing the cause of science through personal intervention. There are academies and universities where all these tiresome researches may be carried out. Why destroy this oasis?"

"You are eloquent, indeed, Mr. Swaffham. But have you no defense, Augustus?"

"None that will convince cousin Carey." Ampthill's tone suggested that he did not consider it worth the effort to make even an attempt to sway his cousin. Then George and Lady Honoria came up the hill, and they continued on their way around the grounds until they were back at the house, accompanied by a ceaseless commentary from Carey. A servant came out to meet them, bearing a message for Lord Ampthill. The earl excused himself, whereupon Carey protested that the effort of their walk had been too much for him and retired to his room to rest before nuncheon. But just as the ladies were about to congratulate themselves the chance for a comfortable cose while Lord George exerted himself intellectually, Lady Evelyn appeared at the French windows and summoned them for ratafia.

Although neither Sybilla nor Honoria particularly cared for the cordial, finding it somewhat sickly, manners required them to attend the dowager. George was sent to fetch his drawings to show her ladyship while his mother and aunt submitted to a genteel inquisition about their habits and sensibilities. Lady Evelyn was determined to make up for the missing years during which she had held back from contacting the Smethwick family for fear of her unruly spouse, who at once declared that he would never recognize Harry's marriage while he simultaneously displayed a somewhat salacious interest in the young bride, particularly once she was left a relict. It was increasingly clear to Sybilla that the late earl had been

possessed of an unpredictable temper which once unleashed was ungovernable, causing his wife and sons
grievous mortification. This, coupled with libertine
propensities, ensured that she led a secluded life where
she might limit her exposure to his fits and starts. Only
now, with the earl nearly one year dead, was his widow
able to contemplate emerging a little from her shelter,
and the unexpected appearance of Harry's family provided a welcome spur.

"I have invited the Hartingtons to join us this evening
for dinner. The squire's land lies to the west, and he is the
leading huntsman in these parts. But it is only recently
that I have come to know his wife and children. They
are a charming family. Tonight, you will meet the two el-
dest still at home, Charles and Sophia. They are excellent
company, although Sophia is a little younger than you.
She has not yet been presented, but she is a very good,
sensible girl. There is another girl, between Charles and
Sophia, but she married, very well, I may say, and now
lives largely in Gloucestershire, I believe. When she is recovered from her confinement, I believe she intends to
bring Sophia out. Charles has spent two Seasons in London with her, so he at least has acquired some town
bronze, though whether that is desirable I do not venture
to say."

At that point, the door swung open and in came
Ampthill with a young man in a somewhat chaotic state,
his jacket shiny at the elbows, his pantaloons clean but
plainly elderly, and his cravat crumpled and somewhat
stained.

"Mother, may I present Mr. Cassidy to you. He has just
arrived from London. And here are my sisters, Lady
Honoria and Miss Smethwick, and my young nephew,
George."

Mr. Cassidy made his bow and launched into speech.

"Not the famous Misses Smethwick, daughters of Mr. Josiah Smethwick?"

"Indeed, we are the same," replied Honoria.

"What an honor!" said Mr. Cassidy. "Why, with scientists such as these at hand, Lord Ampthill, you scarcely need me. Here you have two of the finest minds of the age, trained by a master. If the ladies are to be in residence, I would be almost ashamed to put my own humble plans forward."

"You exaggerate, Mr. Cassidy," said Sybilla.

"No, I only wish I did, Miss Smethwick. You put so many of us to the blush, and to think that a mere female could have come up with the calculations you put forward for the Clitheroe Canal is mortifying to those of my fellow engineers who maintain that a woman mathematician is as mythical a creature as the unicorn."

"I had no idea that such genius was come amongst us," commented Ampthill icily. "I can only wonder at the impulse that drove the ladies to conceal their prowess."

Sybilla and Honoria glanced at each other. The earl was clearly horrified by the discovery that his newfound relatives were bluestockings.

"We concealed nothing, my lord," responded Sybilla with a militant lift to her chin. "We were not asked, so it did not occur to us to supply such information. It is hardly a serious offense."

"No, of course not." Ampthill's reply was curt.

"I should say not. Why, it was difficult enough when your father's position ensured the respect due to you as scientists. I should imagine it is even harder now." Mr. Cassidy's tone was sympathetic. "But perhaps you are sufficiently established in the world of engineering for those desirous of your expertise to overcome any foolish scruples about your womanhood."

"So you do not believe in the innate superiority of men, Mr. Cassidy?" inquired Ampthill.

"By no means. As the only male in a family of six, I was left in no doubt of my innate inferiority to the fairer sex in every sphere. My father died early and my mother took over the management of his affairs with consummate skill, ably assisted by my three elder sisters."

The earl was not in fact particularly outraged by Mr. Cassidy's revelation. What did irk him was the notion that either of the fair sisters had decided to conceal their abilities from him. It could be that he had appeared toplofty when they first met, but he hoped that they had seen enough of him to banish that perception. Then his natural sense of justice prevailed, for he realized that there had scarcely been time for him to find out—it was scarcely a week since his visit to their rather dreary menage in Fitzroy Square, and so much had happened since then. So Ampthill's good sense reasserted itself and the cloud which seemed to cast a pall over the proceedings was blown on its way.

Luncheon was a cheerful affair, rendered more so by the absence of Cousin Carey who sent a message declaring himself too enervated by the morning's exertion to come down for the meal. Afterwards, while the dowager retired for her rest, George was finally set some sums and the sisters took up their current projects also, relaxing in the room where they had earlier taken breakfast. The afternoon passed swiftly until Sybilla announced that she felt stifled and must have some fresh air before getting changed for supper. George wished to accompany her, and they explored the formal gardens near the house until Tabitha called out that it was time for his lordship's bath and supper in the nursery. The thought of a nursery supper aroused outrage in George's bosom, until Sybilla pointed out that he had much the best of it, with a candle and plenty to read while the rest of them must put on their finest clothes and talk to strangers about dull stuff like the weather and the loveliness of the landscape.

Of course, dinner was not nearly so dull. First of all, there was the curious absence of Carey Swaffham, who had precipitately remembered a vital engagement in town and excused himself from Swaffham Park. His absence came as a relief to Sybilla following their mild contretemps earlier that morning. She had not relished the prospect of his unquestionably frivolous and ill-informed ramblings. Then the Hartingtons arrived. Mrs. Hartington was a buxom woman who prided herself on her good sense, with a straightforward manner and a warm laugh, while her husband, a slim, ascetic-looking gentleman, soon displayed a wry sense of humor and an easy way with all the company, neither too formal nor too familiar. Their children were similarly pleasant, although both were somewhat in awe of their host.

Sybilla was led in to dinner by Charles Hartington and seated next to him. A slender young man who clearly emulated the earl's dress in spite of being dumbstruck in his presence, he thawed under Sybilla's gentle inquiry as to his favorite pastimes and his impressions of London. He declared that he had liked nothing more than the theater, which had seemed to him redolent of every enchantment, and it was now his avowed intention to become a playwright. Indeed, he had got up several entertainments which had not been ill-received. At the moment, he and his sisters were trying to get a marvelous play ready for the dowager's forthcoming birthday. Perhaps Miss Smethwick was familiar with *She Stoops to Conquer?* Before she knew it, Sybilla found herself engaged to participate in the production, in a starring role hitherto played by Miss Sophia who pronounced herself quite unable to learn her lines and much relieved by the possibility of an alternative actress for the role of Constance Neville.

So engrossed was she in Charles's eager description of how he planned to stage the play that she failed to observe the glower of disapproval Ampthill sent in her direction. Mrs. Hartington, however, did notice.

"Come, Ampthill, do not feel put out that my young people should be planning such an entertainment for your mother's birthday. When Charles came up with this idea, we feared you would be too occupied with the London Season to spare her much time and of course, I asked Lady Evelyn if the notion was agreeable to her. If you wish to celebrate her birthday in some other fashion, then tell us now and we may put an end to this project, although it is an innocent enough piece of fun."

Ampthill felt trapped, knowing of his mother's affection for the Hartington family and reluctant to appear the ogre to the entire company. Since she had given her consent, there was nothing to be done other than give his imprimatur. He watched Sybilla chatting animatedly to his young neighbor and felt a twinge of resentment. She seemed so at ease with everyone she encountered, with the glaring exception of himself. Then he remembered her obvious delight at the supper before the ball, in his plans for the cascade, then their conversation only this morning. She had been so frank and then apologized so handsomely for doubting him. As she had done for the incident at the ball, which Carey had managed to suggest was still the talk of all London. He had seen that tear, and the fierce defiance with which it had been brushed away. She was spirited as well as beautiful.

Lady Evelyn laughed, drawing his attention. She was clearly enjoying herself. The need to retain the Smethwick girls in the family engulfed the earl. To see her wearing once again her 'Harry dress' was further evidence of the deep regret she clearly felt. She had been deprived of the company of her grandson and daughter-in-law far too long. Ampthill cursed the memory of his father, vowing to do all he could to make up to his mother for the long years of loneliness. To give his approval to a simple entertainment was the slightest of amends.

# NINE

Life at Swaffham Park began to take on its own pattern over the next few days. To their delight, Honoria and Sybilla found themselves fully occupied, what with George's lessons, Lord Augustus's great plans, both for the improvements to the grounds and for the establishment of his laboratories, and generally learning the ways of a Great House. Their days fell into an easy rhythm: a timetable of lessons was established for George, with the sisters each taking turns at the subjects they knew best. Between lessons they set out preliminary drawings for the waterworks and cascade, unless they were required to interview an aspiring scientist attracted to Lord Augustus's laboratory. The mornings thus flew by.

Lunch became rather a technical affair with a review of the morning's activities, George always taking first place, since he could not abide anyone to remain ignorant of what he had learned that day. The sisters then reported on their progress with what became known as the water circuit, while Ampthill himself told of his activities connected with reading applications to join the laboratories, and the myriad tasks, decisions, and responsibilities connected with the day-to-day running of the estate itself.

"Mother," said Ampthill one day after a particularly convoluted discussion of the water circuit, "if you would rather talk of higher things at luncheon, instead of all this engineering and mechanics. . . ."

"My dear boy," replied the Dowager Evelyn, "this is the first time in my life that I have really seen Swaffham Park truly alive. To be sure, it is not at all the sort of lunchtime conversation that I ever imagined enjoying, but if I could have George sit beside me, then we can talk of castles when your science overcomes me. And he is so very clever at explaining the details to me later."

"And I like hearing what Uncle Gus has to do to keep a place like this going," interrupted George. "It all seems to work perfectly, but someone must be in charge of it all. I love to hear about decisions about things like the trees and the planting and the landscaping and keeping the game stocked and so on."

"Those are certainly things that should interest any householder, whatever the size of their property," said Honoria, "since they have effects which go beyond their immediate boundaries. The countryside of England reflects the care taken by generations of estate owners."

So by common consent, luncheons became key meeting times for them all.

Weather permitting, the afternoons were spent outdoors. Since the Smethwick girls were enthusiastic and accomplished horsewomen, Lord Augustus had found them suitable mounts, a spirited bay mare for Sybilla, rejoicing in the unlikely name of Norah, and a handsome chestnut gelding for Honoria. While the sisters rode out for pleasure, accompanied either by a groom or by Lord Augustus, George's riding was a far more serious affair. Ampthill had suggested that he should learn the whole range of equestrian skills, including both driving and riding, as well as some basic veterinary science. He therefore spent most of the afternoon in the charge of the Laxtons.

Mr. Laxton was too old to teach the racier parts of horsemanship, being well-advanced in his sixties, but was known throughout the county for his skill in driving, his strictness when it came to matters such as seat and hands, and above all for his knowledge of how to care for horses. Young Bob Laxton who was one of the local huntsmen, was in charge of the more adventurous parts of George's training. George adored them both and was busy hatching a plot that when he was well enough advanced in driving skills, which he confidently anticipated would be any day now, that he would take his grandmama for a spin around the Park in the dog cart.

Sybilla had an extra engagement, namely, her undertaking to play a major role in *She Stoops to Conquer*. The day after she had committed herself to the role of Constance, she had re-read the play. She had seen it put on once by a touring group of players and been mightily amused, but faced with performing the part herself she was somewhat put out of countenance by the deception involved in her role.

"The whole plot is built upon duplicity," she complained to her sister, during one of their late-night chats. "I think I might have felt easy doing it at home, but here? I don't feel we are sure enough of our ground. The whole plot revolves around deceiving parents and lovers. And while it is very good fun to watch when others perform these roles, I don't know that I want to do it myself. Miss Neville is besieged by an ignorant and foolish aunt who wishes her to marry her utterly coarse son; oh, I can't tell you how many ruses and contrivances there are in the plot. And Miss Neville connives at it absolutely. I know it has been a good deal put on in private theatricals, but I am not sure I wish to appear in it myself."

"But you would seriously disappoint the Hartingtons," said Honoria, "and the thing with a play is that the lack of taste you perceive depends very much on the way it is put on. I think you should at least go to the first few rehearsals and find out quite what tone is going to be used. After all, the entertainment is in honor of Lady Evelyn's birthday; I doubt very much that her close neighbors would be likely to put on anything that she might find offensive. Particularly since she reads such a great deal herself."

"But I particularly do not wish to put Lady Evelyn out," said Sybilla, "and above all, I would hate it if your position and George's might be compromised."

"Dear Sybilla," said Honoria, "the way George is getting on with his new grandmother, we have little to fear. If you feel that the way you are asked to play your part is at all discomforting to you, let us ask her. She will surely know what is suitable for you to do."

And so the matter had been left.

One of the new pleasures of taking part in the play, was the ride across to the Hartington's each afternoon. Although the play would eventually be performed at Swaffham, it had been agreed that the early rehearsals should take place at Hartington Court. Hartington Court was just the right distance from Swaffham as far as Sybilla and Norah were concerned. The first two or three times, young Barnes had accompanied Sybilla to make sure she knew all the easy rides, the drier routes, should it rain, and all the places between where it was safe to let the mare have her head and go for a good gallop. Sybilla had observed all these routes carefully, and was now planning where she might have some extra practice at country jumps. Norah was such a delightful and willing ride, surely, come the autumn, they should hunt! Except that the realization that she would not be here in the autumn struck her with a sudden sense of dismay.

For the first few days she had been extra careful to follow everything that Barnes, assigned to her by Laxton, Senior, had told her. But at last she had earned her freedom. Laxton was such a clever manager of his stables that he disliked giving a groom "the afternoon off to sit around gossiping with the Hartington lads." And by appearing very dutiful, obedient, and safe, Sybilla was at last given the freedom to ride by the way she chose to Hartington Court. On this particular afternoon, she thought she would ride decorously to the Hartingtons, and then have a tremendous gallop home. As she went, she planned her routes and fences.

Planning routes and fences was one thing. Playing the part of Miss Constance Neville was quite another. Although, towards the end of the play, Miss Constance might be revealed as having the truest heart, Sybilla was ashamed to hear her described as a "dear dissembler." She was further embarrassed by the way Charles Hartington had changed his own role from Marlowe to Hastings so that he could address his "playful" attentions to her. On that particular afternoon, they rehearsed the scene where all is explicit between Miss Neville and Mr. Hastings. She found the combination of young Charles's heavy breathing and beseeching eyes all too much, and was at last relieved to be reseated on Norah's slim and accommodating back at the end of the afternoon. They had a wonderful gallop on the way home and practiced jumping over some very neat brooks and fences en route.

While she walked the mare the last few yards home, and Norah snuffled about her pockets for the ends of carrots, sugar lumps, and other treats, Sybilla decided quite finally that she was not going to take part in the play. At least, she was not going to play it if Charles Hartingdon should appoint himself as her stage lover. Wondering how she might extricate herself from the predicament, her ears were assailed by a vociferous "Halloo, cousin," and she found herself confronted by the loathsome Cousin Carey. Sybilla was surprised at herself. Why should she, all of a sudden, find Cousin Carey so loathsome? Hitherto, he had always seemed nothing more than a fop and a baboon. Of course, a full curtsey was demanded, and she performed it with good grace.

"Dear Cousin Carey, how nice to see you. Are you . . . ?" Her query was cut short.

"My dear cousin, what an honor to find you! Chaff such as myself are rarely allowed the infinite pleasure of greeting a lady who has been the subject of an exchange!" at which point he bowed deeply.

"What on earth do you mean? An exchange?"

"Why of arms, of course. You don't mean to tell me that you don't know?"

"Know what?"

"You don't know that Ampthill was so enraged by Venables's behavior at his ball that he called him out the very next day, and that after pinking the devil, he needs must stay at home? My dear lady, I had assumed that you knew. The whole of London knows."

Sybilla was horrified. Luckily further conversation with Carey was averted by the appearance of Barnes running up to take charge of the horse and discussion of how much longer the mare needed walking to cool her off after her rather energetic trip home. Instantly bored and careless of such matters, Carey took himself off, leaving Sybilla to ponder this latest revelation. She wondered where she might find Honoria and decided to try the library, where the main plans for the water circuit were laid out.

But as she walked through the double doors into the library, it was Ampthill rather than Honoria that she found bent over the plans. Before she could stop herself, her outrage erupted.

"How could you? Oh, Augustus, how could you?"

"How could I what?"

Lord Augustus looked up from the table, smiling, but his expression changed when he saw the drawn look on Sybilla's face. "My dear Sybilla, you look distraught, what can I have done to upset you so?"

"Why fight that odious Venables, on my account and then keep the whole thing from us in this way. How could you let us bumble on in ignorance of the fact that you had called him out, and are now rusticated down here when you should be gracing the drawing rooms of London? And suppose you had been hurt yourself? Oh, it is too awful to think of."

"Sybilla, my dear, let us sit down and discuss this calmly."

He drew her to a window seat and pulled over a chair so that he was facing her. He thought how truly lovely she looked, despite her obvious concern, her cheeks slightly flushed and her eyes wide with anxiety.

"Let us take things in the reverse order," he said. "Although I do not like to boast, I can assure you that there was little personal danger involved in the fight, if, indeed, what transpired could be dignified by the word. I had excellent masters in India and always kept myself up to form out there, while poor Venables cannot have touched a blade for decades. I regret to say I felt almost sorry for the fellow when we met that morning; he was in a great panic. Second, I am far happier being rusticated, as you call it, than being crushed at balls and soirées and gatherings of empty-headed people all scrabbling to marry me off to their over-dressed daughters. And finally, my dear, although you bore the brunt of Venables's insults, they encompassed us all, especially George, his late father, and your dear sister. But the honor of the whole family had been assailed, as you yourself showed you felt at the time."

Ampthill had often remembered with wry amusement the scene at the ball and had dwelt in his inner thoughts on the loveliness of Sybilla's revealed form. He cherished the contrast between the apparent frail slenderness of her body and the savagely effective blow she had given Venables. He smiled now at the recollection. Her outrage had not been wholly dispelled, and, as she was about to continue her objections, a thought occurred to Ampthill.

"How did you hear of the affair?" he inquired. "I had made sure that no one down here knew of it, except for Brockley."

"From Cousin Carey, of course. He was positively crowing about it, booming out the story in the stable yard so that half the household must have heard. If no one here has heard, then perhaps you had better warn your mother or she, too, may be distressed."

"I had, in fact, mentioned it to my mother. She corresponds from time to time with London people, and I made sure she would not be alarmed if word of the affair should reach her."

"I see. . . ."

Augustus was dismayed to watch Sybilla's features contract in fury; he almost recoiled at the anger in her eyes, but he was struck at the same time by how magnificent she looked.

"So it is only we poor Smethwicks who are to be kept in ignorance?" said Sybilla. "Not being of the *ton* there is no need to tell us, your *sisters*—" the sarcasm with which Sybilla spat out the word was indeed considerable—"that we are such country bumpkins, or such bluestockings, that there is no need to tell us anything at all, I suppose. We should never understand or appreciate the finer points of the honor of the Ampthills, of course.

We are far too humble folk to be allowed to congratulate
you on your success, or to thank you for having undertaken the inconvenience of early rising in order to prick
holes in an unworthy opponent. Really, Lord Augustus,
I had not expected to find that my *brother* is such a dissembler!"

Unconsciously, she found herself using the vocabulary
of the play, and could not have chosen a better word to
anger Ampthill.

"Sybilla," he shouted, determined to stop her tirade,
"there was no deceit involved, at least no more than your
own in hiding from me your eminence as scientists. For
goodness sake, girl. . . ." In exasperation he stood up and
strode about the room. "We are all trying to make new
lives for ourselves. I am doing the best I can to make
amends for the cruelty with which my family treated your
sister. But when I neglect to tell you the details of a tri-
fling dawn affair, you accuse me of dissembling, whereas
your *modesty* about your scientific abilities and the well-
deserved recognition this has earned you and your sister,
actually led me into embarrassment the other day in front
of Cassidy. Which of us then is the greater dissembler?
Tell me that if you please!"

At his words, Sybilla blushed. She almost hung her
head, but she thought herself too fine a creature for that.
Ampthill felt that blushing was as near an apology as he
was likely to get and immediately felt remorse that he
might have caused her pain. Her impetuous tongue made
quarrels seem inevitable, but if only they could find a
way to make peace, there might be some way of keeping
her by. For of course, if she were not at Swaffham, neither would Honoria and George remain at hand.

He stepped toward her. "My dear Sybilla, I did not
mean . . ."

His arms reached out to her, but whatever he might or

might not mean was lost as Brockley opened the door to announce Lindsay. Sybilla immediately rose, gave her hand to Lindsay and, muttering about the need to change from her riding clothes, she excused herself.

"What was that all about?" asked Lindsay. "Miss Smethwick did not appear quite herself, I fancy?"

"Indeed not. It seems that that fool Carey has reappeared and was unable to contain himself from reporting the hot gossip from town. In short, within five minutes of arriving, he contrived to tell her about my meeting with Venables and she was most indignant that I had not seen fit to inform my dear sisters of the matter. Lindsay, is there not some way that I might call out that dreadful bounder of a cousin? There can be few people on this earth whom I would more cheerfully run through!"

Lindsay laughed. "Little chance, I fear, of running Cousin Carey through. If matters were to come to a head between the two of you it would have to be firearms. Carey only practices sports which require standing still."

After a sour frown, Ampthill smiled.

"You do me good, Lindsay, as always."

"Tell me how things are going with the fair sisters?" asked Lindsay.

"Well enough, I suppose. You should have warned me better about their renown. I was fairly embarrassed by that young Cassidy and his respect for the Misses Smethwick."

"I did try to warn you that you were taking on a pair of women of strong character," Lindsay smiled, "but I suppose you had too many other things on your mind at the time. How are you making out in the day-to-day run of things?"

"Well, of all the Smethwicks, the easiest and the most entertaining by far is my nephew, George. He has quite made his mark with my mother who seems almost rejuvenated by his presence. They are the closest of conspirators! I have never seen her so animated. You are staying, I suppose? At luncheon tomorrow you will see. Lunch has become a sort of business conference. First, George regales us with whatever he has learned during the morning, then the girls weigh in with incomprehensible discussions of elevations, then I come in with questions for Mother about pruning and planting. The Glovers claim that she is an utterly reformed person."

"So the additions to the family are a success?"

"A devilish prickly success, apart from young George. The mother is charming, of course, unless you happen to question any of her calculations, but the aunt!"

"The aunt is very beautiful, Ampthill."

"So she may be, but she is the most uncommonly sensitive girl. Try as I might, there is no way of settling her. Everything I do seems to cause offense. Also, I fear they hanker after their former life of freedom. I had no idea women were brought up in such a way. It is not that they have no modesty. They are very proper in that sense, but the freedom of using their heads is what they value most. They are accustomed to using their heads for financial gain! It is a very novel idea at Swaffham, you will admit."

"But your mother does not disapprove?"

"If only she did! Unfortunately, she is entranced. It is as if she were making up for all the years that she spent under the shadow of my father."

"But surely, Augustus, you would not criticize her new vitality?"

"Not at all. I am delighted. But the devil of it is that I must contrive to convince those two young women to make this place their home."

Lindsay wondered at this point, which of the two "young women" his friend had in mind.

"You could marry one of them," he teased. "I believe it is quite common for royalty to marry their brother's widows; you could marry Honoria and adopt George, and then they would have to stay."

"I suspect that Honoria is far too attached to Harry's memory for that, even if I were to consider such a thing, which I do not," replied the earl somewhat heatedly.

Delighted to see that Ampthill had taken the bait, Lindsay decided to play his fish a little longer.

"Then marry the younger one, although she is, I think, the less handsome of the two."

"Nonsense, Sybilla is far the prettier; she has such spirit in her eyes and her expression changes so enchantingly with her every mood."

"Does it, by Jove? I see which way the wind is blowing, my friend," Lindsay laughed.

"You see no such thing," said Ampthill crossly. "Besides the girl spends all her time at the Squire's place, playing amateur theatricals with young Hartington."

"Amateur theatricals?"

"Yes, the Hartingtons have had the absurd idea of presenting my mother with a performance of *She Stoops to Conquer* in honor of her birthday. And they easily persuaded Sybilla to join in their nonsense. She is to be Miss Neville, I understand."

"A-hah, I see, and young Hartington has no doubt cast himself as Hastings." Lindsay laughed. "Augustus my friend, I see it all; you are taken with Miss Smethwick, and jealous that she should enjoy a stage flirtation with your young neighbor. Though why you should worry about such a youngster as that I cannot imagine. Miss Smethwick is surely more likely to attract one of your resident scientists, than fall for an inexperienced youth like Charles Hartington."

"I have no interest in Miss Smethwick, Lindsay; do not leap to such a ludicrous conclusion," protested Ampthill, a little too warmly and emphatically to Lindsay's way of

thinking. "I do not approve of amateur theatricals because in India I so often saw respectable married women
in the Hill Stations for the summer, making fools of
themselves in that way with junior officers. They caused
no end of trouble and I should be sorry if they were to
become a common entertainment in this part of the
world. But let us be serious, Lindsay, for goodness' sake.
Come, let us arm ourselves with some liquid refreshment, and then I have a matter of some gravity that I wish
to discuss with you."

Lindsay smiled to himself as Ampthill poured them
both a generous measure from the decanter on the table.
Despite the earl's disclaimer, he suspected that his friend
was indeed smitten by Sybilla's beauty. He could never
imagine Augustus settling with one of the conventional
London heiresses or fortune-seekers, whose sole ambitions in life revolved around the attending and giving of
parties, in seeing and being seen. Sybilla would make
an admirable countess, thought Lindsay, resolving to observe the two closely at dinner. But after handing him his
drink, Ampthill stood before him with a serious frown
clouding his expression.

"The source of my concern is the safety of young
George."

"What on earth can you mean?" inquired the mystified
Scot.

"On their way here, George was nearly run over by a
curricle." Ampthill tried to communicate to his friend the
way in which young George might have met with his end
or at best an unfortunate accident. He then described the
episode of the cider vat.

"Lindsay, tell me I am raving. Who would want to
harm the boy? I could not bear it if my bringing them
here should entail risk for the boy."

"Ampthill, until you yourself marry, he is your heir,"

said Lindsay drily. "If you fear for the boy, then you must fear for yourself."

"It had never occurred to me to do so."

"And the accident with the curricle occurred at Farnham, you say?"

"Yes, Lindsay. Why?"

"Well, on my way down from London yesterday, I traveled as far as Farnham myself, having business in the town there this morning. And as I set out to visit my client, I saw Carey standing in the public bar, deep in conversation with one of the most disreputable and felonious-looking characters I have seen in a long while, quite the footpad. I thought it strange at the time, most out of character for one so high in the instep as your cousin. But then my Farnham business and anticipation of a few days here, put it all out of my head. What is Carey's position regarding Swaffham Park? Does he not inherit the title and the property if you should predecease him and leave no heir? I wonder if he might not be at the bottom of these incidents?"

"Oh surely not, Lindsay. He is perfectly well off; he has shown not the slightest interest in running the estate. Surely if he had ambitions in that direction, he would have made himself more useful in the time between my father's death and my return. Besides, he is so idle and effete that I cannot imagine him summoning up the energy to plot anything so complicated. I admit he is a malicious gossip, but I doubt if he is really wicked enough to try to get rid of young George."

"I would not be so certain, in your place. I can think of no one else who could have even the remotest interest in harming the boy."

"But he certainly cannot be held responsible for the incident here in the stables. Why, the Smethwicks had only been here about twenty minutes when it happened, and Carey himself only appeared just in time for dinner."

"Maybe so," said Lindsay thoughtfully, "but he comes down here with some frequency, does he not? There may be some disgruntled person about the estate who is in his pay. Have you had to turn off any men for some reason, or has anyone been made to leave their cottage?"

"Not that I am in any way aware," said Ampthill. "But you are right, he has many connections with people hereabouts. His valet, Mortley, I understand from Brockley and Carstairs, was born and bred around here. He has a drunken, disreputable brother, who looks villainous enough, but it was he who saved George's life at Farnham. Lady Honoria persuaded me to allow him back here in the stables, and he is devoted to her. He still looks a ragamuffin, but Laxton keeps a strict eye on him and says he appears to have turned over a new leaf. But the bow he produces whenever he catches a glimpse of Honoria is most comical. He sweeps off his crumpled old hat to reveal a most disgustingly shaggy head and bows to the ground after the manner of a courtier in a play. I saw him at it yesterday."

Ampthill smiled at the memory, and his tone was more cheerful when he spoke: " I am sure I am just imagining things, Lindsay. Do not trouble your mind about it further. The two events were just accidents, they cannot be related."

"Will you at least let me have a word with Carstairs and Brockley in the morning, Augustus?" asked Lindsay. "Unpleasant though it be, I think we must look into any possible resentments there might be smoldering about the place. They are in a better position than we to learn of any discontent."

"I suppose we had better, though it is disagreeable."

"And I shall also keep an eye on Carey's doings in

London, I think," Lindsay went on. "We retain one or two men of complete discretion to watch out for villains. If Carey comes up with a clean bill of health, then no harm has been done."

"Thank you, Lindsay. I certainly feel easier after sharing my fears with you. But for heaven's sake be careful. I do not wish to alarm the ladies, nor do I wish my household to know that I am fretting like an old woman over a little boy getting into silly scrapes. But, speaking of the ladies, we must change for dinner; they will be waiting for us in my mother's drawing room. Lady Evelyn is greatly looking forward to your visit and will no doubt quiz you about Edinburgh authors at dinner."

While he changed, Lindsay pondered his conversation with Ampthill. The disturbing image of Carey deep in conference with an obvious villain stuck in his mind, and he resolved to start on his inquiries in the morning.

# TEN

That evening, Carey continued to sow dissent and dissatisfaction by making veiled references to Ampthill's duel and the reputations of his dearest cousins, vowing that they would all make an appearance at Ackermann's, the notable gallery on the Strand, where cartoonists such as Gillray sold their wares. Even Lady Evelyn was shocked by her old companion's twitterings and simperings, sufficiently so that she dressed him down in a severe undertone as the party retired after their dinner to the drawing room where Lindsay immediately demanded the pleasure of hearing the ladies sing to his accompaniment. The dowager's scolding did not inhibit Carey from quizzing Ampthill about his intentions for the estate.

"Instead of scientists, dear Augustus, you should strive to become a patron of the arts. The latest thing is to keep an orchestra. You must set up one here at Swaffham. It would provide us all with much amusement, and far more tunefully than the explosions wrought upon us by all these theoreticians you propose to install."

Lady Evelyn rolled her eyes in despair as she saw her son stifling the impulse to eject his cousin from the drawing room.

"Carey, do listen to the girls, they are singing quite delightfully and seem well up on the latest songs from Paris. As for your suggestion, I myself would not care to share my home with professional musicians when we have such fine local talent as these two and the Hartingtons. Why, Sophia's skill on the harp is remarked on through the county."

When Honoria and Sybilla pleaded for respite, Carey decided it was time to regale his cousins with a ballad hot from the press and very popular in the London theaters. Lindsay swiftly commandeered the dandy for a game of backgammon, naming a high stake to distract his attention entirely, while Ampthill organized the ladies into a foursome for whist at a penny-a-point. Lady Evelyn was astonished to find that her new relatives had never learned how to play any card games, and she took great pleasure in training them. The earl proved to be a proficient and patient partner to Honoria, while Sybilla grasped the mechanics of the game very easily, finding it simple. Once they were sufficiently expert to play each rubber without tuition, Ampthill brought up the notion of identifying a room that might be suitably equipped for George's studies.

"Once we know which room to fit out, I wish to supply it with every necessity for his full education, so that you may never hesitate to bring him here for fear of his missing any schoolwork," he said.

"Just so." The dowager was emphatic in her endorsement of Ampthill's plan.

"That is doing a great deal too much for him," protested Honoria. "He may study anywhere, provided there is room to open a book and lay out his drawings."

"I am sure that your father must have made room for the pair of you. If you will only let me know the details, I will be sure to provide an environment equally stimulating for my nephew. And perhaps, before you depart on your travels to the Continent, we should discuss his progress in classics with some of the local clerics, to see whether any of them is able to supplement the work of your Reverend Hardisty on your return," said Ampthill.

"You are planning too far into the future for my taste," responded Honoria, trying to deflect Ampthill's enthusiasm as graciously as possible. "For now, we are content to organize only our travels. I am sensible of your desire to include us all in your life here at Swaffham Park, and both Sybilla and I are much honored, especially after relations have been so delicate in the past. But let us not arrange every detail of George's existence just now. There will be plenty of time on our return."

The dowager and her son recognized that this was not the moment to pursue their plans to bring Lord George firmly into the Swaffham household. Soon, the party retired.

The next day, Ampthill rose early and went immediately to the estate office in the West wing of the big house, so that he might expedite all necessary business. He was expecting Cassidy to return to Swaffham with a contingent of colleagues to be shown round the facilities and interviewed with regard to their suitability for a prolonged sojourn in the country.

Five scientists arrived just before midday and were greeted by the whole family, with the exception of Carey Swaffham, who made it his practice to emerge from his ablutions only at the luncheon gong. Sybilla and Honoria were delighted to find that among Cassidy's friends was their own intimate, Samuel Compton, a chemist at once well regarded for his research into organic properties of a host of materials and widely mocked for his tendency to cause explosions wheresoever he set up his laboratory.

"Why, Ampthill, you will have to create an entirely separate laboratory to house smoldering Sam," said Sybilla, fondly tucking her hand into the chemist's arm as they took a turn about the knot garden before sitting down to lunch. Ampthill regarded it as unfortunate that Mr. Compton's looks were as smoldering as his reputation. All the scientists seemed improbably young and good-looking, but the earl hardly supposed he could blame either Lindsay or Cassidy for that, since he had specifically requested them to seek out young practitioners who were not too set in their ways. Although the Smethwick sisters would be safely distant from the scientists' attentions during their travels, there would certainly be ample opportunity for one of these dashing intellects to capture either of their hearts when they next brought George to visit. He found the idea strangely irksome.

Lunch was a riotous affair, with the ladies flirting, as Ampthill thought, quite outrageously with the men of science, which ladies included, to his astonishment, Lady Evelyn, who had clearly taken in far more than she realized in the past week or so of working lunches. Her intelligent queries and quick witted ability to connect different theories and concepts drew warm applause from the assembled company, although it was obvious that Carey felt disgruntled by her refusal to participate in his baiting of Ampthill or the prospective residents of Swaffham Park. His barbed remarks took flight, but found no real target, particularly as they multiplied in frequency and viciousness.

It was with some dismay then that Sybilla found, when she had Norah brought round after lunch to ride over to the Hartingtons, Cousin Carey already in the saddle on Blaze, a somewhat temperamental gelding. Mr. Swaffham did not show to advantage. His claret-colored morning coat, teamed with a virulently ochre waistcoat, seemed garish, the proportions of his hat overlarge, his breeches over revealing of his slack shanks. The exertion of propelling his over-corseted frame onto the horse's back had left him breathless.

"Miss Smethwick, I hope I do not derange you by attending the rehearsals. You artistic souls do, I know, need freedom to loose your creative spirit, but I venture to think that my presence will not inhibit the thespians."

"Of course not, Mr. Swaffham." Sybilla could not bring herself to say any more to her unexpected escort.

"You are kind. You understand my dilemma. I cannot remain here while Lady Evelyn and his lordship squire about these tiresome scientific fellows. It is not to be borne. To see Swaffham reduced to ashes by the likes of—what was his name—Smoldering Sam? It is utterly repugnant to me."

Upon which pronouncement, Sybilla resolved to lead him a merry gallop. "Shall we be off?" she inquired, tapping Norah's side with her crop a little more smartly than usual. The responsive mare started and broke into an immediate canter down the drive. Carey was left to dig his heels into the gelding and follow, elbows flapping, jiggeting around in his saddle. He was not a competent horseman, and nearly flew off at a low fence. Good manners prevailed, and Sybilla slowed her pace somewhat.

The rehearsal was a torment. Charles Hartington was more pressing than usual, and Sybilla was conscious of Carey Swaffham's beady brown gaze absorbing the sight of the young man clasping her hands, then her waist. Consequently, although everyone was as kind as they could be, it was clear that her performance had been lackluster and this caused some concern. When Carey seemed at the point of settling in for a protracted tea with the Hartingtons, Sybilla abruptly signaled her intention to leave, whether he would or no. She set a cracking pace back to Swaffham Park, finally forgetting all constraints as they crossed into the grounds and urging Norah into a gallop, leaving Carey squeaking ineffectually behind her.

Norah was overheated when Sybilla dismounted, so she walked the mare around the stable yard to cool her down. Just then, a shabby figure emerged from the tack room.

"Here, miss, let me do that," he said.

"There's no need. It was I who pushed her too hard, so it is I who must make sure she does not catch cold." Sybilla eyed the groom. "I have seen you before. I remember! Abel Mortley, who saved George at the inn. What are you doing here?"

"It's thanks to you and your sister, miss. Your recommendation secured me the position here. I must thank you, miss, for it's rare as the quality remembers their dues, but you have treated me right handsome. Right handsome." And so saying, he took Sybilla's gloved hand and bent to kiss it in gratitude.

"Dog! Unhand that lady!" came a furious yelp, and a riding crop whistled down onto the bared nape of Abel Mortley's neck. Both Sybilla and the unfortunate groom leapt apart, turning to gaze at the mottled features of Carey Swaffham, already raising his arm to make another blow. "How dare you despoil this lady?"

"How dare you, sir!" Sybilla pushed between the two men, shielding Mortley from the dandy's ire. "Mr. Mortley was in no way molesting me. He has behaved in a way that was entirely proper, unlike you, leaping to vile conclusions and resorting to violence."

"Out of my way, Miss Smethwick, you have no notion of how to treat these bounders. A good thrashing is in order." He tried to move round Sybilla, but she stood her ground. Then something caught her eye just past Carey's

shoulder, and he took the opportunity of her distraction
to push past her and brandish his crop once again over
Mortley's cowering head. Sybilla turned and was about
to grab at Swaffham's arm when a lazy drawl came from
the stable.

"Dear coz, what are you at? Is this really a sight suitable for a lady's eyes? It seems to me that a true gallant
would make it his business to escort the lady away from
the brute. Then one might return and give the peasant his
due." Ampthill was leaning against the brick, examining
his nails as he spoke. "Might I suggest, however, that
since this is my stable yard, you leave it to me to discipline my unruly groom in my own way?"

Carey's arm dropped. "Of course, Augustus. *Mea
culpa, mea maxima culpa.* Do forgive me, Miss Smethwick." He turned on his heel, and left the stables without
further comment.

"Here's a sovereign, Mortley, which I adjure you to
save rather than spend in the local tavern. And might I
suggest that you find a less effusive way of thanking your
benefactors."

"That's very kind in you, m'lord, and I'm sure I won't
be in his way again, nohow."

"I hope not. Now, perhaps you will take the horse in
hand while I escort Miss Smethwick back to the house.
I am sure that Mr. Swaffham will not be this way again."

Mortley took the mare to her quarters and Ampthill
tucked Sybilla's hand into the crook of his arm and led
her away from the yard. She found she was shaking.

"I am forever finding you in the midst of a scene, Miss
Smethwick. You have a talent for excitement." The earl's
tone was mildly amused, but it undid Sybilla entirely. She
was not able to forget Carey Swaffham's fury, nor the
look of blazing hatred he had directed at Ampthill himself. She pulled her hand away and folded her arms tight

across her body. She found she could not walk another step. She was shivering quite markedly.

"There. There, there." The earl's voice was quite different, no longer light, and much closer. First, slowly and calmly, he removed her bonnet, then took her in his arms and held her tight, just as her father had done, so that all she felt was the warmth and comfort of the embrace.

They stood quite still for what seemed long minutes until her shivering subsided. She sighed, and in doing so, inhaled deeply, so that she was suddenly conscious of the cologne he wore and the slight scent of sweat beneath it and then she realized that his light breath was stirring the curls at her temple, and that his thumb was gently stroking her neck.

Softly, his hand cupping her face, he tilted her head back so that she could look into his eyes. She swallowed. It was clear that he intended to kiss her. And then he brushed his lips against her forehead and pulled away from her abruptly. He handed her bonnet back and waited while she retied it, then said, "Come, Miss Smethwick. We must to the house and dispel any vicious tale that my dear cousin is no doubt spinning." Brusque, unsmiling, he escorted her back to the house without another word.

At once affronted and relieved, Sybilla headed for her room. But going through the antechamber, she came across Honoria, whose normally placid features were marred by a frown.

"Hono, what is vexing you?"

"Oh, George complains of stomach pains and wishes just to sleep. It is most unlike him. He did not even stir with excitement at the prospect of riding out with Augustus. Now, I must find the earl and make George's excuses."

"Let me, if you wish to stay with George."

"Would you, dearest? I daresay he will be right as rain by dinner, but I own I should like to be near."

And so Sybilla went in search of Ampthill, whom she found in his library.

"I understand from Honoria that you were waiting for George when we met at the stables."

"Yes. There is no sign of the young scamp."

Sybilla explained about her nephew's indisposition, provoking a scowl. "Should I send for the doctor?" inquired the earl.

"By no means. Honoria thinks he is likely to be quite well by supper."

"Let us hope so. Perhaps I may go up and see him later."

Sybilla nodded, and feeling dismissed, turned to leave.

"You are none the worse for Carey's display of ill temper, I trust."

"Not at all. I only hope that he and Mr. Mortley may avoid each other in future, for they are sure to come to blows again. Does Mr. Swaffham frequently explode?"

"I cannot say. It is many years since I had the pleasure of his company in quite such a dose, and he never before struck me as the sort to fly off the handle. My only concern is that this unsavory episode did not worry you unduly. You seemed . . . a little overset once Carey made himself scarce."

"Perhaps. I am not normally so susceptible, I do assure you."

"I can well believe it."

Sybilla curtseyed and withdrew, perturbed by the earl's calm acceptance of the situation. She could not help but feel baffled by his detached manner, and a little hurt. He had been quick enough to comfort her this afternoon, but now he seemed aloof and she could only conclude that he considered the Smethwick family somewhat beneath him. She could not even confide in her dear sister, for Honoria was at George's bedside, reading a treatise on canal construction while checking his brow for fever. Sybilla joined her sister and while she observed that her nephew did indeed appear pale, found him relaxed in his slumbers.

The boy roused around six that evening, and pronounced himself quite restored, indeed, ravenous. Sybilla and Honoria smiled with pleasure as he bounced about his room while they summoned Tabitha and asked her to ready his bath and supper. His delight knew no bounds when the earl came up, and he gave his uncle a warm hug and demanded the earl's opinion of his latest sketch in preparation for the great work for Grandmama. Sybilla excused herself, wishing to change before dinner. George's enthusiastic explanation of his work was interrupted by Tabitha, bearing a tray of steaming food and two footmen bearing hot water for a pre-prandial wash.

"Honoria, might we leave George to his ablutions and speak privately for a moment?" requested the earl with a warm smile. His sister-in-law could not refuse. He led her down the corridor to a landing bathed by the glow of the sun gradually sinking in the west.

"He seems lively enough. Sybilla explained that he was troubled by stomach pains and weariness. It may simply be that we have provided a little too much excitement these past few days."

"That may be so, but he has never been a sickly child, so when he is under the weather, I am unduly apprehensive. He slept very soundly this afternoon, but I shall keep a watch on him, for we cannot travel far if excitement does wear him out so readily."

"Well, you have some weeks before you need make any firm decisions on that score. Enough time, indeed, to design for me a proper watercourse, if you and your sister have a mind to do so."

"Is that truly what your lordship wishes? You are not simply asking us to be kind?"

"Where is the kindness in setting you to work when you should be enjoying a respite before your travels? No, it will be you and Sybilla who are doing me a kindness, for I am sure that with a Smethwick watercourse, I shall be the envy of every engineer in Britain. It is very likely that I shall be able to use it to attract men of science the length and breadth of the country, at the very least for a call, if not for a more permanent sojourn here at Swaffham."

"It is a very tempting prospect. The lie of the land and the artesian wells are situated so aptly, I feel we could create a marvel worth at least the trip from London. Let me speak of this with Sybilla. Certainly, we want for no attention here, but it would be a delightful way of passing the time."

"Is it such a hardship to be at Swaffham?"

"By no means, Augustus. I must confess that we had reservations about lengthening our stay, but both you and Lady Evelyn have made us so welcome here that we shall be hard-pressed to remove ourselves once her birthday is past."

"You seem surprised to find yourself so at home."

"Well, I am. You must know that Harry was always very frank about his unhappiness at home. He did not speak of it often, but when he did, it was clear that neither you nor he had enjoyed the felicities of a happy family, as has been our privilege. I was frankly dreading any extended sojourn here, but I find that I am far happier than I ever expected to be."

"I only wish Sybilla felt the same," responded the earl, his face impassive, his tone noncommittal.

Honoria was tempted to press Ampthill about what he meant about Sybilla, or at least to say something in her sister's defense, but the earl had turned away and was making his way down the stairs. He turned toward her, to say, with what looked like a carefree smile, "I am so glad the little man is himself again," then left swiftly.

# ELEVEN

Later that evening, Honoria came into Sybilla's room, leaving the door to her own room ajar, to be within earshot of George. "Sybilla, my dear, this evening Augustus invited us formally to take over the complete design of the watercourse. Of course I could not promise him that we should do so without consulting with you. Let me confess that I am very drawn to the idea, but I do not want us to undertake anything with which you might not be happy."

Sybilla frowned lightly in thought. Her sister went on, "He was very complimentary in his asking," she smiled, "saying that a Smethwick watercourse would make him the envy of every engineer. . . ."

"So it would," said Sybilla. "Your work in that area is unparalleled, Hono. Of course we must do it. You must design it, and I shall be your assistant."

"And severest critic, no doubt!" laughed Honoria.

"But we shall hardly have time before we leave for the Continent, that is why I was slow to reply. We were planning to leave in early June, and that is but four or five weeks away. I calculate that the full plan will take six or seven weeks to complete."

"I think we could manage in a bit less. I have been thinking, just occasionally, about what could be achieved."

Sybilla laughed out loud. "Oh Hono, I declare, you

have been plotting this all along. Are you sure Ampthill asked you, or have you been quietly persuading him all this time?"

"No, not at all. His request to me came from out of the blue. It is true, I was not very complimentary about that young man who presented himself as an engineer last week, but that is because his training was obviously so incomplete, and his knowledge of hydraulics only of the most rudimentary. But with such a project in the air, one cannot help just thinking about it. I was beginning to hope that we should be away when the designs were made, because otherwise, I am not sure I could have prevented myself from interfering."

"It will be a splendid way of repaying Ampthill for his hospitality. I shall feel less of a beggar at the rich man's table if we make him a present of a really first-rate design. Normally, we should receive quite a large sum for a work of this scale."

"Indeed we should," said Honoria, "but there can be no question of charging money in this case. Though I rather wish we could. I miss our old independence. That is the only real difficulty I feel about staying here. But I fear you do not share my pleasure in seeing the growing affection between Georgie and his new relations."

"Hono, I do. Really, I do," countered Sybilla indignantly. "It is the greatest fun to watch him and Lady Evelyn together and even I will admit that the presence and example of a gentleman like Lord Ampthill is of the greatest benefit. George needs a firm man's hand to steady him, and one whose manners and goodness to all whom he has in charge are so exemplary."

"But you are still unhappy here?"

"I would not go so far as to describe myself as unhappy. But I cannot bring myself to trust Ampthill completely. I find it impossible to be at ease with him. At one minute he is affectionate and easy, just like a brother should be, the next he is cold and haughty; I never know where I am with him."

Sybilla did not mention the incident in the stable yard that afternoon; she had not told her sister of Carey's extraordinary turn of temper with poor Abel Mortley, as she had decided that she had helped provoke his anger by the fine gallop she had led him on the way home. And there had been something not quite brotherly in Ampthill's comforting embrace that she felt unequal to explain.

"Perhaps, my dear, it is your own quick temper that may disconcert him?" suggested Honoria. "I find his behavior to me is unvaryingly kind and gracious."

"How can you say such a thing? I know I am quick to leap to conclusions, and I was furious about that awful duel because I am still so discomfited when I remember that dreadful moment at the ball. But he always makes me feel I am in the wrong and that we are beneath him. Did you not see his expression tonight when Lady Evelyn inquired about our rehearsals? He positively scowled."

"I am afraid that Augustus disapproves strongly of amateur theatricals. According to Mr. Lindsay, he took a dislike to them in India, where some of the flightier wives seem to have used them as an opportunity to flirt."

"I suppose I cannot blame him for that, Honoria. Charles Hartington was far too enthusiastic this afternoon, and that horrid Cousin Carey was watching it all, in that sneering way he has. I really would give it up if I could, but I do not want to let Ampthill feel that he owns me, and that I must automatically renounce any pastime of my own of which he might disapprove. We are to have our first full-length rehearsal in the next day or two, and Mrs. Hartington has agreed to watch and offer her opinion. I shall ask her particularly to watch for any improprieties that we in our thespian enthusiasm may have ignored. I cannot ask her openly to criticize her own son, so it is difficult. Honoria, will you come too? That would make me easier. And if we feel there is anything improper, perhaps I can use the watercourse as an excuse to get out of it."

"But surely the thing is too far advanced for you to pull out now. The Hartingtons are quite set on it and Lady Evelyn also seems to be looking forward to your performance. Poor Sybilla, why do you get yourself into such scrapes? Why can you not learn to think before you act?"

Sybilla's face flushed with annoyance. While she may have said these very words to herself a thousand times, it still hurt to endure the same criticism from her elder sister. But before she could think of a suitable reply, they were interrupted by a piercing shriek from George's room. They found him doubled up on his bed, clutching his stomach, and moaning piteously. Honoria felt his forehead.

"Sybilla, quickly, dampen a cloth, he is burning with fever." Fortunately Sybilla brought the cloth in the bowl from the washstand, just as George struggled to sit up under his mother's administrations and was violently sick.

"I shall fetch Ampthill immediately," said Sybilla, "this is not normal. We must ask him to send for the doctor at once."

Luckily Ampthill had only reached his room a few moments before he was disturbed by the frantic knocking at his door. He gasped in dismay at Sybilla's distraught expression.

"My dear girl, what can be the matter? It must be George?" He guessed the reason for her distress at once. "Oh, the devil! I wish I had insisted on summoning Doctor Truscott this afternoon."

"He suddenly gave a great shriek of pain, he has a high fever, and has been most violently sick. I came straight-away."

"I shall send Carstairs immediately for the doctor; he was with me but a few minutes ago, so he can be off at once. May I join you when I have done so?"

"Please, Augustus, he is so fond of you, it will comfort him I am sure if you sit with us."

"Tell your sister that it will take at least half an hour to fetch Truscott, and that as soon as I have made the arrangements, I shall come up to you."

As he hurried away in search of Carstairs, he suddenly realized that this was the first occasion that Sybilla had spontaneously called him Augustus. Despite his concern for his nephew, he felt a surge of pleasure at the thought.

Ten minutes later, he joined the anxious sisters. Honoria was kneeling by her son, holding a cooling cloth to his forehead. George was flushed and restless, and was still moaning softly, in between the complaint, "Oh, Mother, it does hurt so." Sybilla was standing like a stone; she was completely calm, but her expression was numb with anxiety. She had fetched a second bowl and water from her own room, and stood by to offer a fresh cool cloth whenever Honoria might need it.

"Poor old man," said Ampthill, "what a miserable business for you."

The boy's eyelids fluttered, and his mouth quivered in an attempt to smile, but instead out came an involuntary low scream of pain.

"I am sorry, Uncle Gus, but it hurts very much."

"Do not try to talk, George. Carstairs has taken the fastest curricle and has gone in search of Doctor Truscott. He will be here in an hour. Would you like me to read to you? When I was ill as a child, my mother used to read to me."

"Augustus, we do not mean to be so importunate. Please do not trouble."

"Honoria, illness is illness, and must be treated seriously. I enjoy reading aloud and it may soothe the poor lad. I was dipping into Coleridge before going to bed and have brought it along with me. How well does he know *The Ancient Mariner?*"

"We have read it but once and he enjoyed it then, but in this case, it will be the sound of your voice rather than the poetry that will calm him best."

Ampthill pulled up a chair on the far side of George's bed and started to read in a low but perfectly audible voice. Gradually George's moans grew less frequent and he lay still, while his mother held his hand, and from time to time changed the cloth cooling his forehead.

Sybilla was agreeably surprised at the skill with which Ampthill read, slowly, savoring the poem's rhythm and meter. He had inherited some of his mother's taste for poetry, and clearly knew this poem well. Although he pointed up the dramatic passages so as to make them exciting, he never raised his voice or over-dramatized his reading in such a way that would excite the now peaceful George. Sybilla enjoyed his finely modulated voice, wondering whether his reading aloud was an innate skill or one that had been nurtured by his tutors at home or at school. But she soon found herself captivated by the tale itself, and the fate of the hapless mariner so cruelly punished for shooting the albatross. When he had finished, he closed the book, and the three of them sat on in silence, waiting for the doctor. Honoria was the first to speak.

"Thank you, Augustus. That was most beautifully read."

She was about to say more, but at that moment they

heard a bustle in the house, steps on the stairs, and Ampthill hurried to open the door to admit the doctor.

Doctor Truscott was a well-built man in his forties, with unruly sandy hair and piercing blue eyes. He looked around, taking in the situation, while Ampthill introduced Lady Honoria and Miss Smethwick.

"I knew you would summon me at this hour only for a grave reason, Lord Ampthill. I think I should like to examine the boy with just his mother here, so would you kindly leave us? Lady Honoria looks a little done in, perhaps some tea for her. We shall join you as soon as we have finished."

Ampthill instructed Carstairs to arrange for tea to be brought to the sick room, and also for himself and Sybilla in George's temporary schoolroom.

"Thank you for reading to us. I know you did it principally for George, but you read so well. I was much comforted, and I am sure that Honoria felt the same. There were moments when I was so gripped by the story that I almost forgot why we were all there. What can be the matter with George? He seemed perfectly well at his supper."

"He most certainly did," agreed Ampthill. "But the subsequent pain seems to have been rather too severe for the usual sort of chill or mild distemper. Has he ever been through anything like this before?"

"No, never. I should describe his as an iron constitution. Of course he has had the odd cold, and has indeed been unwell after eating too much of what he should not, but this is quite different. Whenever he has been upset before, the pain always goes as soon as he has got rid of whatever it was that did the damage, usually unripe fruit from our orchard at home. He complains of a stomach ache for about half an hour, is then sick, and within ten minutes is roaring around as before." Sybilla shuddered. "Oh, that awful first cry! I can still hear it."

"What happened exactly?" asked Ampthill.

Sybilla explained how she and Honoria had been chatting. "Let me try to remember my manners for once," she interrupted herself, "we were talking about your magnificent proposal that we should design the watercourse. We shall be honored to do so, and will do our best to make you something truly noteworthy. But as we were beginning to discuss some of Honoria's preliminary ideas, George gave a most piercing shriek." She shuddered again, again hearing the awful sound, and then described how they had found the little boy convulsed with pain and burning with fever.

"Did you keep the slops?" asked Ampthill. "We may as well have Mr. Compton have a look at them in the morning."

"What a good idea," said Sybilla admiringly. "I should never have thought of that." She almost laughed, "Poor Sam, he may be rather upset that his first task will be to examine the rejected contents of a little boy's stomach. It will not be the most salubrious of tasks, poor man. Perhaps I should offer to help him, so that he does not feel himself too put upon."

As they sat sipping their tea, Ampthill found himself admiring Sybilla's self-control. In contrast to the episode in the stable yard when she had been so shocked by Carey's behavior, she now seemed very calm and almost relaxed in her manner, although her eyes were clouded with anxiety. He was surprised too at her concern that the chemist should not feel put upon by the suggestion that he analyze the remnants of George's rejected supper, but of course she was right; it was rather a sordid task compared with the research into dyes and textile treatments that he had been engaged to undertake. Thinking it best to keep Sybilla distracted with matters of business, he decided to ask her advice.

"You are right, of course, it is not at all the sort of thing he was engaged to do. Who do you think we had better get to persuade him to undertake the analysis? Your sister would be the best person, perhaps."

"She is certainly more tactful than I am," agreed Sybilla. "If she does her best she'll have him thinking it's the greatest privilege to be analyzing yesterday's dinner and tea."

"Will he have the necessary skills, do you think?"

"There is no doubt about that. He has had the most excellent training and has indeed already worked with a group of physicians in London, so I have no doubt he will be able to perform a thorough and accurate analysis."

"And what do you plan so far for the watercourse?"

"We really had no time to go into any sort of detail but Honoria does have some ideas. I think she is extremely pleased to be asked to do it; I suspect she has been having great difficulty not thinking about it in case she should disapprove of whatever any other person you might have appointed may have come up with. But you will have to wait a week or two for us to get the design right. Even with pumps, we can only do what the terrain and the natural water pressures allow. And we must plan for all kinds of weather conditions. There is nothing so unsightly as a dry watercourse. So the first step is a great deal of measurement and working out of pressures that determine the overall nature of the design. The embellishments come rather toward the end."

Sybilla wondered if she dare ask him where he had learned to read so beautifully, and decided that the sudden intimacy of the circumstances of the night allowed her to satisfy her curiosity. For the first time she felt really fond of Ampthill. His concern for George was so obviously genuine, his affection very deep.

"May I ask, have you always read so beautifully, or is it an acquired skill? I wonder Lady Evelyn does not insist on you reading to us of an evening."

"I regret to say it is an acquired skill. We were drilled in verse speaking at school, both in Latin and Greek. There were prizes for the best recitations. But I beg of you, don't mention it to my mother. I do not at all share her taste in verse, and it is one thing to read a poem I have long admired for people of whom I am especially fond, in special circumstances of need, and quite another to be asked to trot out the latest bagatelle from some ignominious versifier who is the talk of the London salons."

"I promise you the secret will be kept. I shall warn Honoria at an appropriate moment." Mention of Honoria brought back all her anxieties and she stood and started pacing about the room. "What can be keeping the doctor so long? We must have been here for at least half an hour."

The next half hour passed slowly. Gradually Sybilla's self-possession deserted her, and she grew increasingly distraught as she paced up and down the little room, flinging herself into an easy chair for a minute or two and then standing again to resume her prowling. Ampthill watched her anxiously, wondering what grisly paths her thoughts were taking. He himself was desperately worried, since both mother and aunt had assured him that George was never ill. The severity of the boy's pain made him fear the worst.

After some time, Ampthill could stand it no longer. "Sybilla, my dear, do try to calm yourself. Either the news will not be bad, in which case we need not fret, but if the doctor diagnoses something serious, you will need all your strength to comfort and sustain your sister.

Meanwhile, I myself feel the need of something a little more heartening than tea. Excuse me while I fetch us something a little stronger. We may all need it by and by."

When he returned with a decanter and four glasses, he found Sybilla sitting on the window seat wiping her eyes. He swiftly poured her a glass, sat beside her, and put his arm around her shoulders. "Take a sip, it may give you courage."

At this, Sybilla burst into sobs. "Oh, Augustus, I was just thinking of Honoria. What will she do if something happens to Georgie? He is all that is left to her of her beloved Harry. She almost never speaks of her grief, but if you had seen them together, they were like a single person. If it had not been for George, I fear she would have died with the sorrow of Harry's death."

Ampthill tightened his hold on her shoulder. "Sybilla, my dear, you must be strong for your sister's sake. You know that we shall do everything that can be done for George. And now that you have come here, your sister is not the only one who would be sadly affected. Your nephew has effected the most astonishing change in my mother. It would I fear destroy her utterly if anything should happen to him. Here, have a proper handkerchief and compose yourself. The doctor and Honoria may be with us at any moment."

Sybilla accepted his larger handkerchief and blew her nose heartily, in not quite the manner ladies normally choose to perform this act when gentlemen are present.

"Of course you are right, Augustus. I had quite forgotten poor Lady Evelyn. She was so distant and languid the first few days we were here, and now she is so full of life, she is a pleasure to behold. As usual I have just been thinking of ourselves and forgetting that Honoria and George are now part of your family too."

Ampthill gently took the glass from her and turned

Sybilla towards him, looking deeply into her eyes which still glistened with tears.

"Not just Honoria and George, my dear Sybilla. You, too, belong here."

And so saying he enfolded her in his arms, willing her to be comforted. He longed to kiss away her worry, but knew that in the circumstances this was impossible. He released her reluctantly, but took her hand in his and raised each of her fingers to his lips in turn. "Dear Sybilla, let us be friends," he whispered.

At this moment the door opened and Doctor Truscott ushered in Honoria and followed himself. Honoria was white as a sheet, and Ampthill hastened to offer her a glass, which she accepted mutely but did not drink. Sybilla drew her sister down beside her on the window seat and faced the doctor. "Tell us the worst, Dr. Truscott, if you please. We do not wish to nurture any illusions."

Truscott coughed, and looked nervously at Ampthill, who said, "Miss Smethwick speaks for us all. There are no secrets here, Truscott. Tell us at once what your diagnosis may be, and tell us clearly what must be done for the best. My nephew currently stands as my heir, and quite apart from the devotion of these two ladies he has secured the deepest affection on the part of my mother. His well-being is of the utmost importance to us all."

"Very well, m'lord," said the doctor. "I shall be as straight as I can with you all. First, I can find no trace of any obstruction in the stomach area, no internal swelling, or anything of that sort. His fever has now subsided and I find no trace of any infection. What is very baffling is the suddenness of the onset of the symptoms. Lady Honoria assures me that he first complained of discomfort this afternoon, but slept soundly, and by six o'clock was naturally hungry and quite his usual self."

"Yes, we all saw him and he was obviously in fine fettle."

"Quite so, m'lord, and according to Lady Honoria, with no trace of that febrile state which one might expect at times when an infection is present but dormant."

"Yes, Doctor Truscott," said Ampthill, not without a touch of impatience.

"I have reviewed most thoroughly with Lady Honoria everything that the boy has eaten in the last two days. It seems to have differed very little from his customary fare. Furthermore, the acute nature of his symptoms is not consistent with the kind of illness caused by overindulgence in injudicious foods." Just as Ampthill was about to urge the windbag to make a firm pronouncement, Truscott declared his own bafflement. "In short, m'lord, ladies, I can find no natural cause for his condition, which has now calmed completely. I am sure you will wish to see the young gentleman before you retire my lord. You will find him sleeping peacefully."

"What do you mean, no natural cause for his condition?" asked Sybilla.

"I am afraid, Miss Smethwick, that someone may have been tampering with your nephew's food. I do beg your pardon, my lord; it is very disagreeable to have to relate such a thing, but it is a conclusion we must consider carefully. Lady Honoria had not mentioned to me that the lad is currently your heir, but now you yourself have told me . . ." His voice trailed away in embarrassment.

"Doctor Truscott, this is a very serious business. But first let me make sure I understand you. In your view there is nothing intrinsically wrong with the boy?"

"Nothing whatsoever that I can observe, my lord. I have of course requested that all stools and liquids from now on be preserved for examination, but on the evidence so far, he seems to me to be in perfect health."

"Well that at least is something. I think we can make sure that this kind of tampering ceases from now on. But Truscott, you must not say a word of this to a soul, not even Mrs. Truscott. It is late to keep you now, but by morning the whole house will know what has occurred tonight. If you would call tomorrow, then I can tell you exactly how we propose to proceed. I suspect we may find it expedient to keep George to his rooms for a little while, in which case you might be thinking of some trivial child's ailment that we might use as an excuse for the household. Something that requires that he is kept indoors, but that is in no way threatening. I would not have my mother alarmed, and of course there is no way that she can be told of your suspicions. Let me accompany you downstairs. I believe Carstairs is waiting to take you home again."

While Ampthill escorted the doctor downstairs, the two sisters tried to collect their thoughts. Sybilla, impetuous as ever, was the first to speak.

"Hono! Can this be true?"

"It seems very likely. I know Truscott was pompous just now, but I think he was fearfully embarrassed by this suspicion that someone is trying to poison George. Still, his examination was extraordinarily thorough. I was surprised that a country doctor should be so knowledgeable and shrewd, but I have every confidence in his judgment."

"In a way, it is rather a relief," said Sybilla. "I had been imagining all sorts of dreadful illnesses, and George having to put up with that appalling pain and you and me having to sit and watch him suffer, powerless to do anything. I would rather deal with a hundred poisoners than a serious illness sent by nature."

"Well that is one way of looking at it certainly." Honoria laughed. "Dear Sybilla, what you say sounds absurd, but I think I agree. Let us see what Augustus has to suggest."

"He has already had one bright idea," and Sybilla explained Ampthill's plan to have the unsuspecting Samuel Compton analyze the slops from George's seizure.

When Ampthill rejoined the sisters, he was white.

"Honoria, Sybilla, I am mortified. What can I say? That this should happen here at Swaffham Park. . . ."

Honoria went over to him and gently took his arm, walking him quietly about the room. She explained her sense of relief that there was nothing wrong with George that a little vigilance would not put right, congratulated him on the idea of securing the services of Mr. Compton as their analyst, and then asked him what steps he proposed they should take to get to the bottom of the matter.

Soothed out of his embarrassment, Ampthill speedily outlined a plan of action. "First, I have been considering who among the staff we can trust. We shall need help from the kitchen. Obviously the fewer people who know what we suspect, the better. I think Mrs. Glover and Tabitha can be relied upon, both for their loyalty and their discretion.

"Second, I have been considering when the poison could have been administered. George takes lunch in the dining room, so it seems that he is safe then. Am I not right in thinking that tonight was unusual in that his supper was served to him upstairs, does he not usually have supper with Mrs. Glover in her parlor?"

"Yes, and it was Tabitha who brought it," interjected Sybilla.

"Yes, but the kitchen is always a bustle at that time of the evening, which is why Mrs. Glover asked me if I would not mind him having his meal in her parlor," explained Honoria. "She usually prepares it for him herself, or tells Tabitha to do it, and he usually has either something from our dinner, if it is ready in time, or Mrs. Glover herself cooks him something. Once the tray is set, the poisoner could pour the powder or liquid over George's food in a trice with everyone too busy to notice."

"I see some things do not change," Ampthill laughed.

"Indeed not. She has a box full of puzzles and toys that you and Harry had when you used to be invited to her parlor and has got it out again for George."

"Has she indeed, by Jove!" said Ampthill. "I must go and see for myself. But to continue, where does George have breakfast?"

"It is brought up to him here every morning at about eight o'clock by anyone who is free at the time and left on the table for him, although I believe he is usually striding about the place in anticipation when it arrives."

"And what does he have?"

"Mainly porridge, which he smothers in sugar and cream, I regret to say," said his mother.

"Then I suggest that breakfast is the most likely suspect meal, and I have a suggestion for tomorrow. The whole household will know in the morning that Truscott has been here. But we shall say that it was a mild stomach upset and that he should have his breakfast as usual. But you must not let him eat it, Honoria. We must have it analyzed by Compton. I have already told Carstairs to wake me early tomorrow, on the grounds that I really must have an early morning ride to inspect the rabbits at work. Apparently they are inflicting enormous damages on certain crops and the best time to catch them at their business is soon after sunrise. On my return, I can easily slip into the kitchen to steal an early bite before breakfast and snatch a confidential interview with Mrs. Glover in her parlor, especially now you tell me that she has re-opened our old box for George's benefit. I shall be back in time to make sure Mrs. Glover can bring him a separate plate of unadulterated porridge by eight o'clock."

Sybilla had been listening to the deftly outlined plan in some admiration. Ampthill is certainly clever, she reflected. No wonder he was so successful in India, for he thought swiftly. But here she spotted a flaw.

"Will people in the kitchen not be surprised when they see Mrs. Glover bring a second tray for George?"

"They won't see her. The third earl's wife was a recusant, and sheltered Catholic priests here in the days before and after the Gunpowder Plot. There is a passage and refuge built by Nicholas Owen, leading, as it happens, from the dining room to this very room. She will take the porridge into the dining room herself, and slip through the passage with a fresh tray for George."

As he spoke, Ampthill rose, and reached up into the chimney. A section of the wall slowly creaked open.

"By tradition, only the master of the estate and one trusted servant know of the passage. The Glovers know, because of course, it must be swept from time to time. Poor old Jonah has the task at the moment. The heir is told when he comes of age, though, if his father dies before that time and without telling the secret to his son, then it falls to the trusted servant to tell the new earl. I only learned about it on my return from India. My father had not told me. Even my mother probably does not know of it. I must beg you both to respect our tradition in this regard.

"Honoria, although George stands as my heir at present, he is far from coming of age. I should not like the secret to be spilt. And although I would trust George with many a secret, I fear this is too exciting for him to keep to himself. Can you contrive to keep him out of the schoolroom while Mrs. Glover brings his breakfast? Heaven knows, I never realized how useful the tradition of secrecy might become. I fear old Jonah will not be pleased that I have told you both."

The sisters gave their most solemn word that they would respect Ampthill's confidence. Sybilla was entranced. She and Honoria had heard of the work of Nicholas Owen since most of his hiding places had been built in the Midlands. Priests had been able to survive in his "holes" for as long as nine days.

But Ampthill had not finished.

"I am sorry, it is now very late. But may we run through the plans for the early morning again. George's breakfast will appear as usual. This we shall remove for analysis by Compton. Mrs. Glover will provide a new, unadulterated breakfast by eight o'clock. It is imperative, of course, that whoever is responsible for this outrage should not know that they are discovered. Truscott will no doubt come up with some suitable medical alibi to stave off my mother's desire for George's company and to lull the villain into a sense of security. But since my inspection of the predatory rabbits means I must be in the stables by six o'clock, perhaps you will excuse me."

Honoria had just a moment in which to seize his hand and express her thanks. Sybilla had no such opportunity, and found herself somewhat piqued as a result. She felt a definite sense of anticlimax as Ampthill left them. Honoria was plainly exhausted, and since the main duty of supervising the complicated business of George's multiple breakfasts would fall to Honoria, she helped her sister to bed with as little fuss as possible.

Lying in bed she found herself unable to sleep. Although she had said it was a relief to know that poison rather than some natural illness was the cause of George's suffering, the thought of someone so determined to hurt the innocent boy was in itself a torment. As she tossed in search of sleep she determined to rehearse to herself the circumstances of all the mishaps that had befallen George: the curricle, the cider vat, and now this latest dramatic threat. What was the name that Abel Mortley had shouted as he dived for George and plucked him to safety? Try as she could, Sybilla could not remember it. It had only one syllable. It was one of those biblical names, like Abel.

Then another thought assailed her. All these events had occurred since they had been publicly associated with Ampthill and Swaffham. Surely the most urgent thing was to get George away, back to Stourbridge. The thought of her own home was intensely beguiling to Sybilla. She thought of Mrs. Gurney, of the house itself, her own room, the offices where they worked, its modest gardens, the blossom in the orchard, the tranquil, albeit busy existence they had enjoyed. Seized with an attack of homesickness, she drifted into an uneasy sleep.

# TWELVE

The next morning Sybilla awoke feeling tired and out of sorts, but early enough to help Honoria with the complicated business of keeping George out of the schoolroom while his breakfasts were changed. This proved easier than Sybilla would have expected as she had fallen into the habit of rising rather late at Swaffham. George was entranced by the prospect of pestering his aunt to wake up, and sat happily with her in her room showing her all his drawings for his Grand Castle for Lady Evelyn while she ate her breakfast.

Doctor Truscott arrived at half past nine and decreed that George could be suspected of having contracted measles, since there was an outbreak in the village. Although Lord George had not yet mixed with the village children, many of the stable lads and outdoor hands had homes in the village and it was to be supposed that he might have picked up the infection from one of them.

Although George started out the day with all his usual enthusiasm and vigor, by midmorning he had become listless, so that Sybilla and he readily gave up their mathematics for the pleasure of just chatting.

"Aunt Syb, was I dreaming, or did Uncle Gus read to me last night?"

"You were not dreaming, George. What do you remember?"

"I remember that horrid pain. I remember being sick. And I remember Uncle Gus coming in. And then I think he started reading, some poem about some wicked sailors shooting a huge sea bird with an arrow. I remember reading it with Grandpapa at home. It's by someone called Samuel something. I remember wondering if he was a relative of Smoldering Sam, but then having the same Christian name means nothing."

"Do you miss home, George?" interrupted Sybilla.

George's answer came slowly and haltingly. "I miss Mrs. Gurney. But it's topping here. And I love my new grandmama. Of course, she is not Grandma, but when I think of home I think of Grandpapa and Grandma, and I know that they will never come back."

This last sentence was said in a whisper, and Sybilla pulled the little boy to her and held him in a long hug. There was a knock at the door and, as George broke free from Sybilla's embrace, he asked, "Aunt Syb, do you think I might ask Uncle Gus to read me that poem again?"

"I should think so, young George," answered Ampthill, for it was he who had knocked. "How are you feeling this morning?"

"Lots better, thank you, Uncle Gus. And Bob told me yesterday that he would teach me all about the different harnesses for curricles this afternoon."

Ampthill looked at Sybilla, who boldly endeavored to explain,

"Georgie, dear. I'm afraid you cannot go down to the stables this afternoon. The doctor fears that you may have caught something called 'measles' from one of the stable lads. No one quite knows what made you have that horrid pain last night, but until we are quite sure, you must be in quarantine."

"What's quarantine? It doesn't sound like much fun to me." George frowned.

"It means you have to keep to your rooms for a day or two, old man," explained Ampthill, "in case other beings catch whatever it is ails you. And since I don't want all my horses shrieking and groaning like you did last night, I'll thank you to keep out of the stables for a day or two."

"But beasts do not . . ."

Ampthill threw an apologetic look at Sybilla and fled, leaving her to deal with a furious George who argued endlessly that animals do not suffer the same illnesses as humans and that therefore his going down to the stables would not put Ampthill's horses at risk.

Sybilla was heartily glad when Honoria appeared, some thirty minutes later, to take on the next lesson, and she withdrew to her own room, thinking to write a note to the Hartingtons excusing herself from the afternoon's rehearsals on the excuse of George's supposed infection. She found a note on her writing desk.

> *Miss Smethwick,*
> *I hope you will forgive the liberty I have just taken on your behalf. Since you were busy with Master George, I have just sent word to the Hartingtons that you are unable to be present at the theatricals this afternoon.*
>
> *Ampthill*

Sybilla was thunderstruck. After last night! The first hurt was the cold address "Miss Smethwick." She retired to the window seat and looked wistfully out over the Park. Last night she had been "my dear" and "my dear Sybilla." This morning she was just Miss Smethwick. Of course all proprieties must be assumed in a note which might be read by any passing servant, but he could have written "Dear Sister," he could have signed himself "Augustus." And although her first and immediate intent on entering her room had been to write the very note that Ampthill had written on her behalf, the fact that he had preempted her intention annoyed her deeply.

For the first time in her life, Sybilla felt herself to be superfluous. Honoria belonged at Swaffham, because she had been married to Harry, and she was mother to Harry's son. *And they really do love George,* she said to herself, *especially Lady Evelyn.* She resolved that, even though Honoria might be bound to make a prolonged stay at Swaffham on their return from Europe, she would go directly home. It was the first time she had really taken in the idea that she might find herself living in Stourbridge without Honoria and George. Would she really be able to live there alone? As George had said in the schoolroom, it was a place marked by the absence of its previous owners. But she was comforted by the thought of Mrs. Gurney.

In between sitting with George and endeavoring to keep him entertained, Sybilla spent the remainder of the afternoon writing a long letter to Mrs. Gurney, forgetting the immediate horrors of the various attempts on George's life, stressing her own unsuitability as a resident of Swaffham Park, and beseeching her lifelong friend to remember that she would soon be home again. As she wrote, her indignation increased. Ampthill had entered their lives and was now using Honoria and Georgie to enliven his mother. Additionally, he was using the Smethwick connection to ensure that his scientific dabblings would be respectable. She put none of her indignation in the letter. But as she wrote simple sentiments that she only half felt, she grew increasingly angry with Ampthill.

For the rest of the house the day passed smoothly, if quietly. Because George's presumed measles were considered so infectious, it was easy enough for Honoria to insist on taking a tray up from the dining room for both her son and herself at luncheon and dinner. While Lady Evelyn was anxious, she was easily convinced that she should keep well away from George until the precise nature of his illness was known. Carey made punctilious inquiries at luncheon, professed himself sad to hear "the little fellow is unwell" and announced his departure that evening for London to attend Lady Jersey's ball the following day.

With only Sybilla, Ampthill, and Lady Evelyn at dinner, the meal was a rather mournful affair and Sybilla was able to retire early without comment. Ampthill noticed that she was unusually silent and preoccupied, but put this down to her obvious concern over George and thought little more about it. He wished he could find some way of rallying her, or at least find some words of comfort, but she had not once looked his way in the course of the evening and he could think of no way of saying what he felt to her without arousing questions from his mother.

Once upstairs, Sybilla went first to George's room where the little boy was fast asleep. Honoria took her sister's hand and drew her into her own bedroom.

"Sybilla, you look exhausted, whatever is the matter?"

"I think I must be taking this business about George more to heart than I at first realized."

"You must be sure to get out tomorrow and have a good gallop. Sitting with George is no trouble for me, and you must not let yourself be pulled down. I cannot be nursing two of you."

Sybilla was amazed at her sister's calm manner.

"Ah, that reminds me. Augustus stepped in to see George earlier. He had a word with Sam this evening who says that he should have the results of the analysis first thing tomorrow. Augustus would like us to meet in the li-

brary tomorrow at eleven. He has engaged Tabitha to be
with George. Between them they found some old puzzle
of Harry's in Mrs. Glover's box which he thinks will keep
the two of them amused."

"I see," said Sybilla shortly. "As usual, Lord Ampthill
has thought of everything." She sighed. "If you can spare
me, dear Honoria, I will go straight to my bed. I am a
little done up."

The sisters parted. Again Sybilla found sleep difficult,
and spent much of the night awake, making mental lists
of projects that she would undertake at Stourbridge. As
she thought of their home, she became increasingly convinced that the best thing for George would be to take
him back there immediately. Perhaps Ampthill could be
persuaded to put it about that he and his family had bro-
ken with the Smethwicks, or at least to disinherit George.
She reflected miserably that if it had not been for her
wretched temper, and the way she had lashed out at Venables, they would not need to be at Swaffham Park at
all. This train of thought made her utterly miserable, and
to put the scene at the ball out of her mind, she got up and
wrote a list of reasons why they should return to Stourbridge at once. At last in the small hours she returned to
bed, resolved to awaken early and persuade Honoria that
they must go home immediately.

The next day it was pouring with rain, greatly to Honoria's relief, since this would make it easier to convince
George that he must stay indoors. The darkness of the
morning also meant he slept longer, and it was almost
eight o'clock before he came sleepily into her room to
wish her good morning. It was thus an easy matter to
check that Mrs. Glover had brought his second breakfast and removed the first while George performed his
morning ablutions. Reassured by the piece of blue ribbon
that Mrs. Glover had threaded through the handle of his

porringer, she happily went to ready herself for the day ahead.

Dr. Truscott came at ten and very solemnly told George that he was definitely sickening with something, although in the absence of spots, it might not after all be the measles. George at first protested that he felt perfectly well, but the doctor insisted that he was running a fever and must be confined to his rooms upstairs until the fever abated. While George set about his lessons, the doctor had time for a brief word with Honoria, as he handed her a small vial.

"Lady Honoria, might I suggest a light sedative for the boy; it will make him feel drowsy and perhaps ease the task of keeping him indoors when there is very little wrong with him. It is not in the least habit-forming, and you may find it useful. A few drops in his milk will suffice."

Honoria's first reaction was to refuse the offer indignantly, but she was unwilling to offend the doctor. She accepted the offered medication graciously, intent on asking Sam Compton to identify its ingredients before administering it to George.

At half past ten, there was still no sign of Sybilla, so Honoria went to rouse her sister. As she opened the door she heard a tremendous clatter and bustle, mixed with some rather unladylike imprecations as Sybilla quarreled with her buttons and fought with her hose.

"Hono, I must speak with you before we meet with Ampthill. I hardly slept all night, and now I have overslept. I meant to get up early and talk to you calmly, and now we have so little time."

But before she could say more, George appeared, insisting that his mother look over the page of calculations he had just completed, and before Honoria returned, Tabitha appeared with a tray.

"His lordship said I should bring you some coffee,

ma'am, seeing as how you hadn't been seen for breakfast. And where should I set out the puzzle for Lord
George?"

Sybilla sent her off to the schoolroom, and glared at
the silver coffeepot steaming on its tray. Wretched
Ampthill! So he had noticed she had overslept. Was she
to have no privacy? Nonetheless the coffee was very welcome as she paced up and down the room trying to calm
her jangled nerves in readiness for what she thought of as
the confrontation to come. In no time at all Honoria was
at the door, saying that it was already past the hour and
they must not keep Sam and Augustus waiting.

As they entered the library the sight of Smoldering
Sam's sturdy back cheered Sybilla somewhat. Here at
least was someone who would be on her side, but as he
turned to greet the sisters, she saw that his normally
cheerful expression had been replaced with a deeply worried frown. Ampthill saw that everyone was comfortably
seated and suggested they start by hearing Sam's report.

"Not good news I am afraid," said Sam immediately.
"Someone is definitely putting poison in Master, er, Lord
George's food. It seems to be some compound of arsenic,
as far as I can tell. The dose seems to vary. There was
very much more in the er, er, matter rejected by the lad
than there was in the breakfast porridge from yesterday.
That probably explains the violence of his reaction at
night, compared to the milder stomach ache and drowsi-
ness you described him suffering earlier in the day."

Honoria and Sybilla then proceeded to elicit all sorts of
details about exactly what tests Compton had performed,
the exact quantities of arsenic and other chemicals he had
found. Ampthill, unable to follow the complexity of the
chemistry, sat listening patiently. Sybilla looked very
drawn, he observed, much more so than Honoria. She had
been almost silent at dinner the previous evening; indeed

they had barely exchanged a word since their shared vigil in the schoolroom. He watched her closely, fascinated by her intense expression as she and her sister questioned the chemist. The downpour outside made the library gloomy, but the halo of lustrous blonde curls seemed, by contrast, to have acquired an especial radiance of its own. Ampthill wanted to lean forward and touch it, but dared not disturb the sisters.

At last the inquisition drew to a close. Honoria put her hand over Sam's.

"Thank you so much, Sam. Dealing with Georgie's vomit must have been peculiarly unpleasant. I am so sorry we had to take advantage of your skills in this way."

"That's all right, miss, er I mean, Lady Honoria. I was happy to help. And I trust that now we know what we are up against, you will not be asking me to analyze that sort of thing again."

"No, I think we shan't need to trouble you again on quite such an unpleasantly intimate level. Nonetheless, I should like to pass by your laboratory later, if you would not mind. I need you to help me specify what analyses we need of the water in order to ensure we use the correct materials in the construction of the watercourse."

"I am always pleased to see you, Lady Honoria, you know that. So I had better do my best not to blow it up today, you reckon?" and Compton grinned mischievously.

"If you could manage to keep it in one piece until this afternoon, I'd be very much obliged," smiled Honoria.

Ampthill ushered the chemist to the door, where he shook hands with the young man and thanked him for his work. Sybilla found herself resenting this. Who was Ampthill to thank a scientist? What did he know of the hours of work that must have gone into the comprehensive report that Sam had just delivered? The sense of being used by this all-powerful aristocrat returned.

Ampthill stood at the window, as the rain poured down. With his back to the sisters he spoke haltingly. "Honoria, Sybilla, I do not know what to say. That George should be attacked in this way, in my own home . . . It is unspeakable!"

Before he could say more, Sybilla plunged in.

"Lord Ampthill, this can be easily avoided. We simply take George back home or abroad at once. These attempts on his life, the curricle, the cider vat, and now this crude attempt to poison him, none of this happened before you so kindly deigned to notice us. If we could go back to Stourbridge and resume our useful lives there, I am sure we should have no further disturbances."

Ampthill studied her face. While she and her sister had been interrogating young Compton, her expression had been intense with keen concentration as she evaluated the information the young chemist had relayed to them all. But she had looked alive. Now, she appeared hard, cold, numb.

"After all, we planned to leave for Europe. If we take George home and follow up our plans to go abroad, we might yet get away by the middle of June. We could resume the modest and purposeful way of life we have always known."

Ampthill interrupted her, "My dear Sybilla—"

Oh, she was my dear Sybilla again was she? How dare Ampthill attempt to pacify her by such false endearments? She knew that he thought of her simply as Miss Smethwick. She tossed her head furiously, but Honoria was holding her hand tightly, so she forced herself to listen to whatever Ampthill might propose. "My lord?" she invited him to resume.

Ampthill walked over to the window and miserably watched the rain before venturing to speak. Although he was at a loss to account for the level of hostility Sybilla managed to compress into her cold stare and concentrated slim body, he could sympathize with her point of view. It was indeed only since he had let it be known that he regarded George as his heir that these misadventures had begun. Summoning all his courage he turned back to the sisters.

"I fear that the damage has been done. Removing George to Stourbridge will not make him one jot less my heir. I cannot undo what has been one of the happiest of my family duties, namely the recognition of Lady Honoria's claim to be considered one of the family. She and George are now fully acknowledged, and George is above all the dearest person to my mother's heart."

Sybilla interrupted, "At the expense of his life!" Her eyes were blazing now. "Just because you have huge estates and enormous properties, you think you can uproot people from their normal lives and force them to dance like puppets on strings at your merest whim. It took but a day or so for you to acknowledge Honoria and Georgie. George's life is now at risk. Why can you not simply unacknowledge him? For pity's sake, tell the world that we are unspeakable bumpkins, admit that you made an error in wishing to include us into your family and let us depart in peace."

Honoria tried to intervene. "Sybilla!" was all she was allowed to say.

"Don't you 'Sybilla' me. Do you not see how this man is using us? He has pretensions to be a patron of science, and so, of course it suits him to have us here, so that he can take advantage of Papa's impeccable reputation for integrity. Lady Evelyn is fond of Georgie, I admit, but what about his lordship? He despises us. And he has brought us here and put George at risk. . . . We do not matter to him, Honoria. We are nothing, except when we are useful in furthering his scientific ambitions. We were happy in Stourbridge; we had our own concerns and our own responsibilities. And this man has brought us here, keeps us here, and now someone is poisoning George. Why, perhaps even he is behind it. He has secured the Smethwick reputation. All he needs to do is polish us all off, one by one."

Sybilla collapsed in tears. She had not meant to go so far, although the wild accusations reflected accurately her darkest suspicions of the last two wakeful nights.

Ampthill and Honoria were speechless. Honoria was embarrassed beyond feeling and blamed herself for not having gone to rouse her sister earlier. She could follow only too well the disordered reasoning that lay behind Sybilla's outburst, for many of the same thoughts had occurred to her, but she had rejected them. If only they could have spoken together earlier that morning.

Ampthill felt utterly defeated. It was not so much that he resented the injustice of Sybilla's accusations; those he could understand and forgive. But it was the sense of her deep distrust that left him in despair. If she was to seek the worst interpretation of his every act, how were they ever to be friends? Wearily he turned back from the window to face the sisters. After all, this was a council of war; the next steps to be taken in order to safeguard George had to be decided.

Honoria had her arm round Sybilla and was doing her best to calm her. Sybilla, between sniffs, was trying to apologize to her sister.

"Oh, Hono, I am so sorry. I did not mean it to come out at all like that. I am so sorry. It's just that all these things coming together, why should anyone want to hurt poor Georgie? That horrid incident with the curricle, and . . ." She stopped, then with a triumphant tone of voice declared, "Seth, that was the name."

"What name?" inquired Honoria, utterly mystified.

"Honoria, remember at the inn, when Abel Mortley saved George?"

"Yes, dear."

"I remembered him shouting out 'No,' and a name. For days I have been trying to remember the name. It was Seth. I distinctly remember him shouting 'No, Seth,' as he dived for George."

"And later Brockley told us that Abel's brother Seth was Cousin Carey's valet," said Honoria, slowly but very distinctly.

"You both heard him?" asked Ampthill.

"Yes, indeed."

"Most definitely," replied the two sisters in unison.

Ampthill sat down heavily at the library desk. For a moment he sat wearily with his forehead resting on his hand. When he looked up, his face was stern.

"Lindsay and I were discussing Cousin Carey just the other day. Lindsay had seen him at Farnham on his way here, conferring with some blackguard at the inn, whom he later recognized as Abel Mortley. I am afraid my despicable cousin may be at the bottom of this."

"Augustus," breathed Honoria, "how dreadful!"

"It is worse than dreadful," said Ampthill. "But you see, Sybilla, why I think George would be safer here, now things have come to this pass. Everyone here knows the Mortleys. The Glovers can keep an eye on them in the kitchens, and Carstairs and Brockley can watch for them above stairs, but in Stourbridge they would be strangers."

"And you know, Sybilla," Honoria went on, "George had complete freedom to go about the neighborhood at home. It would be extremely difficult to confine him to the house and garden."

"Yes, I suppose you are right," said Sybilla quietly. She took a deep breath. "Lord Augustus, please try to overlook my outburst just now. I am afraid I have hardly slept the last two nights. I regret to say I allowed my feelings to get out of control."

"We are all desperately worried, Sybilla," answered Ampthill. "I am only sorry that you feel so unable to trust my motives in having you and your sister here."

His voice was distant. In the confusion of the moment, Sybilla could not remember exactly what she had said, but she knew she had spoken in utter rage, determined to wound this man in his pride. She also knew she had gone too far and perhaps made herself ridiculous into the bargain. There was no way she could redeem herself, so she kept silent.

"Whatever our feelings, we need to set a strategy for the next few days," Ampthill continued. "Might I be allowed to outline a possible plan of action?"

"Of course, Augustus, pray do so," said Honoria, while Sybilla nodded miserably.

"It seems that so far we have been able to make sure we get George's food to him safely."

Honoria and Sybilla both nodded their agreement.

"And it seems to me that the best way to put an end to this is to try to catch the poisoner at work. Once we catch whoever is directly responsible for tampering with George's food, I have no doubt it will be easy to persuade him or her to confess who is behind all this, whether it be Cousin Carey or some other person or persons as yet unknown. The penalties for attempted murder are severe enough to elicit a full confession."

"I am reluctant to suspect Abel Mortley," said Honoria.

"I share your feelings about Abel," agreed Ampthill. "He had a poor reputation hereabouts, but since Lindsay recognized him, I have told Laxton to keep him on a very short rein, and he definitely seems to have turned over a new leaf. His gratitude and devotion to your good selves seem entirely genuine; he hasn't been seen drinking heavily in any of the local public houses, he has even had his hair cut and endeavors to look respectable."

Ampthill's expression lightened momentarily as he remembered the sight of poor Abel's crudely trimmed hair from the previous morning. "But, the fact that you heard him call out to Seth that morning at Farnham suggests to me that his brother may be too much my cousin's man to absolve him of suspicion."

"But Seth cannot be here." Despite her vow of silence, Sybilla could not prevent herself from interrupting. "Surely he must have gone to London with Carey to attend Lady Jersey's rout?"

"Quite so. Even Carey is not entirely stupid. Once he was assured that the poison was reaching its target he took himself off to London in order to allay any doubts we might have about him. But there is a Mortley sister who works in the laundry. She is of necessity about the kitchens a good deal, removing dirty linens and returning those cleaned. She would have ample opportunity to get at George's food, especially in the mornings. The laundry girls all come into the kitchen for a breakfast around about eight o'clock."

Ampthill sighed. He had hoped to keep the more unsavory results of Lindsay's inquiries to himself, but faced with Sybilla's rage, he felt that he must tell the sisters everything.

"It transpires that there was a. . . ." He searched helplessly for words, "a misadventure concerning the poor girl, for which my father was responsible. It is more than likely that she deeply resents us all."

There was a long silence. Honoria felt deeply for Ampthill. She had learned how fastidious he was, how careful of the well-being of the people who earned their keep by their duties in the household and on the estate.

She could easily imagine the shame and disgust he must feel at the unscrupulous behavior of his predecessor.

"What then do you suggest, Augustus?" she prompted gently.

"I fear that the best way forward must be pretense. If we give out that George is getting worse, the poisoner may grow overconfident and become careless. But that means the hardest task falls upon the two of you. It is plain that George is already pretty much recovered. However, if we can keep him to your rooms upstairs . . ."

"But what about Lady Evelyn?" Again Sybilla found herself unable to keep quiet.

"Thank you, Sybilla," said Ampthill softly, grateful to her for remembering his mother's love for the little boy. "She will be much distressed, and while you are guarding George, Mrs. Glover and I will have the equally difficult task of preventing Mama from coming to see George. Like you, I have slept little these last nights, but I do not believe we can risk sharing our fears with her until we are certain. She was able to ignore my father's abominations while he restricted himself to London. For years, in Harry's and my absences, Carey was her main comfort, albeit a false and perfidious one."

Ampthill fell silent. Sybilla watched his face, as it showed fleeting expressions of rage, bitterness, and profound sorrow. "She has built a fragile wall between herself and the outside world, from which she felt only harm could come. These few weeks that you have been here have given her a brief experience of the everyday content and fulfillment that is the right of every human being. How can I tell her that we suspect her longtime confidant and friend of attempting to murder her grandson? How can I tell her that at the end of his life my father began to seek the pleasures he previously found in London amongst the young girls working about the estate? All those years I abandoned her, in India. . . . I should have found some way of staying here to support her through the misery my father imposed on us all."

"Augustus, stop this." Honoria's tone was absolute. "You have nothing with which to reproach yourself. While Harry used sometimes to envy you your 'escape' to India, he always spoke of you as the savior of the family honor and fortune. He knew and understood why you went, he supported you through and through."

She paused. "Of course it will be difficult to keep George indoors. Let us hope this rain keeps up. But you are quite right that we cannot tell Lady Evelyn of our suspicions." Her tone of voice became entirely practical. "We shall have to give up the measles. Everyone knows that once the spots appear the worst is over and there is no danger of infection to visitors. I think we must give out that Dr. Truscott is baffled about what might be ailing George. Poor man, it hurts me to suggest this, he is the most thoroughly expert physician. Perhaps we might allow him to find a solution; he must be able to think up some version of agues and fevers that would satisfy our need for bafflement without harming his local reputation. Meanwhile, Sam will test each of George's breakfasts that come up from the kitchen to measure the dosage used."

Sybilla longed to be away. She glanced at the clock which plainly showed that it was now long past twelve.

"It is time we relieved Tabitha," she declared. "Let me go upstairs, while the two of you work out the last details of what is to be done."

So saying she rose and left the room, summoning what little dignity she felt she had left at her disposal. There was a silence after she was gone, which Honoria eventually broke.

"Augustus, I am so sorry, I had no idea that Sybilla . . ."

". . . hated me so thoroughly," said Ampthill dryly.

"Honoria, I honor and respect your sister, but I am not about to be deflected from our main business, which must be to stop Carey, if indeed he is the person responsible."

Ampthill's voice had resumed its natural tone of authority and purpose. Honoria was about to leave the room, but Ampthill called her back.

"Lady Harry." Honoria stopped where she stood. Ampthill had called her "Lady Harry" when they had first met, but never since. What was he about to say?

"The other night your sister said something about you and Harry; she described how the two of you had seemed like one person. As we get to know each other better, it is my deepest regret never to have seen you and my brother together. He must have been very proud to have you on his arm."

"Harry's love touched all of us. It was not that he belonged to such a great family," and at this point she simply bowed her lovely head, "it was, as my ever fiery young sister told you, that we knew we belonged together. In its way, it was the most terrifying emotion I have ever experienced. Yet it was also the most exhilarating. We were complete only with one another. We brought out the best in one another." She paused. "Augustus, you must know. Of course Sybilla's outburst just now was unforgivable. But I have had the very same thoughts myself. And do not dare to let that firebrand of a sister of mine ever know that I have told you so. But I trust you implicitly and forever, because Harry told me that you were utterly trustworthy. Were it not so, we should have been well on our way to Stourbridge long since."

On which decisive note, she dropped another curtsey and left Ampthill to ponder the mysteries of the female mind, and the Smethwick sisters' minds in particular.

# THIRTEEN

Despite the absence of Lady Honoria and her lovely sister, Cassidy, Samuel Compton, and the other scientists provided Lady Evelyn with enough entertainment to take her mind off George's quarantine. While she had wished to assist with her grandson's nursing, the combined force of objections from Ampthill, Mrs. Glover, and Honoria to the notion that she might expose herself to whatever sickness afflicted the boy overcame her determination to play a grandmotherly role. Ampthill engaged to occupy his mother for the rest of the afternoon, first requesting her assistance on a tour of the glasshouses with the scientists and then sitting with her to prevent her from lingering outside the sickroom. Fortunately, Mrs. Hartington came to call, and Ampthill took the opportunity to withdraw and visit the sickroom in person.

There he found the fair sisters at their wits' end, with a mutinous George all set to explode from the exigencies of his confinement in a single room. The earl scooped up his nephew, bade the ladies follow him, and headed out into the corridor, round a corner and through a door leading onto a spiral staircase.

"Where are you taking me, Uncle Gus?"

"Wait and see, sprig. And don't squirm while I climb the stairs."

They climbed up to another doorway, exiting onto another corridor, but this one was bare, with no runner along the floor, no tables with Italian marble tops or ornate statuary, no pictures. Blinds covered the windows and the dingy weather made the corridor seem even darker. Along they went, round more corners and up a shallow step into another room, shaded from the day with shabby curtains. Ampthill set George down, drew one set of curtains back, then another, to reveal a bare expanse of parquet with occasional chairs, chests, and tables dumped indiscriminately around the edges. The furniture was missing legs, drawers, arms, corners, while springs and horsehair, stuffing and feathers spewed from torn upholstery. In the middle of the room stood a rocking horse larger than George himself, complete with horsehair mane and tail, leather saddle and bridle, with bells on the reins. It was a dapple gray thoroughbred. George hurtled toward it, inspecting it minutely before turning and saying, "May I?"

"Of course you may. And then I thought we would play Round-the-World, just as Harry and I used to on rainy afternoons."

"What is Round-the-World?" inquired George, already in the saddle and galloping over an imaginary plain.

"Why, it is when you go round the room without touching the floor. We shall all play. You can watch and join in when you have finished riding Bucephalus."

"But Bucephalus was all black."

"That was Alexander's Bucephalus. This one is Harry's and mine."

"Are we to play, too?" asked Honoria.

"Of course. One of us must be the ogre who is chasing the rest round the world."

"Let me be the ogre, let me," cried George, dismounting abruptly and dashing over to stand on a rickety dining chair. His uncle, aunt, and mother obligingly climbed into position, and they started a riotous game, climbing round the room, teetering precariously on the arms of sofas, crawling across gaps between tallboy and table, leaping from chest to armchair, laughing helplessly. George captured Sybilla, hampered as she and Honoria were by their skirts, in short order. She chased her fellows round, tagging her sister easily.

Honoria made Ampthill her target, and proved surprisingly nimble, so that the earl was forced to close in on Sybilla, who had reached the most precarious crossing in the assembly of furniture, moving from a silk-covered ottoman, perched on its side, onto the top of a scratched Italian cabinet. Ampthill had offered his arm to her for assistance when his foot slipped and he tumbled to the floor, taking Sybilla with him. She landed flat on her back and cracked the back of her skull on the parquet.

"Sybilla!" Then softly, "Sybilla." His hand caressed her cheek, then slipped to cradle the nape of her neck. Winded and dazed, she looked up at him. He met her gaze, and whatever he would have said died on his lips as he continued to hold her as his other hand sketched a gentle path down her bare arm. He tugged softly and she came up. He released her then.

"You are all right?"

"It was the merest bump." Honoria and George crowded about her, and she volunteered to sit out the next game, instead taking to the rocking horse sidesaddle and gently rocking as the others carried on rampaging round the wreckage. But the aim of Ampthill's romp had been achieved—George was tiring fast.

Sybilla's name was also spoken downstairs, where Lady Evelyn and Mrs. Hartington were discussing the progress of the play. With the familiarity of long friendship, there was no need to fence. Mrs. Hartington went straight to the heart of things.

"My Charles is in a fair way to making a cake of himself over the lovely Miss Smethwick. Although she looks exactly right for the part, I cannot help wishing that she had not shown any interest in participating."

"Do you mean she leads him on?"

"Not at all—quite the reverse. She is as nervy as a scalded cat when he must make up to her as Hastings. But you know how men are. Opposition only makes them more determined. On occasion I cannot help think that we would have been much better off letting him have his head and going for a soldier. After all, there is not much mischief to be had in peacetime, and he'd come back in a trice if there were any cause at home."

"Is there anything to be done?"

"Nothing that either you or I might do. We cannot cry impropriety now after letting them start their rehearsals; indeed, it would draw even more attention to my lovesick looby."

"What about Sybilla? Perhaps if I spoke with her?"

"That could serve no purpose either. She is doing all she can to evade my son's die-away airs. It would only make her even more self-conscious in the part. No, we must see this beastly play through to its performance and then perhaps we can send Charles off on some expedition, or up to town for a little polish."

Then Mrs. Hartington asked after George and became the recipient for all the dowager's worries and fears. As the squire's wife tried to calm her, in came Ampthill, looking grave. "George is resting quiet now, but I don't think Honoria or Sybilla will be joining us this evening."

"What ails the lad? I hear you've had Truscott in and he's unable to make a diagnosis." Mrs. Hartington was clearly astounded by Truscott's apparent failure.

"Not for want of trying. He has several theories, but we must wait it out until George's symptoms give further indication of the cause. The one thing we wish to avoid is the rest of us coming down with it, should it prove infectious."

"Quite right. We want no measles doing the rounds of every house in the neighborhood. Does this mean that Miss Smethwick will be unable to attend any further rehearsals?" inquired Mrs. Hartington.

"I shall ask when I next see her. I understand from Lady Honoria that both girls have had the disease as children and they are both inoculated against smallpox. But she may not wish to be away from her sister and her nephew at so anxious a time."

"Well, she knows many of her lines, for she's a quick girl. We shall have Sophie read in for her. Tell her not to fret in the slightest. We still have a fortnight or more before the performance, after all."

"I shall pass the message on," said Ampthill. This he accomplished on his final visit to the sickroom for the day, just before dinner was served. He appeared slim and resplendent in a bottle green jacket and white silk waistcoat embroidered with golden thread, and immaculate linen, checked briefly on George's condition, passed on Mrs. Hartington's reassurances to Sybilla and let the girls know that Lindsay had returned from London with further information about Carey. As he made to leave, Sybilla accompanied him.

Pulling the door so that her words could not be heard by George or her sister, she said softly, "I did not have the chance earlier to apologize properly for my rant this morning. You must know that we are deeply in your debt and it was the grossest folly to harangue you so. Please believe me when I say that my rash words were the product of lack of sleep and worry for my sister and my nephew." She bit her lip. "I seem always to be apologizing to you, Lord Ampthill. In future, I shall contrive to hold my tongue until I am sure of my facts."

He took her hands and dropped a light kiss on the back of each. "Do not do so on my behalf. It would be a shame to see you stifling your thoughts and bottling up your notions." His smile was warm, his eyes alight with laughter. "I am only glad to know that you do not hate me."

"By no means," Sybilla muttered. Just then, all around the house, the clocks started chiming the hour and both man and girl started. Bowing, Ampthill made his apologies and went down to dinner in an effervescent mood. Lindsay, just returned from London, was reminded of Ampthill at his most carefree, keeping Lindsays young and old alike in stitches with his jokes and games.

Later, when the household had retired, the earl led his friend into the library. Having given no instructions to light the room, Ampthill found it dark, although moonlight spilled through the windows. He took a spill from the fireplace, lit two tapers and the men went round the sconces setting the candles aflame until the gilded leather book spines were clearly readable. On a silver tray atop a mahogany table sat a decanter of brandy and several glasses. Ampthill quirked an eyebrow at Lindsay, who nodded in assent. They took their glasses and seated themselves on an immense sofa covered in maroon brocade.

"What is your news from the metropolis?"

"Carey's behind with his bills—and not just the tradesmen. His estates are heavily mortgaged and he has missed numerous payments. It looks as though he may be at *point non plus*."

"His whole fortune gone?" Ampthill was astounded. "But his mother was a Croesus. Or the female equivalent."

"They play deep at Brooks's."

"He has nigh on thirty thousand a year. Certainly more than I."

"You can drop over five thousand in an hour at the

gambling tables. Besides, he doesn't only play at Brooks's. There are plenty of hells where he's welcome. And he'll gamble on anything. He has wagers in half the betting books in London that you'll be setting up your nursery within a twelvemonth, and in the other half, that you'll never marry at all. One of my men reports that in the last month, he has bet on the color of the waistcoat Elvanston would wear one evening, the selection of wines that Prinny would serve at a banquet, and whether Lady Harriet Anstey would be brought to bed of a son."

"The man is mad. What does he hope to achieve?"

"Nothing. That is his misfortune. He has no ambitions and a hunger for risk that has never been exorcised by any worthwhile activity. Now, he owes money on all sides. He has gone to Howard and Gibbs, and the interest alone is crippling."

"I cannot understand it."

"Because you have never gambled." Lindsay chuckled. "Let me rephrase that, for you took a huge gamble in departing for India. You have no taste for games of chance. But I tell you, Carey has made chance his mistress, and she appears to be a fickle jade."

"That is still no reason to make an attempt on George's life. For heaven's sake, he need only apply to me. I would do the necessary for a relative. I could not let my cousin, and even more, my mother's friend, go to the wall."

"He has made so much of his independence from the earldom. He has mocked your plans for Swaffham Park in every drawing room in London. He has contributed significantly to the gossip surrounding Miss Smethwick. How could he come cap in hand to you now?"

"But all this is nothing compared with a child's life!"

"I am not sure he intends to stop with George's life. I believe that you are in as much danger from him as

George. Perhaps more, for he actively detests you. You have not dealt softly with him, Gus."

"He is so egregious in his speech, in his dress, in his manner. A man milliner. I have always found him to display such a want of sense. He is no lackwit, but he does nothing with his mind and less with the other gifts with which he has been endowed."

"The difficulty is not what you think of him, but that you have not concealed it, and since your return from India, you have been more impatient with him than ever. At times, scathing. No red-blooded man would have tolerated your scorn, it is true, but it seems increasingly clear that if Carey has any blood at all, it is thin and cold. I fear in crossing him, even unwittingly, you have unleashed a fury."

The two men sat in silence, sipping at their brandy. Lindsay's words carried no reproof, but Ampthill felt their weight nonetheless. If he had been slower to find fault, less brusque, more accommodating, Carey might never have resorted to making any attempt on George's life.

Then he remembered Harry, who had always been wary of their cousin, treating him with a respect that Augustus found himself hard put to understand. Harry had once commented on it one afternoon when they were boating, just before Ampthill left for India. The brothers had sculled from Chelsea to Kew against the river and were resting there before letting the Thames carry them back to town. Harry had announced his determination to keep an eye on Cousin Carey and look after their mama. Then he told a tale of going on a shoot and seeing Carey emerge furtively from some coppice in the park and making his way back to the house, complete with shotgun. Two or three years later, after Augustus had left for school, whitened bones, presumed to be those of a well-known poacher had come up from the pond. Harry had later said, "I have always feared that our cousin was somehow responsible for that man's death. I know you regard him as an idle buffoon, Gus, but I cannot help feeling that there is something more dangerous than we know about Cousin Carey."

Ampthill tried to fix the year that Harry had spoken of.

"Lindsay, have you heard any word of Carey's accomplishments and pastimes? Does he shoot, or fish? I know he will not hunt."

"I will send to my men to find out what they can. Why?"

"Just something that Harry saw as a boy. It was one autumn. I think it was the year before I started school. Harry claims to have seen Carey carrying a gun, but he has no reputation as a shot. None that I am aware of. Perhaps it is nothing, but I am persuaded that if we can pin him down in some lie, some fabrication, we shall be able to unravel this sorry business before he can do more harm."

On this determined note, the gentlemen retired, Lindsay to puzzle over the question of Carey's guilt, Ampthill to ponder Sybilla's words. "By no means" did she hate him. He wondered whether she could be brought to care for him.

Unfortunately, their next meeting was by no means auspicious. He had not troubled the sisters in the morning, but knew that by midafternoon, young George would almost certainly be restive once again. Unaware that Lindsay had inveigled Honoria out on a walk in the grounds, ostensibly to start work on the watercourse, Ampthill went upstairs hoping for a repeat visit to the old nursery. But the sisters' rooms were empty. Quelling a flicker of anxiety, he wondered whether they had already gone up to the nursery and proceeded there, only to find it similarly deserted. Now concerned, he ran downstairs using the servant's staircase.

All was still. It being a fine afternoon, the chances were that anyone temporarily free of duties would be found gossiping in the courtyard between the scullery, the laundry, and the brewhouse or on the lawns leading to the kitchen garden, as had been the habit of Swaffham's domestic staff for many years.

The earl was prepared to wager that George had made for the stables. Sybilla by now certainly knew of at least one of the more protected entries by which she might smuggle her errant nephew back into the house. Ampthill plumped for the chapel door as the most likely, mostly because it was least likely to lead to discovery. Although the chapel was kept open for any that might care to use it, it was by and large deserted. With long strides, he easily covered the yards, slipping through little-used rooms to evade voices until he reached the interior door to the chapel. With well-oiled ease, it swung open, just as the latch to the external door dropped back into place.

It was hard to make out anything in the dim light, the high, ornate stained glass windows admitting little light into the miniature cathedral a devout fifteenth-century ancestor had ordered in the vain hope that his blood-stained deeds might be expunged from his soul. But a scuffle behind one of the columns of the central nave was followed by Sybilla peering round before heaving a sigh of relief and coming forward, holding her recalcitrant nephew in a firm grasp.

"Thank goodness it's you. When I heard the door open, my heart stopped. I caught him before he had time to reach the stables."

"George." His uncle addressed him with winter in his voice. "This is no prank to be laughed off. You are under strict instructions not to leave your room. You put at risk of illness anyone who might encounter you. Have you no thought for anything other than your own impulses? Your father would never have acted in so willful and inconsiderate a way."

The boy hung his head. Sybilla, who had been ready to pour a diatribe of much the same substance into George's mischievous ears, felt defensive of the lad and bristled visibly.

"We shall go up to your room and there you will stay until you are told by Truscott that it is safe for you to come downstairs. Is that understood?"

"Yes, Uncle," came a chastened whisper.

Ampthill led the way, Sybilla pushing George along as they attempted to keep up with his brisk step, the first damp tears trickling down George's face. By the time they reached his room, the boy was awash, his face puce with shame and rage. He disengaged his arm from Sybilla and ran to the window seat to gaze out, gulping as he strove to stifle his sobs.

The earl tugged fiercely at the bell. The seconds stretched into small eternities as the three silent figures waited for Tabitha. Ampthill instructed her to keep watch over George and then requested an interview in his library with Miss Sybilla. Immediately. He held the door open for her and she led the way, daintily scooping up her skirts, her chin at an ominously militant angle as she descended the stairs, swept along the gallery and into the library leaving the door ajar.

There was a firm click as Ampthill closed the door behind him. Sybilla, her rigid back to the door, was perusing the shelves with intensity.

"Miss Smethwick." She plucked a book out before turning to face him. She appeared unruffled.

"My lord."

"Miss Smethwick, how is that George came to be

scampering his way to the stables?" The earl kept his distance.

"He tricked me. Shaming, I know, but that is what happened. At least he has displayed both wit and efficiency." Sybilla opened the book and started leafing through its pages.

"How could you let him do it? What folly is this, with his attempted murder so nearly accomplished not once but thrice!" So battle commenced.

"Do you think I did not realize that?" Sybilla, equally frightened and infuriated by George's activities, vented her anxieties, her knuckles white as she clutched the volume in an effort to prevent herself from throwing it at Ampthill's head. "How do you think I felt when I found the room empty? And yet we cannot tell him the real reason for his incarceration."

"Not for much longer. The end is in sight, if Lindsay and I can just secure some evidence. And yet you jeopardize all this with your carelessness."

"Stop this hullabaloo. You blame yourself and for once you have the right of it."

Ampthill came over to Sybilla and plucked the book from her fingers, tossing it aside before grasping her by the shoulders. "There is but one way to silence you. You may have the last word. But I shall have the final pleasure." Then he took her head in both hands and, holding her still, kissed her. He was beyond fury. His lips met hers with an impact. Their eyes met, both pairs sparking and defiant. And then his lids drooped so that she could no longer read his intentions, and his lips gentled until her mouth opened, then his lips were drifting over her face until her eyes too had closed and she was only conscious of his mouth and hands, stroking, caressing, demanding. He took possession of her mouth, and then her hands were on his chest, not pushing him away but pulling him closer, crushing the lapels of his jacket, climbing until she held his face.

His hands smoothed down over her shoulders, around her waist, and now the two of them were dueling silently, panting slightly as they drove each other on. He broke away only to trail light kisses from her hairline down past her ear, taking the lobe between his teeth and tugging, then continuing down her jaw line until her head was thrown back, her neck exposed. He carried on downward, until he was nuzzling at the curve of her breasts, drawing a line with his tongue along the silk and cotton ridge of her bodice, tantalizing her unbearably. His mouth trailed upward until he tasted her again. One hand stroked downward, down the length of her backbone until every vertebrae seemed charged with life and she could feel him pulling her closer to his body, closer until their clothes seemed hardly able to keep them from each other. Thought had been dispelled, sensation ruled them as they strained together.

A low moan broke from her, a sound she had never known she was capable of, guttural, eager, to be stifled by his tongue. His hands were moving over her once again, awakening every nerve until she was clinging to his shoulders to stop herself from shaking. He cupped her right breast and then his thumb passed delicately over her nipple. She gave a stifled whimper. Pulling back slightly, he looked down, found the ribbon that would loosen her bodice, and pulled it, so slowly, so softly. They both watched as the bow disintegrated, as her breath caused the material to rise taut and then relax and then as he slipped his fingers under the soft cotton to free her and give him greater access.

He dropped a kiss just above her nipple, then stepped back, pulling her with him as he sat in an armchair, easing her onto his lap so that lingeringly, he could caress and sip and love her shoulders, her neck, her bare breasts, her throat, the nape of her neck. Her skin was so soft, so fine, the down upon it feathery and golden. Then he brought her face round so that they could again drink from each other's lips. And like someone tasting water in a drought, Sybilla curved herself around him and gave back kiss for kiss. Now his hands were at her hips, his fingers circling and pressing. She shifted uneasily on his lap as unfamiliar sensations coursed through her. And then slowly, gradually, she started to pull away from him, as intellect overcame ardor, holding his hands away from her clamoring body, willing herself to break away from the spell of his mouth.

Then she pushed away his importunate hands and jumped up to rearrange her bodice and look frantically round in search of her shawl puddled on the carpet. She shook it out then swirled it about her shoulders decisively before shaking out her hair.

Ampthill remained seated, watching her delicious confusion with interest as an enigmatic smile crossed his lips.

"What did you mean the end is in sight?" demanded Sybilla, grasping at any topic to distract from the sight of the pleased beam on his face.

So she was determined to evade the consequences of their embrace. Augustus grinned. He was prepared to play whatever games she wished, if only they ended up as the last one had, with her in his arms.

"There's no need to sit smirking at me. What has Lindsay found out?"

Without delay, Ampthill detailed the financial disaster that had come upon his cousin and the need for further proof.

"You seem very sanguine for someone whose cousin may very well make an attempt on your life."

"While George must still be done away with, I am safe. Or so I believe. Except perhaps from his aunt."

Sybilla decided against dignifying this with comment. Having collected herself, she refused to behave like some *ton* miss. Ampthill had manhandled her disgracefully, but that was no reason to sink to his level. If she ignored his unbridled passions, he would surely understand that she was a woman of intelligence and as such, uninterested in the baser emotions. In the ensuing silence, Ampthill watched her carefully, while she looked intently at anything other than him.

"Yes, that cabinet is a very fine piece of chinoiserie. I believe my grandfather purchased it in the Low Countries for my grandmother. We think it is ebony, inlaid with gold and ivory. The animals are said to represent—"

"How fascinating. I must return to Honoria." Biting her lip, Sybilla left the library, holding back tears. The earl, in addition to all his other manifold faults, was an unprincipled trifler. As she trailed upstairs, Sybilla wiped the tears away. What had she hoped for? A declaration, perhaps? What nonsense. He was piqued by her refusal to be taken in by his charming ways, unlike her sister and her nephew. He had kissed her as a punishment, and a more effective scourge Sybilla had yet to encounter.

She had imagined her first kiss as a chaste, elegant business, the sealing of a contract or partnership with a fellow scientist to make their way through life together. But that fond hope was quite stifled by the wanton way in which she had given Ampthill kiss for kiss in their torrid exchange. No man would want so easy a creature. Except that she had an even more uncomfortable inkling that no man would ever be so desirable.

Later that evening, Ampthill and Honoria had a conference with Mrs. Glover. They agreed that if they were to catch the poisoner, he or she must be presented with more opportunities to tamper with George's food. They agreed that a lunch tray for George should be prepared in the kitchen, to be replaced by Mrs. Glover in the same way as the breakfast tray. All three were determined to smoke out the malefactor without further delay.

# FOURTEEN

Two mornings later, the sun woke Ampthill before Carstairs could. He luxuriated, as he lay in his bed, in the recollection of his passionate encounter with Sybilla. He had not imagined that any English girl would be capable of such ardor, such a delicious, untrammeled response to his kisses. In India, he had been careful to avoid the bored wives and occasional misses dangling for marriage, preferring uncomplicated liaisons with local courtesans who were well aware of the limits of his affections. Lakshmi had been the most recent in a line of charming, practised, and detached women, ready to offer an array of delights, but no ties. Now, he found he wanted more, and in Sybilla, perhaps he had discovered what he had scarcely known he was seeking.

His behavior had been beyond the bounds of what was acceptable in the standard formal courtship. She had every right to expect a proposal and he would not shrink from offering one. Lindsay had chaffed him before, but his mischievous suggestion that he marry one of the Smethwick sisters was more attractive than Ampthill would have believed possible only a month earlier.

Sybilla was no debutante, schooled in winsomeness and wiles. She was certainly stubborn, but her outbursts had been occasioned, he understood, by uncertainty and outright fear for the safety of her nephew and the happiness of her sister. Of course, there was that ridiculous nonsense she had spouted at the ball about never falling in love. She had managed to break off their embrace. There were obstacles before him, but he felt sure that he could overcome them. There could be no objection to their marriage. Miss Smethwick might not be from the aristocracy, but her family was entirely respectable. Still, he did not intend to broach the subject until his nephew was entirely safe. Carey must be caught out and prevented from ever bringing harm to any member of the family.

In this resolute state of mind, Ampthill rose and dressed, quickly, almost carelessly, despite Carstairs's attempt to discipline his hair, his cravat, a fob, a seal, the crease of his linen into the most perfect of ensembles. Brushing aside his valet, the earl attempted to placate him. "I am sorry, but I must speak with Compton. We have not yet heard the latest results of his analyses. I haven't time for all this frippery."

"You never do," replied Carstairs lugubriously.

The earl laughed and ran lightly down the stairs to the breakfast parlor where he demolished deviled kidneys and toast before retreating to the estate office. A message had been delivered to Samuel Compton, requesting his presence in the study at the scientist's convenience. Ampthill did not have time to go through more than two of his papers before the scientist was knocking on the door.

"Come in, take a seat." Ampthill indicated a rather battered sofa, where they both sat. "Lady Honoria and Miss Smethwick will be with George, but I can convey any message you have for them. What are the results of your analysis?"

"The amounts of poison and the frequency with which it is added to George's food are erratic. There is no particular pattern. It is as though the poisoner is adding the powder—for that is how it is dispensed—whenever he or she has an opportunity. I do not believe it is someone living in the house, but rather someone with irregular access to the house."

"That would fit with my suspicions. But why do it in this slow manner? Why not just make one or two attempts?"

"Too much in a single dose might cause an overreaction, in which case, it would be reasonably easy to treat—one needs to drink an abundance of milk. As it is, if you had not had a chemist at hand, I think the arsenic would have been well nigh impossible to detect, except for yesterday's breakfast. That had an unusually high level of the substance. That may have been caused by a slip of the hand or it may have been because George is not failing as fast as the poisoner expected."

"What does the powder look like?"

"Fine white grains. Finer than salt. Why?"

"Is the poison thoroughly mixed in with the food George eats?"

"Yes. It is least detectable in things like porridge or a thick soup. In those it dissolves. I have noticed that when George's food is more solid, less is used, unless there is a gravy or sauce."

"It seems to me that the only way to stop the poisoning is to catch the poisoner in the attempt. But I do not see how to do that without alerting this villain. Those servants who are trustworthy will almost certainly alter their behavior once they know of this plot, and we shall lose any chance of securing proof of this creature's malice."

"Do you have any idea of who it might be?"

"I do. But this person is merely the cat's-paw of another, someone ignorant, bearing a grudge against my family, and little knowing how to distinguish right from wrong."

"If there is any more I can do," said Sam Compton,

"please let me know it. I have long held the Smethwick family in the highest esteem, and anything I can do to preserve their comfort and safety, I will do." Then he withdrew, leaving Ampthill to wonder whether it was the whole family or just one particular member that the chemist so revered.

It was sometime later that the earl noticed a tentative tapping at the door.

"Come." It was Bob Laxton, who had been endeavoring to pass on some of his skills as a whipster to George.

"I came to inquire after Master George."

"He is doing as well as can be expected. We have hopes that he may be able to emerge from his quarantine in six or seven days. It is good of you to inquire after him, Bob."

"That was not all, m'lord." Laxton looked unexpectedly uncomfortable. Ampthill rose from behind his desk and indicated to the huntsman that he should take a seat, before leaning on the edge of his desk.

"You have something serious to report?" asked the earl.

"Abel Mortley, your lordship."

"What of him? Not taken to drink again, I hope."

"No, sir. It is just that I overheard him speaking with his sister, and it seems a sneaking, mean thing to come a-carrying tales. But I think you must know what I heard, though I did not mean to."

"I am quite sure you did not mean to, Bob. Let me hear of this. Does it treat with Master George?"

"As to that, I am not sure. Yesterday afternoon, Agnes Mortley came down to the stables, in search of Abel. He was grooming Norah for Miss Smethwick, and I was in the stall next door, cleaning out Blaze's hooves."

"Yes," prompted Ampthill, for Bob, fallen silent, was chewing at his lower lip.

"She started in on him, sharp as a burr under a horse

blanket, worrying at him for his following of you and the
ladies, saying as how it was a wrong that had been done
her that caused her to take this path, and he should be
helping her along it, 'stead of standing in her way. He
give her a right rollicking, telling her it was nigh on
twenty year that old master had had his way with her, she
ought to leave off festering on it or leave Swaffham altogether, as he had told her often enough. And if she hurt
a hair on any head at Swaffham, she need no longer call
him brother. Then she says, well it's too late for that, for
if the plans have gone aright, more than a hair on Master
George's head was well hurt already. And he ask her what
she means, and she says as how Master George's illness
is all along of her. So he says that's the end on it between
them and he would be up and telling of what she had said
to him soon as he had finished his work. So she swanned
off in high dudgeon and he start crying."

"He has not yet come to any of us."

"No sir, that's my father's doing. Because of the drink,
and all the regular suspicions of Mortleys in general,
Abel never does finish his work until he's too tired to go
anywhere but bed. He's up in the stable now, has been
since six, mucking out and polishing tack. Old Pa says
there's no better cure for the dismals or the drunks than
work, and work is what Abel must have, for he's in the
dismals and if he's let off, he'll be on a drunk sooner than
you can say horse brass."

Despite the serious implications of young Laxton's information, Ampthill had difficulty in smothering his
amusement at Bob's colorful rendition of his father's receipt for a sober life.

"I thank you, Bob, for telling me this. May I ask you this
favor? Will you counsel your father to let Mortley groom
my stallion this morning, ready for me to ride this afternoon? Mortley needs to tack him up at half past two, and I

want him standing by, ready to show me the work he's done. This will give him the opportunity to speak with me."

"I shall do that, m'lord. And I hope you'll excuse me for eavesdropping."

"I do not see what else you could have done. Has Agnes always held this grudge?"

"It's deep, sir, for when the earl—beg pardon, the old earl—made free with her, he left her with a babe. And she had a man, but he was sore and went for a soldier, or so my father tells me. Then the babe died and the man never came back and she has been left alone with nothing to console her and Abel turning out worse and worse and Seth scorning them both because he is a gentleman's valet now. This is what I've heard, but I was only a boy when it all turned up. I remember my mother and father and all the servants' hall talking it up, but it was the sort of thing they'd hush at if they saw a nipper listening in."

Despite his anger with Agnes Mortley, Ampthill could not help feeling for this unfortunate woman, who had been dealt such bitter blows by the rash and selfish acts of his own father. Dismissing Laxton, he returned to the papers the steward had readied for him the previous evening and worked steadily through certificates and bills of lading and requests for the purchase of seed and livestock, invitations to buy neighboring land, and offers to take on acres he might care to sell. Realizing there was sufficient correspondence to keep him occupied for hours yet, he penned a note excusing himself from formal lunch with his mother, secure in the knowledge that Lindsay would act as host in his stead. He summoned a footman and requested a simple lunch of a trencher with meat and ale before vowing that he would find himself a sensible secretary by the month's end. There remained business outstanding from before his father's death and his plans for improvements to the estate would create an even greater weight of communications and organization to be managed. He added yet another task to the seemingly endless list he had thus far amassed. Every day seemed to bring to light some area of neglect that demanded immediate expenditure and action.

The earl scarcely noticed the clouds amassing, the sun disappearing, and the drizzle which descended over Swaffham Park around midday. It was not until the old clock on the mantelpiece struck two that he looked up and noted that the weather had closed in and that he had sent no message to the stable canceling the arrangement with Abel Mortley. He stood and stretched, tidied up his papers, and left for the stables, eager for fresh air, however damp.

After calling for a stout coat, he left the house by the nearest door, which took him round the exterior of the chapel and the back of the house. To his surprise, walking toward him was Charles Hartington, looking somewhat muddy and disheveled. Bidding him goodday, he inquired as to Hartington's purpose.

"I am hoping that I may help Miss Sybilla run through her lines. I thought if Lady Honoria did not mind, we might rehearse a little, and keep the words fresh in her mind, as well as some of the movements. There are one or two that I have rehearsed with Sophie that are new."

Ampthill gritted his teeth. He did not intend that this puppy should spend any time with Sybilla without a chaperone. Then it occurred to him to enlist Lindsay's help. He knew he would find his friend in the library, particularly on so miserable a day. Provided the Scot was prepared to sit through the ineffable tedium of a rehearsal, that would be protection enough for Miss Smethwick. As he escorted Hartington indoors, he asked, "And how does the play go?"

"As with all such ventures, we have one mishap after another. Apart from Miss Sybilla's absence, Dr. Truscott's nephew must leave unexpectedly, which means we must fill not one but two parts. And the curate has sprained his ankle, so he is hobbling about."

"These affairs are too much effort for too little reward in my view. There are always alarums and it is for one night only that you exert yourselves. Certainly, I cannot see Miss Smethwick repeating the experience."

"I do not see why not. She seems to be enjoying herself as heartily as the rest of us, and we have a great deal of fun in assembling ourselves, practising, and finding our costumes. If she is to be a regular visitor at Swaffham, she will be very much in demand, you know, for she remembers all her lines and is so lively and has us all toeing the scratch simply to keep up with her."

"Of course she will be a regular visitor here. Indeed, I have every intention that she should make her home here. But I do not imagine that she will be able to spare the time for such japes."

"No doubt she will have her own views," replied Hartington warily. The earl seemed to him verging on the proprietorial.

"No doubt she will also take into account those of her betrothed on such activities."

"Her betrothed?" Charles Hartington was astonished by this turn of events. "To whom has she become betrothed?"

"As yet, she is not formally contracted. However, she will be promised to me in marriage within the month, I can assure you," announced Ampthill calmly. "Ah, here is the library. You can rehearse in here, I suppose. And I see Mr. Lindsay is ensconced. He will help you find Miss Sybilla. Lindsay, my friend, I am sure you are longing to see for yourself how well my young relative performs her part. Perhaps you might do us the kindness of warning her that her stage beau awaits her here."

The earl excused himself, well pleased with his warning shots across young Hartington's bow. He marched away to the stable, leaving Hartington gasping behind him. Lindsay left him for George's room, where he found Sybilla and Lady Honoria and George assembling a collection of hideous monsters that they had drawn as a result of a lively round of picture consequences. He explained his errand, and Sybilla grimaced.

"I do not want to go, but Charles is quite right to come over. I do need to run through my lines. We need not actually enact the play, after all."

"If you will allow me to replace you for a round or two at consequences, I shall be down directly after that to rescue you and preserve the proprieties."

"It is agreed. But no more than a quarter of an hour, I beg, otherwise he will be trying to persuade me to take all the parts in the play while he runs through his role." She left the room reluctantly, taking with her her copy of the play, convinced that it would be a good deal longer than fifteen minutes before she saw Mr. Lindsay, who looked at once engrossed in the creations they had so far sketched.

Charles Hartington was gazing out of the window, which overlooked the Park toward the lake, fiddling incessantly with the links of his watch chain in a fussy manner that suggested considerable disquiet. Sybilla had to suppress her own discomfort on her first visit to the library since her encounter with Ampthill.

"Good afternoon, Charles. I beg your pardon for keeping you waiting, but I found a girl and asked her to bring us some tea, for it is so tiresome to be practising and find one's throat dry. Are you all quite well?"

"Why, yes, Miss Smethwick." He came towards her. "That is, apart from Mr. Roberts, the curate, you know, who has sprained his ankle, had you heard?"

"No. Dear, dear, perhaps our endeavors are cursed." She withdrew a pace or two to seat herself in an armchair well away from the sofa or the easy chair where she had sat with the earl the day before.

"Don't jest, please! We all so much want to make this a happy occasion for Lady Evelyn." He took a seat at some distance from her, paying close attention to the crease in his breeches as he sat, and then an invisible mote of dust which he kept flicking away from his knee.

"Of course. Let us start as soon as the tea arrives."

"Yes. Yes."

Sybilla was baffled by her guest's quite distracted air. "Charles, you are not worried about catching George's disease?"

"No. Not at all. By no means. That is to say, well, no."

"Then what is troubling you?"

"Miss Smethwick, I do not know how to tell you."

Then it came tumbling out, Ampthill's chilly demeanor and his astonishing pronouncement that she and the earl would be marrying. Sybilla was about to utter a vehement denial when the door opened and in came a parlor maid with the tea.

"Thank you, Jenny, I shall pour. Please would you ask Tabitha to go up to Master George and ask that Lady Honoria come downstairs immediately. Without fail."

Jenny, quite overawed by Miss Smethwick's flashing eyes and firm tone, ran to do her bidding. Sybilla poured tea for herself and Charles Hartington, struggling all the while to contain her urge to hurl the teapot across the room. She wondered where the earl was and why he had seen fit to reveal his intentions to poor Hartington.

"Charles, let me assure you that I know nothing of the earl's intentions, but my own are quite clear. I am looking forward to playing the part of Constance Neville enormously, and I fully intend to participate in every dramatic production that comes my way." Sybilla smiled, unaccountably reminding Hartington of a painting at home of a lioness preparing to pounce. She continued, "Beyond that, I do not look."

"But he seemed so sure."

"I fear that while the earl may know his own mind, he is not sufficiently acquainted with mine to be at all sure of anything I may decide." Or perhaps it had been a tigress in the picture, he was not sure.

"Miss Smethwick, if you need any refuge, any assistance, any port in a storm, please, remember that I am ready to stand by you."

"You are very good, Mr. Hartington. But do not forget that I have a sister who will guard my interests. If you do not mind, though, I am really not equal to rehearsing after hearing such news. I am quite overset. Will you forgive me?"

"Of course. Naturally."

"Do let our fellow actors know that I shall attend rehearsals from tomorrow. And let us try to run through the whole play without our scripts. That should be very exciting."

"Why yes, Miss Smethwick." Stunned, Charles found himself drinking up his tea and making his bow just as Lady Honoria arrived. Scarcely knowing if he was on his head or his heels, he left, praying that he might not bump into the earl on his way.

"Syb? Lindsay is with George. I thought you wanted me because he was being importunate, but it looks quite the reverse."

Sybilla stood up. She scarcely knew where to start.

"He said that Ampthill said that we were going to marry."

"Charles Hartington? He's forcing you to marry

Charles Hartington? I never heard of anything so pre-posterous."

"No, Ampthill told Charles that he, Ampthill, and I were to be married. And that I would be much too busy to be in frippery plays."

"You'd be a countess, Sybbie."

"I shall be no such thing. How dare he, Hono? How dare he tell such things to some stranger we scarcely know, when he has made not the slightest push to court me, let alone putting the question of marriage to me. He is monstrous. He is determined to eat us for breakfast. He is not beyond the pale, he is nowhere near it, he has over-leapt it."

"Sybilla, has he given you no cause at all to think that he might harbor tender feelings for you? Really none? Think carefully."

Sybilla looked her sister in the eye, caught her unmis-takable grin, and blushed. "But he has not asked me. And even if he had, I am not sure that I would—that I could accept."

"Why not? It seems to me that you have come to care for him. When you are with him, you are volatile in a way I have never known before."

Sybilla was flustered by this shrewd remark and de-cided that George's well-being required them both to return to him without delay. While Honoria's blunt speak-ing gave her pause, she did not wish to dilute her outrage with further discussion.

Fortunately, on their return to their rooms, Lindsay dis-tracted both ladies with the news that his partner, a Mr. Hugh Gordon, had received a letter from a cousin in the Jerez region of southern Spain, with news of a possible courier. The man, Rackham, had performed sterling ser-vice for more than one acquaintance of the Gordon family, and better still, was currently in England. If the sisters were agreeable, Lindsay proposed to interview Mr. Rackham at the first opportunity.

"Yes, indeed." Honoria considered carefully. "Let us hope he is able to wait until this miserable difficulty with George is settled."

"Let us hope that this will all be over before Lady Evelyn's birthday," said Lindsay. "I understand you are committed to Swaffham until then. I shall tell him you propose to leave early in June."

"Yes, do approach him, Mr. Lindsay. If he seems suitable, secure his services and assure him we shall pay him for any additional time should he have to twiddle his thumbs awaiting our pleasure."

Having imparted this news, Lindsay went downstairs in search of Ampthill. There had been a suppressed mischief about Augustus's demeanor reminiscent of his schoolboy days and Lindsay was curious as to the cause.

George was thrilled by the news of Rackham. "Grandmamma's birthday is only twelve days away. We could be off in a fortnight! There will be ships! I shall miss Uncle Gus and Grandmamma, but we have been planning this for so long. Should we start packing up now?"

"Not yet, George. It is unlikely to take more than a day or two to pack our things," said Sybilla, smiling at her irrepressible nephew. It was a considerable relief to her as well. A mere fourteen days and they might be away from Swaffham. Surely his lordship would be easy to avoid in the interim.

When Lindsay finally found Ampthill in his study, the earl was fuming with rage and frustration as he pulled off his heavy coat and hurled it across the room where it dripped over the hardwood chair.

"Come, man, there's a decanter and decent fire in the library."

Lindsay followed meekly, reluctant to say a word until

he and Ampthill were both installed in armchairs before the fire.

"I was on the brink of discovering the truth of Carey's villainy, but I've been frustrated by the reforming zeal of the head groom of my own damned stables."

"What do you mean?"

"When I went down to the stables to try to talk to Mortley about his brother and sister, I found Bob Laxton instead of Mortley tacking up my mount. Old Laxton had set off as Bob was talking to me, Mortley in tow, to collect two young carriage horses I bought in Salisbury last month. It was too late by then to send after them."

"Why should Laxton take Mortley?"

"He seems to regard the rehabilitation of the unfortunate drunkard as a sacred trust. He's been driving the poor creature fairly hard." Ampthill relaxed and regaled Lindsay with Laxton's cure for the dismals and the drunks. "Poor Mortley, hacking across country to Salisbury and back with Laxton lecturing him all the way and never allowed so much as a draught of beer at day's end!" laughed Augustus. "I suppose all we've lost is a little time. They are due back in three or four days. Abel will deserve some sort of compensation for enduring four days of Laxton's lectures."

"It sounds like a monstrous tonic. Perhaps we should patent it as a cure for unreliable servants. We'd make a fortune."

Ampthill smiled warmly, but the mirth faded as another thought occurred to him. "I do not think we should say anything to the ladies. They have suffered enough without our raising hopes of a solution when there is a serious risk that Mortley may abscond and leave us without any evidence for our theories."

"You could tackle Agnes Mortley," suggested Lindsay.

"No, although I have considered it. But she's an ignorant woman and there's little to be gained in browbeating her while both brothers are absent. All we will get is a mishmash of incomprehensible lies and contradictions." Ampthill sighed. "I cannot find it in my heart to detest her, although her actions are iniquitous. All this is my father's doing more than hers. I dread further bitter legacies of this sort as the years go by."

Lindsay could think of nothing to console his friend. The late earl had been so loose a fish that it was likely there would be numerous calls on the Swaffhams. Ampthill drained his glass of brandy and stood, sighing.

"I suppose I had best return to my study. I must beg one further service of you too, my friend. You must find me a secretary. I have a mountain—no, not a mountain, a Himalayan range of correspondence on my desk and I need a young man of judgment who can remove from me some of the more routine burdens of correspondence. Carstairs is able, but already has more than enough to do. Come with me now, take a look, and form a sound view as to what sort of qualifications any amanuensis will need."

"With pleasure," responded Lindsay, having forgotten entirely to satisfy his curiosity as to Ampthill's earlier impishness.

# FIFTEEN

The rehearsals of *She Stoops to Conquer* intensified as the small company strove to double up roles and learn additional lines. This, along with George's continued malaise, effectively allowed Sybilla to avoid her host from daybreak to nightfall for nearly three full days. But on her return to the stables that third evening, she noticed that Carey's equipage and matched bays were installed in the yard and a shiver of apprehension shook her.

Upstairs, Honoria awaited her sister's return. She was reading to George, but jumped at every sound until her frustrated son plucked the book from her fingers and took up where she had left off. It was a relief when Sybilla came in, followed shortly after by Tabitha with George's supper. Honoria hauled Sybilla into her bedroom as George greeted the prospect of food with unbounded enthusiasm.

"You have seen? Carey is back. Of course, I have been up here all the day. Please, Sybilla, go down to dinner tonight, watch him, see how he is. I know it is folly in me to think that we can tell just by looking at him whether he has had anything to do with George's sickness, but somehow I feel that if one of us sets eyes on him, it will protect George."

"Of course I shall go down. It may not be rational, but I share your sentiments."

Sybilla took pains with her ensemble that evening, determined that Carey Swaffham should find no fault in either her appearance or her demeanor. As the layers of chemise and petticoats and underskirt and overdress were assembled under Honoria's careful eye, her hair dressed into a shining mass of ringlets tumbling from artlessly placed ribbons, the string of pearls from their mother fixed round her throat, the bracelets their father had brought back from Paris for her eighteenth birthday slipped over her evening gloves, and an ivory and ostrich feather fan set to dangle at her wrist, she felt like a knight buckling on his armor and girding up his weaponry. Carey was not the only man against whom she wished to secure her defenses.

On entering the yellow drawing room, Sybilla realized there were two camps—Lady Evelyn, seated on a chaise lounge with Carey and Ampthill, and on the other side of the room, Lindsay and the scientists. She was the last to join the company, and her entrance caused a hush to descend as both groups waited to see where she would head. She went first to Lady Evelyn, who indicated that Sybilla should sit beside her before dismissing both her son and her cousin-in-law. While Ampthill joined the scientists, Sybilla noticed that Carey skulked by the open windows of the salon, gazing out on the Park in a brown study.

As Sybilla had expected, there followed an intense interrogation regarding the welfare of George, which she met with gentle confidence. Eventually, Lindsay rescued her, leading her over to speak with Compton and his associates. Carey, Sybilla noticed, made his way back to Lady Evelyn and sat listening to her with every semblance of profound interest. Ampthill's eyes followed his cousin then he turned back and met Sybilla's glance. She was the first to look away. It was going to be a long evening. She wondered where she would be seated at dinner, but found to her relief that she was well away from the head of the table, seated between Lindsay and Compton.

After dinner, Lady Evelyn summoned Sybilla to withdraw quite promptly, leaving the gentlemen to their port. The dowager led Sybilla into the music room and they chatted amicably of nothing in particular for only minutes before Carey joined them. Shortly afterward, the rest of the company, led by Ampthill, arrived, and immediately importuned Sybilla for a song. Thereafter, try as she might, she had neither peace nor leisure to observe Carey Swaffham, for the scientists were determined to make the most of this rare glimpse of youthful feminine company.

There was a sad lack of substantial matter to report to Honoria, thought Sybilla as she climbed the stairs on retiring. Carey had certainly seemed aloof from the company, but that was only to be expected given his emphatic distaste for the men of science. As for Ampthill, insofar as he could, he had ignored her. Now the evening had passed, Sybilla was assailed by a sense of anticlimax. She was not sure what she had expected, but certainly not so uneventful an evening.

Rehearsals began at ten the following morning, and Sybilla, having breakfasted with her sister and nephew, left the house promptly at nine, without seeing anyone. Both Sophia and Charles Hartington were waiting for her in the receiving room that had been chosen for the dramatic performance, eager to show her the progress that had been made in painting scenery and sewing costumes. Their straightforward enthusiasm helped her cast off her glooms and throw herself into the rehearsals with enthusiasm. The Truscotts and the curate all appeared and under Mrs. Hartington's eagle eye, they ran through the whole play before lunch.

After lunch, they were all sent for a turn about the garden with instructions not to return for an hour, to clear the wool from their heads that they might go through the play once again that afternoon. While the rest of the party raced about, Sybilla found herself walking through the rose garden with Charles Hartington, who naturally asked after all at the Park. Once the courtesies had been done, he fell silent, clearing his throat from time to time. It took some minutes for him to come to the point.

"Miss Sybilla, it is my hope that you have not been discommoded by what I said yesterday afternoon. If you are in any way unhappy or put upon at Swaffham Park, it would be my privilege to assist you."

"You are good, Charles, but as I mentioned, I have Honoria to care for my interests and between us we are quite capable of dealing with his lordship's more outrageous suggestions. I am only sorry that you have been placed in so difficult a position. Ampthill has quite overstepped the bounds and I find it distressing that he should have troubled you with his rash expectations."

"Are they rash?"

"And unprompted. I do not know how he could ever have thought that I would be brought to accept his hand in marriage. He has made no suit for it, I can tell you freely."

"Your affections are not engaged?"

"Not at all." Sybilla looked away at the roses. Charles sank to one knee.

"Miss Smethwick, may I hope . . ."

She took his hands and pulled him up gently and shook her head.

"I thought not." Charles Hartington blushed. "You must think me foolish."

"No. Certainly not. It is simply that I do not wish to marry anyone. My home is with my sister and my nephew." She noted that he did not appear utterly down-cast.

"I will not importune you again, Miss Smethwick, but if you should ever change your mind, I will be ready to offer you my hand and my heart."

"Dear Charles, you have done me a signal honor, but please, do not hold out any hopes that my sentiments will alter. If it doesn't make you miserable, I should be very proud to count you amongst my friends."

"It is you who do me the honor. I will strive to be worthy of it."

On this amicable note, they found their fellow actors and headed back to the house, Sybilla convinced that while Charles believed he was in love, he was in fact more enamored of the role of thwarted suitor which would give him license to take on a wounded, soulful air that would be romantic without being unduly painful. He was still, despite his Seasons in London, a youth with some distance to travel before he would become a man. Which brought back thoughts of Ampthill, who was unquestionably too much the man.

All thought was driven out by the appearance of Carey Swaffham at the rehearsals, ready, he claimed to accompany his fair cousin back to Swaffham Park. The rehearsal mercifully seemed to extend but finally, she could put off her return no longer.

Once they were clear of the Hartington home, Sybilla intended to use her crop to spur Norah homeward as quickly as the lovely horse could manage. She was forestalled by the appearance of Bob Laxton standing by Norah as she and Carey rounded the gateway into the stable yard.

"When you weren't home by five, Lady Honoria and the earl instructed me to accompany you home, miss, sir, with the evening drawing in. There's been rumors of foot-pads abroad this fortnight."

"Why, how thoughtful!" exclaimed Carey. "I am reas-sured. I was going to urge you, cousin, to make all haste for home, for I had heard the same tales on my way down from London."

As it was, Sybilla was forced to travel sedately be-tween her escorts, leaving Carey ample opportunity to quiz her on the sorry subject of George's health.

"The effrontery!" she snapped, as she dressed hurriedly for dinner, attended once again by her apprehensive sister. "He went on and on about digestions and persistent ail-ments and congenital diseases, trying make butter and cheese of me by tracing the source back to some great-grandmother in Harry's family, all innocence. I would have shot the cat, but for Bob. That was well done of you, Hono, to send him to escort us."

"Shot the cat! You have been spending too much time in the stables, Sybilla." Honoria's amusement faded. "I had hoped Bob's presence would save you just such an audacious performance, but perhaps it is as well that we have a witness to Cousin Carey's excessive interest in George's health."

"Mr. Swaffham is not so simple as to give anyone any tangible evidence of his villainy. I am confounded both by his boldness and his elusiveness."

There was a tap on the door and Tabitha peeked in. "Ma'am, miss, his lordship is here to bid goodnight to Master George and he begged a word with you both in private. May he be admitted?"

The sisters' eyes met. Sybilla looked away first and Honoria signaled to Tabitha to let in Ampthill. He closed the door and made his bow.

"I do not mean to intrude on your toilette, but I wished to hear of Carey's demeanor this afternoon."

Sybilla made a brisk report and thanked his lordship also for allowing Bob Laxton to meet her. "I'd as lief not be with Carey on my own, for fear that I'll give the game away with my impetuous tongue," she said, grinning at her sister, who quirked an eyebrow in response.

"I fear your impetuous tongue far less than I fear Carey's capacity to do harm to you," responded Ampthill. "He is cunning as smoke and even more dangerous. Desperation is taking him to the brink, and we must all exercise the greatest vigilance in his vicinity."

"Is there no way to precipitate a confession?" asked Honoria.

"His inquisition of Miss Sybilla this afternoon suggests that he feels no remorse for his attacks on George, only frustration at their failure. But might I suggest that George officially experience a relapse. This may lead Carey to drop his guard, and more important, it is sure to keep George safe."

"I just do not know how I can keep George quiet. He is so lively and the prohibition on going out makes him restive in the extreme."

"Hono, I know that it is something you resist, but what about the laudanum that Dr. Truscott left? If we can drug him for a day or two, it may give us the time to establish Carey's guilt without question."

Lady Honoria sighed deeply. "It goes against my every principle, my every instinct. A mother should not resort to such measures to keep her child quiet."

Going over to embrace her sister by the waist, Sybilla smoothed back a lock of Honoria's tumbled hair. "But this is not some regular habit. These are extraordinary circumstances. It will give us all peace of mind if we know that George is asleep and genuinely unable to encounter Carey accidentally. In this instance, dearest Hono, no one could question your motherly inclinations."

Lady Honoria agreed wearily, and Ampthill escorted Sybilla downstairs for supper.

"That was well done," he said in low tones as they descended the staircase, his hand at her elbow. "I do believe that we shall be able to uncover Carey's machinations very soon, and then we may all be comfortable again."

Sybilla longed to shake off his touch and shout that she certainly would never feel at ease while in his home or indeed, anywhere near him, but a footman, looking up, caught sight of them, and opened the door to the drawing room before her wayward mouth could frame a single sentence revealing her true sentiments. So she and the earl appeared to join the assembled company in perfect harmony.

It was not long before Carey came over to her. "You seem to be great friends with Cousin Augustus. It has been otherwise during my absence, I hear."

"I do not know who you hear it from, Cousin Carey. The earl is a generous host. It would be churlish in me to behave in an unfriendly manner towards so gracious a gentleman." Sybilla hoped that the grinding of her teeth was not audible as she uttered these words so palpably at odds with her true estimation of the earl. She was determined not to let Carey discover how very deeply she mistrusted the earl's intentions. The earl's smooth voice at her ear caused her to start visibly.

"You flatter me, Miss Sybilla. With guests as eminent and easy to please as you and your sister, it would be a poor host indeed who incited you to be anything less than friendly."

"Dearest cousins, I hope you do not take my words amiss." Carey retreated in some confusion to take refuge in Lady Evelyn's company. Crossing the room to greet Sam Compton, Sybilla effected an even swifter escape from Ampthill's sole company. He looked after her wryly, all too conscious that to shadow her through the length of the evening was not possible. When he teased her, with every sally and every barb, they each gave too much away. All he wanted was to remove her from the company, and then to remove her every garment and his until there were no barriers between them, only passion. To remain in her company under such conditions was a refined form of torture which he could not long endure.

The stables were customarily a peaceful place by mid-morning. The stalls were mucked out and the horses all groomed by then, and the stable lads were to be found in the paddock exercising those mounts not required by any rider from the house, or buffing harnesses and saddlery. On this fine morning, all were up at the paddock, admiring a new pair recently delivered from Tattersalls, excepting Abel Mortley, who had volunteered to finish polishing the tack.

Seth Mortley chose carefully his moment for accosting his reprobate brother. No one was present to witness his barbed instructions to the man he had hoped never to see again, nor the blunt refusal he received from the reformed drunkard. When the valet left the yard only minutes into their meeting, fastidiously flicking at invisible motes of dust on his velvet livery, the groom shook his head, spat out the hay he had been absently chewing and continued his work, shaking his head and muttering from time to time. When the lads brought the hunters and carriage horses back to their stalls, there was no sign of Abel. No one missed him until the whole stable staff was assembled for supper, and even then, no one made anything of his absence, for he had often enough gone to visit his sister when his duties were done.

It was only when Mr. Laxton burst in on the loft where

the groom slept, ready to remonstrate roundly with Abel for countless failures, including raising his fellow workers promptly, that anyone realized that Abel Mortley had not been seen for nigh on twenty-four hours. Laxton went immediately to the earl's office to ask that the man be dismissed—an eventuality Laxton had been anticipating daily these four weeks, for in all honesty, it was more of a surprise that the devil Mortley had been as steady as a lady's palfrey for even that long.

"Dismissed?" demanded the earl, who had been anticipating an interview with Abel that morning. "But Laxton, you've taken the man across country and back. The carriage horses are safely home. What is your complaint?"

"He'm gone, m'lord."

"Gone? What do you mean gone, man?" It was with some difficulty that Ampthill restrained his impatience.

"Ain't been seen for near on twenty-four hour now. That's what I mean by gone."

"Laxton, I want that man found. Mount up every lad you have and send them out to inquire in every ale-house in the county. Don't make a fuss. Tell them we think Abel must have stolen something. All I ask is that you find him!"

Laxton looked at his master in astonishment. Ampthill saw the look, and with some effort, leveled his voice. Reluctantly, he decided to elaborate on his story.

"A bracelet given to Lady Honoria by my brother has gone missing. Now get on with it. And as you go, pass by the kitchen and ask Mrs. Glover to have Agnes Mortley brought to me without delay."

As it happened, Mortley's sister was already asking to see the earl to complain of her brother's disappearance. Ampthill summoned Lindsay to witness his interview with her. The hefty woman looked far older than her years, her hair strained tight against her scalp, her chafed fingers tweaking at a loose thread in her apron. She seemed at once enraged and resigned, contradicting herself often in her account of how often she saw her brother and when she had last seen him. The great red fists twitched and tugged until the whole apron threatened to unravel on the earl's prized Bokhara rug.

Augustus was revolted, not by the woman herself, but by the thought of his father abusing this unfortunate creature. Surely privilege meant one should protect innocent, ignorant people, not destroy their lives. His sense of disgust was heightened by his thoughtless lie to Laxton about the jewelry. To blacken a man's name went against every principle.

Once the unpleasant interview was concluded, the earl went upstairs to read to his nephew, whom he found dozing and irritable in the window seat of the boy's quarters, while the Smethwick sisters were drawing plans for the watercourse with a grim and silent determination. Work was a welcome distraction from the oppressive sense of menace that seemed to have descended on Swaffham Park.

Opening his volume of Chapman's Homer, the earl began reading, and the poet's cadences poured forth like balm on fresh wounds, sweeping the occupants of the room to a distant time and place when Achilles sulked in his tent and Hector still strode the walls of Ilium. When it was quite clear that George was fast asleep, the earl led the women apart and told them of Abel's continued absence.

"You think Carey is in some way responsible?" asked Sybilla.

"I fear so. There has been a previous disappearance. A poacher. Over twenty years ago. There is no reason to suspect Carey, but I cannot help doing so. It was Harry who first suggested it. He said he had seen Carey frequenting the place where this man's body was found. We know that Carey detests poor Abel."

"I never heard Harry mention Carey, let alone this poacher. But then, our time together was short," commented Honoria.

"What if we ask him about Abel? A simple inquiry?" suggested Sybilla. She was twisting a lock of hair about her finger absently, her brow furrowed with perplexity. "We may be able to read his reaction in some way. Perhaps it will provoke him into some folly."

Ampthill's first impulse was to keep Honoria and Sybilla away from the man who he now felt sure was responsible for at least two murders and who had so callously plotted George's death. He was furthermore doubtful that confronting Carey would resolve anything until there was inescapable evidence to prove his guilt. But he could find no plausible suggestion to dismiss Sybilla's suggestion without disclosing every detail of his father's squalid involvement with Agnes Mortley and his own shameful tale about Abel and the bracelet.

Sybilla's determination was not to be countered. Her rehearsals had been canceled that afternoon to allow those unexpectedly doubling up their roles to learn their additional lines, but the following day, she was expected at the Hartington's promptly at nine. It was just over a week until Lady Evelyn's birthday supper and the performance. This was their one chance of confronting Carey all together. Wearily, Ampthill conceded. Carey should be invited to join them for tea.

Tabitha was happy to sit with George, still soundly asleep following a dose of laudanum taken with his lunch. Honoria, Sybilla, Ampthill, and Lindsay met in the music room. They sat quietly, waiting for the footman to announce Carey Swaffham. On a side table, the teacups, the cakes, the sandwiches all remained untouched. A clock chimed the quarter hour, and the four inhabitants of the room sat as still as the porcelain statuettes on the mantel.

When Carey came in, he wore an air of ineffable weariness. He stood at the sidetable, gazing at the tea as though to lift the pot might break his wrist. Sighing, he put a sandwich on a plate, carried it across to a vacant seat and dropped into it. He nibbled at the sandwich, then left it half-finished on the plate and pulled out a kerchief with which he wiped his fingers most carefully.

"You are all very somber this afternoon. What can have occurred to put you all so deep in the dismals? Master George has not worsened, I hope?"

"You have the right of it, Carey." Lindsay rose and went to kick at the logs laid but not lighted in the fireplace. "And besides that, Miss Sybilla informs us that her protégé has quite vanished, putting her to shame before Ampthill and his whole stable."

"Your protégé? Not that vicious ruffian who tried to paw you on our return from the Hartingtons?"

"He has never shown me the slightest discourtesy, sir. He has until this point, behaved in an exemplary fashion, amply repaying the trust I put in him." Sybilla fired up easily enough in defense of Abel Mortley.

"Is this a habit of yours, Miss Sybilla, to collect strays from the gutter and inflict them on your hosts?" Carey's jocular tone could not diminish the venomous glare he gave her as he spoke.

"Only when her host asks if he might help her. I am sure that Miss Sybilla would have come to some other arrangement to place Abel Mortley in suitable employment if I had not offered my assistance. For I am as grateful to him as she is."

"Why do we waste our breath on this fatiguing topic? Let us talk of something other than the stable and its occupants." Carey picked up his sandwich once again, bit it in two with a clenching of his ample jaw and swallowed, reminding Sybilla of drawings she had seen of croco-diles. She could well imagine Carey basking in the waters of the Nile.

"Before we comply with your wishes, Carey," came Lindsay's calm voice of reason, "might we inquire as to whether you have seen Abel Mortley since your return to Swaffham? Since you remember him so vividly."

"Not at all. He, like all the lower orders, is beneath my notice, and as such, I am not able to tell you whether I have seen him or not. There we have it."

Thwarted, the assembled quartet gave way and allowed Carey to dictate the direction of the conversation, which deteriorated to the usual level of ignorant condemnation of Ampthill's projects, until Honoria and Sybilla excused themselves.

It was a parlor maid who noticed the body bobbing in the great lake as she went about her daily duty of open-ing all the shutters and curtains on the north side of the house at half past six. In the clarity of the early morning light, the uneven surface of the water was an affront to her notions of tidiness, so she opened the French win-dows onto the terrace and walked out into the crispness of a May morning, wondering who she should tell about the deer or upturned boat that marred the view. It was hard to make out the precise details, but if she went closer, it might be more obvious as to whether it should be one of the gardeners or the gamekeepers who should be alerted to the pollution. But then she realized that nei-ther deers' bellies nor the hulls of rowing boats were quite so pink and she gave a whimper and ran back to the house to find Brockley.

Brockley went down to the lakeside and summoned the Laxtons and then his lordship, feeling that the earl would certainly wish to see the body as it was extracted from its watery surroundings. He had a fair idea that it was Mortley, who had no doubt gone on a bender and stumbled on his way back to the stables. Though it was odd that he should stumble into the lake since that was nowhere near either his sister's cottage or the stables or indeed on any direct route to or from the nearest tavern.

When the body came out of the water, it reeked of pondweed and brackish water and mold, and the fish had been at the eyes, certainly. This could not conceal that Mortley had taken a mighty blow, one that had stoved in the left half of his skull, so far as Brockley and his lordship could tell.

Later, no one could tell how Seth Mortley came to be at the lakeside when his brother was pulled from the water. But none would forget his anguished cry when he saw Abel's poor wounded head nor his retching sobs nor the way he had gone off at a disjointed lope in the direction of Agnes Mortley's home. Lindsay looked after him, then looked at the earl, grim-faced and distant.

Ampthill insisted on taking one end of the stretcher on which they had laid the body and carrying it back to the stables where it would lie until Sir John Hartington, in his capacity as the local magistrate, and Dr. Truscott would be able to inspect it. The earl instructed some men to bring blocks of ice from the ice-house to keep the body from decomposing too swiftly and instructed the carpenter to prepare a hardwood coffin for the unfortunate. Then he and Lindsay returned to the house to change and carry the news to the ladies.

"My family has brought nothing but ill fortune to the Mortleys." The earl was calm in the way of men beyond fury. "We shall have Carey for this, you know. Nothing could have given poor Abel such a dent without being marked itself. We shall search the house, every room, but we will start with Carey's possessions. He will not escape justice for this deed."

By early afternoon, the formalities had been completed. It was clear that Abel's death could only be pronounced murder, but both the squire and the doctor were reluctant to noise this abroad, for fear of causing a panic in the area. There had been nothing like it in living memory, or indeed in any of the annals of that part of the world. While they inquired of his lordship whether he knew of any who might have launched the attack on Mortley, they quickly dismissed this notion, pointing out to the earl and one another that, after all, he had scarcely come back into the country, so how was he to know anything of its villains and their deeds.

Lindsay looked at the earl, but he was steadfast in his determination to deal with Carey directly. He would not have his family's name, so bruised by the previous earl's misdeeds, dragged further in the mire. Somehow, justice must be done, but it would have to be a rough and informal justice. On Ampthill's fastidious unwillingness to see any member of his tribe in the dock, Lindsay suspected, Carey himself was counting.

There had been a blunder. The executioner had failed to take into account Abel's own family and its name. Seth and Agnes Mortley came forward and told all they knew to the earl, all they knew of Carey's earliest attempts on the lives of Harry and Ampthill himself, on the disappearance of the poacher who had been similarly battered by the stock of a shotgun, of the debts and the interest payments and the failure to pay any salaries for months past, of the opportunist instruction to run George down with the curricle, then the chance that had taken Agnes to the brewhouse on George's first exploration and finally, of the cold-bloodedly planned, carefully orchestrated arrangement to poison George gradually so as to finish him off during one of Carey's frequent excursions to London. Thereafter, as Lindsay had surmised, the earl himself would have become the next target.

Ampthill, with Lindsay as a witness in his study, listened to this catalogue of vicious hatred and asked the Mortleys if they were prepared to tell Carey to his face that they had betrayed his misdeeds. They nodded, both still knotted inside with horror at the death of their brother, a murder partly of their own making, for if he had not opposed their participation in Carey's plots, or if they had not revealed that opposition to their master, he might yet be in the stables, finally earning a regular wage and finally able to respect himself. And so, when Ampthill asked them if they would confront the man who had destroyed so much and sought to destroy still more, they nodded, strengthened at least a little by each other's determination to see the villain brought to book.

# SIXTEEN

A little after four, Lindsay and Ampthill convened in the library, this time accompanied by Seth and Agnes Mortley. Carey was asked to join them. A footman opened the door to admit him. He checked and examined the inhabitants of the room one by one.

"My misdeeds have found me out, I surmise," said Carey. He was calm and his manner, usually so orotund, was brief. "What shall we do, I wonder?"

"What do you suggest, cousin?" asked Ampthill, equally direct.

"My suggestion is this," replied Carey, flicking his coattails out of the way, hitching his pantaloons and seating himself. "You give me sufficient funds and a passage to the Continent, where I shall trouble you and yours no longer."

"You are at outs, Carey."

"Am I? Are you so willing to parade the Swaffham name through the courts? I imagine not." He made a steeple of his hands and gazed into the distance.

"Sir John has inspected poor Mortley's corpse. I now have in my keeping your shotgun." Carey looked up suddenly at Ampthill. "Your valet was still trying to clean away the traces of blood and hair on the stock when he realized they were his brother's. He passed the gun to me. We also have his testimony in this matter and that of his sister regarding the plans to poison Lord George. They have made statements. Lindsay and I have witnessed these. If you do not accept my suggestion, then we must keep you here until Sir John can send over some men from the watch who will remove you to Winchester, along with the evidence of your violent outburst against Mortley under the gaze of Miss Smethwick. You will be kept in a cell at Winchester gaol until the next assizes. Then, I imagine, given the weight of evidence against you, it will be a matter for the hangman."

"I see. And what of my conspiratorial aides? These turncoats? Surely they will be punished also? Or are they free since they have betrayed me in the end?"

"Turncoat!" screeched Agnes Mortley. "You killed our brother!" Seth hushed his sister.

"The Mortleys have agreed to take passage to the Antipodes. They have no wish to remain here, nor anywhere else in our isles. A fresh start. I regret, Carey, that I cannot offer you the same. If you wish it, you may prolong your life briefly, albeit uncomfortably, and we shall all suffer some temporary unpleasantness as the Swaffham name becomes common currency."

"Or?" The abrupt question was forced from the dandy.

"We have your dueling pistols here. We shall take you to the gun room, Seth Mortley, Lindsay, and I. There, the course open to you would be to choose the gentlemanly end. We may then report that you met with an unfortunate accident while cleaning your pistols, and at least then, you may rest in the family vault, your own name unsmirched."

It was Lindsay who was most astonished by this curt decree. He had not imagined his friend to be capable of such ruthless determination.

"May I have some time to think it over?"

"I think not, Carey. You must choose now. The gun room, or the magistrate."

The older man had paled, but Lindsay could not help admire the way he stood, bowed his head in acquiescence and murmured, "The gun room it is."

"Miss Mortley, you may return to your cottage. I suggest you start ordering your possessions, for you are going to Portsmouth by the first stage tomorrow."

The woman curtseyed and left. Seth turned and lifted the polished wooden case carrying the pistols and led the way out of the library. Ampthill escorted Carey after him, followed by Lindsay. They quietly progressed down to the gun room where Seth placed the case on a leather-topped table, opened it, laid out the cloths and tamps and twine used to clean the guns, then handed one to Ampthill. The earl instructed the valet and Lindsay to throw up the long sash windows and step outside. Then he turned to his cousin.

"I shall be outside the door. You are left with the one pistol. Both are loaded. Do not try and run. If you do, I shall hunt you down. You have taken certainly one life in the most cold-blooded fashion, perhaps more, and you were attempting to do away with a child, even though you knew that to kill George might well inflict a mortal blow on your dearest friend, for so you have always called my mother. There is no place for you here, Carey. It is better to end it now, cleanly. Don't you think?"

"If I agree with you, it will not make you feel any better. You have no taste for this. I think you would almost prefer to see our family's reputation and honor destroyed in the courts, our name a common byword and slanderous tales mounted against us in the press and throughout the *ton,* if it would absolve you of the onerous duty of sitting in justice over me. But you may rely on me, if no one else, to do what is expected of me. Thereafter, you may all go to perdi-

tion in your own way, with your pumps and your engines
and your other follies. I have no wish to remain amongst
such a set of vulgarians, and if the life you propose for
Swaffham Park does not send your mother reeling to her
grave, I do not know what will."

Ampthill withdrew. Standing outside the gun room, the
seconds drew out until finally, there was a single shot, the
thump of the gun as it fell to the floor, a thud as a body
slumped over and a faint moan. Ampthill went in. Carey,
seated in a leather wing chair at the table, had fallen forward. The shot had not been clean, but Carey Swaffham
was dead. Ampthill lay the second, gleaming gun in its
cradle, as though it had already been cleaned by his unfortunate, clumsy cousin.

Lindsay and Seth Mortley came in. Ampthill was gazing at his cousin. Lindsay went over to him, lifted a hand
to comfort the earl, then let it fall. Ampthill turned to
Seth.

"Mortley, Bob Laxton will accompany you and your
sister to Bristol. He will give you a sum of money, and he
will buy your tickets for you. I could wish that my family had dealt with yours more wisely, but that will not
undo the harm. Let this be an end to our association."

"Yes, my lord."

"You are satisfied?"

"Your lordship might have dealt with us much more
harshly. We have both tried to bring harm to your nephew.
That I regret. But, with Mr. Carey, it was as though there
was nothing one might not do and escape the consequences. Playing at his games seemed to give us the
chance to pay back all you Swaffhams for the injury done
to Agnes and Abel being a drunk along of her disgrace
and all the rest. Mr. Carey could be most persuasive." The
valet retired to arrange his effects upstairs.

Outside the door, a group of footmen were already assembled with Brockley. After ushering Lindsay into the hallway, Ampthill closed the door behind him firmly and locked it.

"There has been a grievous accident, Brockley. Please send for Sir John at once. Have the ladies been disturbed?"

"They are upstairs, sir. What should I tell them?"

"There is no need for you to say anything. I shall go up to them."

"They are in Lady Evelyn's sitting room, sir. Tabitha is with Master George."

"Thank you, Brockley. Now you may all be about your business. Oh, and Brockley—"

"Yes, my lord?"

"Please ask the carpenter for a coffin. We shall need it as soon as possible."

Leaving the servants gaping behind him, Ampthill hurried up the stairs, closely followed by Lindsay. As the earl lifted his hand to knock at his mother's door, his friend finally touched him.

"Have you thought of what you will say?"

"I have. It will be an accident. Sybilla and Honoria may have their suspicions, but I would give anything for them to remain in ignorance as to the truth of what passed with Carey today."

"You may rely on me."

"As I so often have had cause to do." The earl tapped at the door, and entered.

The shock to Lady Evelyn was great, but she was not prostrated by it, as Ampthill had feared. Once Sir John Hartington had pronounced the death as accidental and agreed that the burial might proceed, she took in hand the arrangements for Carey's interment in the family vault at Swaffham, requesting Sophie Hartington to play the harp and organize the order of service. Besides, George was now officially well enough for visitors and delighted to be reunited with his grandmother.

Lindsay made a brief trip up to London on Ampthill's instructions, to settle with Carey's creditors. The Hartingtons sorrowfully, but understandingly, canceled the planned performance of *She Stoops to Conquer*. Lady Evelyn's birthday would be spent quietly at home with her family.

Honoria and Sybilla were quite sure that Ampthill was behind Carey's death. While Honoria, passionate with maternal outrage at any attempt to harm her child, felt that Ampthill was to be congratulated on this efficacious outcome, Sybilla was chilled, partly by what she saw as a perversion of the course of law and partly by Ampthill's apparent tranquillity, having propelled his cousin to his untimely demise.

Carey's funeral took place on a glorious summer afternoon, three days after his death. Apart from the family, only Lindsay, fresh from the capital, attended. Carey's gambling cronies were not interested in posting down to the countryside at the height of the Season for a dreary day with no gaming to be had. A prizefight in Winchester might draw them, but nothing less. The Mortleys had been safely seen aboard the *Augusta* bound for Botany Bay.

During the walk from the family vault in the village churchyard and the house, Lindsay accompanied Honoria and Sybilla, determined to pass on his news.

"I have met with Rackham. He struck me as a capital fellow. His father was an Englishman visiting Spain to inspect horseflesh when he met and married a Spanish lady, so Rackham is fluent in both languages. He has a good deal of experience escorting travelers around Spain and comes with a recommendation from several military men whom he assisted during the Peninsular wars."

"What more can you tell us?" inquired Honoria, her eyes agleam with interest.

"I asked Gordon to write immediately and engage his services. What I suggested was that Rackham meets you at Cadiz, accompanies you to Jerez and Sevilla, and then if you all find you suit, you may engage him for the rest of your trip. I hope you do not think me forward."

"Forward!" exclaimed Sybilla. "Why, Mr. Lindsay, you are a true friend. How long must we wait before we set off? Do we need to wait for a reply from Mr. Rackham?"

"No. For Gordon has also written to several of his acquaintances in the south of Spain, and informed them all that you are expected to take ship in the next two to three weeks, so will be there by the end of June. There will certainly be people to meet you. These letters are leaving by the Cadiz packet today."

"How exciting. It makes it seem much more real, doesn't it?" Sybilla took Honoria's hand, smiling broadly. "I am readier than ever for the off."

"Lady Evelyn will be sadly flat without you, though."

"Never fear, Mr. Lindsay, if you continue to propel scientists through her drawing room, she will be fully entertained." Sybilla's admiration could not be suppressed. "She does so well at drawing them out and grasping their ideas. If you can contrive to keep a steady flow of possible residents through Swaffham over the next few months, by the time we come back, she will have started up her own avenues of research."

"It is such a shame she has had no formal education. For she is sharp as a needle when it comes to understanding theories." Honoria sighed. "It seems such a waste. Still, if her interest can be sustained, it will assist the work the earl proposes considerably. I remember how our own mother used to smooth over all sorts of upsets and frets, and if Lady Evelyn will take even half the in-

terest she took in such matters, it will contribute much to
the smooth running of the workshops."

Lindsay was not slow to pass this tribute on to Lady
Evelyn, sitting with the earl while Lady Honoria and her
sister went upstairs to see George.

"That is generous indeed. I feel very much the fool
when I talk to these charming men, but I certainly know
far more than even a month ago. Interestingly, the ones I
have most enjoyed speaking with seem to be the ones Augustus most favors also. Is that not so?"

"I think, Mama, that despite your retired life, you are
as fine a judge of character as any East India man—better than many, indeed. But I did not realize that our guests
were still so set on leaving."

"We must let them go, Augustus. The sooner they are
gone, the sooner they will be back again. Honoria must
visit Badajoz, I quite see. Once that has been accomplished, I believe she will be more equal to making plans
for the future, perhaps plans which will include residing
with us at least part of the year. Until this voyage is done,
though, I think she will be restless and unhappy."

Lindsay noticed that his friend still looked discomfited
by the imminent departure of the Smethwicks, however
emphatically he endorsed his mother's viewpoint. But no
trace of unease did the earl show to his guests.

The need to complete at least the preliminary outline
for the watercourse was pressing, so the sisters were elu-
sive, apart from a daily walk with George in the
afternoons, and dinner. They would not discuss their
progress, laughingly evading inquiries about the work,
insisting instead on playing duets and singing cheerful
songs for the entertainment of Lady Evelyn.

It was three days before Ampthill managed, not entirely accidentally, to encounter Sybilla, who was rather
furtively restoring several volumes to the depleted

shelves of the library. She was balancing on the library steps, straining to slot Euclid into his proper home when the latch clicked open and then firmly closed. She did not look round, for she was teetering already and any additional movement was bound to send her in an ungainly clump to the floor. Firm hands grasped her waist, swung her to terra firma and took the book from her.

"Allow me." Nimbly, the earl stepped up, returned the book to its home and jumped from the steps to face her.

"My lord."

"My pleasure." He bowed slightly. "How much longer shall we be denied your company? Have you any idea?"

"The plans for your watercourse should be completed by tomorrow."

Ampthill grinned, his austere features appearing almost boyish. "I am less excited by the prospect of seeing the plans than I am of enjoying a little more of your presence before you depart for Spain."

This invited a suspicious glance from Sybilla. She stepped away from him. It was with some effort that he did not follow her.

"You must excuse me, my lord, I should return to Honoria."

"Will you not spare me a moment longer?"

It would seem unduly impolite to deny so mild a request. The earl came across, lifted Sybilla's hand to his lips and then led her to the sofa. He released her hand and moved away. She sat, stiff, poised for flight. He cleared his throat, then walked over to the window. He turned and walked back again to stand by the empty fireplace.

"Miss Smethwick. Sybilla." A dreadful premonition overtook Sybilla. She did not respond. The earl plunged in. "I think we should marry."

"Marry!" Sybilla stood up. "Marry?" She sat again. "I see. You think we should marry." She could barely contain her wrath, but calmed herself to the point where her tone was merely witheringly sarcastic. "I had been wondering when you might have the courtesy to inform me of a scheme that so closely concerns me, since it is now over a week since you saw fit to announce your intentions to Mr. Hartington."

Ampthill had clean forgotten his encounter with the young pup. Ruefully, he realized his mistake, for it had never occurred to him that the boy would tell Sybilla. He stumbled on, wrong-footed.

"Obviously, we must leave a suitable period of mourning for the loss of my poor cousin, but no more than six months." He avoided her gaze.

"Six months?"

"I would have it sooner, but I quite see that that would be unacceptable in society's eyes, and perhaps it would not leave you sufficient time to prepare yourself, bride's clothes, securing those possessions you have left in the Midlands, adjusting to the role of countess. So November, or early December. But before the year is out." He was kicking idly at the logs stacked by the side of the fireplace, his gaze fixed on the neat pile as if he were intent on reckoning the number of logs.

Sybilla's indignation increased. He had made no mention of the Smethwick journey to Spain, now barely a week away, much less their plans for a prolonged tour of Europe. Surely even so insufferable a man would not expect the cancellation of all their plans on account of his proposal!

"My lord, I do not believe that I have yet agreed to this unexpected proposal."

Augustus looked at her, his eyebrows quirked in astonished query. "Have you not? I understood that you had."

"How so, my lord?"

"You have raised no objections."

"You have scarcely allowed me to voice an opinion."

"Miss Smethwick, I would be very much obliged if you would favor me with your opinion on this matter without delay."

"My opinion is that I could not—I would not marry you if you were Arkwright and Thomas Telford rolled into one." Sybilla looked down and started toying with the gold braid edging her navy sash.

An unmistakable tension about his jaw and neck was the only evidence that Ampthill was restraining his temper.

"Of course. I cannot compete in scientific matters. But in another arena, I think there is sufficient reason for us to marry." Sybilla looked up. The earl appeared perfectly composed as he approached her. He sat beside her and his eyes swept over her until their gazes met and locked. The corners of his mouth curved upwards as she returned his calm stare, unable to conceal the slight increase in her breathing brought on by his nearness. He leaned forward. She refused to give way, duck back or evade him.

When his lips touched hers, light as a whisper of wind, she did not recoil. He teased the curves of her mouth with his own. He trailed his lips over the curve of her cheek and up to her brow, over her eyes, and down her nose before once again tantalizing her lips. Her eyes closed and her head involuntarily tilted, allowing him greater range as he continued to tease her, his kisses dropping onto her neck and collarbone. What strange chemistry was this, she wondered, that liquified her solid flesh. When she could endure it no longer, she found that of their own volition, her hands had risen to grasp the lapels of his riding coat and pull him closer to her and her mouth had opened and she was now kissing him.

Ampthill ran two fingers along the fine line of her jaw, as if to coax her on, while his other hand slipped to her

waist, holding her steady, guarding against the moment
when she might decide to pull away. But Sybilla did not
wish to pull away. Before long, she was stretched alongside him, cushioned deep in the sofa, as they exchanged
lingering caresses, luring each other on first to delicate
explorations and then to more urgent tusslings with cravat, waistcoat buttons, ribbons and laces, petticoats and
garters, punctuated by deep, draining kisses. When
Ampthill's hand reached the tender skin on the inside of
her thigh, Sybilla gave a slight gasp of shocked pleasure.
His stroking fingers progressed further, eliciting an ac-
quiescent murmur of delight. But Ampthill drew back.

"Sybilla. Say yes."

"Yes, you may make love to me." She stretched lan-
guorously. Then she opened her eyes, and raised her head
to look him directly in the eye. "But you will not make
me your wife."

"What do you mean?"

"I will be your mistress. On our return, if you still wish
it, we should be able to arrange it so."

Ampthill pulled away from her and sat, his elbows on
his knees, his hands knitted deep in his dark hair. He ex-
pelled a deep breath, shook his head and stood up.
Sybilla sat up and began, extraordinarily calmly in his
view, straightening her dress and reknotting the myriad
bows and trimmings that had been loosed—that he had
untied and unraveled.

"You do not wish to marry."

"By no means. I thought I had made that clear on the
night of your ball."

"And how should I make you my mistress? What sort
of insult is that to your name? How can you propose so
calamitous a route?"

"Calamitous? You exaggerate. Many women are mistresses. You would be doing very well out of it, for I

should not demand any money from you. I have quite enough of my own and the means to earn more should I so wish."

"But who will come to you for plans if your reputation is destroyed?" Ampthill went to the mirror over the mantel and started rearranging his neckwear in an attempt to appear as nonchalant as his companion.

"Why should it destroy my reputation to become your mistress? On the contrary, I imagine it will bring many advantages. If I were under your protection, no one would think of making untoward advances themselves, and your recommendation would assuredly bring many additional commissions. It is true that I should not be eligible to attend many *ton* gatherings, but since most of those appear to be a deadly bore, I do not see that I shall lose anything by it."

"What of your sister, your nephew? Don't you think of the damage to them?"

"They are safe. My sister is a respectable widow, my nephew heir to one of the finest names in the country. I could name you scores of women who are mistresses and none the worse for it. As far as I can gather, quite two-thirds of ladies in society give most generously of their favors once they have been safely brought to bed of an heir for their lords. I am simply proposing that we do not tread the wearisome path of conformity."

Ampthill swallowed. It had not occurred to him that his suit would be so firmly rejected, still less that Sybilla should propose in its stead so outrageous a notion as her own ruin. Looking at her, her hair rumpled, her lips still swollen with his kisses, her cheeks flushed with unfulfilled passion, the swell of her breasts above her chemise rising and falling as she attempted to bring her breath under control, every instinct urged him to return to the sofa and complete her seduction. But something held him back.

Reassembled to her own satisfaction, Sybilla looked up at Ampthill. She caught a glimpse of some stark, raw emotion in his dark eyes, but he veiled his expression as soon as he met her gaze and she looked away. He watched her, somewhat disheveled despite her best attempts at ordering her person, and the silent seconds lengthened. It was as though they were standing on opposite sides of a chasm which was gradually, inevitably widening and soon, too soon, it would be too broad to cross with a simple step and then even with a jump.

"Augustus?" His name fell from Sybilla's lips for the first time, wonderingly, fearfully. He was conscious of the constriction of his clothes which had fit perfectly well and a sense that the fabric lay on flayed skin, stripped of a layer, sensitive to the slightest pressure.

"You need no protection from me, Miss Smethwick. Rather it is we men who require preservation from you, I think." He bowed, and left. Sybilla turned to watch him go, white and suddenly very cold.

# SEVENTEEN

Leaving the library before the impulse to shake some sense into Sybilla overtook him, Ampthill strode through the hallways of his house, directionless and conscious of the sound of his footsteps on the wooden floors echoing his every pace mockingly. Never had any woman inflicted such humiliation on him. Never had any person scorned him so thoroughly. Yet she had not seemed to relish her triumph so very greatly.

Without realizing where his feet had taken him, Augustus found himself in the music room. It had scarcely seemed a mere matter of weeks since the Smethwicks had arrived here at Swaffham Park. The memory of Sybilla fluently playing a sonata by Beethoven lingered in the room, and it brought home to the earl how much he would miss her, how much she had imprinted herself already on the house, and what a gap there would be in his life once she had gone to Spain.

He stood by the piano, his long tapering fingers pressing the keys so that slow random notes filled the room. Abruptly, he withdrew his hands and shut the lid over the keyboard, then left the room and headed for the terrace outside. He was at an impasse. He loved, but was not, as far as he could tell, loved in return. He wished to honor the object of his love with his name and his home, but this had been spurned and mocked. But honesty prevailed; he had given Sybilla no indication of how deeply his own emotions were engaged, and she had been right to accuse him of high-handedness in his pronouncement to Charles Hartington that they were already betrothed. To amend things between them before the Smethwicks' departure for Spain seemed nigh on impossible.

A cough behind him made the earl turn round. There stood his sister-in-law.

"Sybilla has been sobbing in her room this half hour and you have been pacing up and down here like a caged bear for as long. May I ask what has passed between you?"

"Honoria, you may ask, but I do not know that I am at liberty to tell you."

"I did manage to extract from Sybilla that you had made her an offer of marriage."

"It was not agreeable to her. She made it clear that she had no intention of ever accepting my suit."

"You know that she speaks without reflecting. She had no intention of ever coming to Swaffham Park, and yet she is here and eager to assist in every project where she can offer her skills. I would not regard her refusal as irrevocable."

Augustus stopped pacing and approached Honoria. "Do you think there is any hope?"

"Tell me exactly what passed between you. I have had a garbled version from my sister, but I could not entirely believe my ears. Then I will tell you if there is any hope."

Ampthill winced. "Neither of us emerges with credit."

"I am not here to assign blame or sit in judgment."

It was not easy to speak of his encounter with Sybilla. But he acknowledged that he had made no mention of the Smethwicks' proposed departure for Spain, nor his own feelings for Sybilla. "Altogether, Honoria, I made poor work of the declaration."

"So I gather. And in return, she suggested an irregular relationship. She is really most exasperating."

"Do you think it was a deliberate attempt to provoke me?"

"I do not imagine that it was in any way planned or considered, but she was inflamed and wished to see you similarly goaded. I believe she thought your honor would be compromised by both her rejection of your offer and by her cheapening of the esteem in which you hold her."

"By heaven." Augustus was rueful. "She certainly succeeded in that."

"But she does not believe that to be the case. You avoided an outright argument with her, and so now she is even more thwarted for she has no way of knowing what you will do next."

Augustus sighed. The truth was, he had no idea what he should do next. He felt that every avenue was blocked by misunderstanding and hurt on both sides.

"Augustus, will you be guided by me?" asked Honoria gently.

"If you can suggest some way of extracting ourselves from this coil, I will gladly accept your guidance."

Honoria hesitated. What she was about to propose seemed, even to her, a great gamble but she was determined that Sybilla should have at least a chance to taste the happiness that she herself had experienced, the joy of loving and knowing one was loved in return. She had no doubt as to her brother-in-law's sincere devotion, and now that she had seen Sybilla's confusion and heartache, it seemed clear that these inefficient lovers should be brought together by whatever means necessary.

"Augustus, you must speak with her tonight. Tell her you have been called away on urgent business, but that if she is still of the same mind, you will accept her offer to become your mistress, on your return in a few days' time.

Do not let her set the date. You must make clear to her that you love her, that you only proceed down this path because it is what she wishes."

"Why need I leave Swaffham? Where should I go?"

Honoria grinned. "You go to your nearest bishop and secure for yourself a special license. If you leave her for two or three days, she will be driven quite wild with confusion. I do not believe that she wishes simply to be your mistress any more than I believe that you would genuinely allow her to pursue that path. However, at the moment, she does not believe that you love her and until you can show her that you will take any course to demonstrate your devotion, she will not bring herself to believe it."

"What of Spain? Can either you or she be diverted from your travels there?" The earl had clearly accepted the initial phase of Honoria's plan.

"No, but we might be brought to postpone them, provided we can still be assured of Mr. Rackham's guidance in the autumn. But if my stratagem is successful, surely you could accompany us to Spain as your wedding trip? For I believe that to see the site of Harry's final months is of as much interest to you as it is to us."

"You are right. But then you plan to travel all over Europe, and that I cannot do. It would be impossible to spend too long away from Swaffham and my mother." The tension was beginning to drain from the earl, who looked more thoughtful than oppressed.

"We might rearrange our travels altogether. If events unfold as I hope they will do, it may be a straightforward matter to plan regular excursions to the Continent from Swaffham."

"I believe you have hit on the solution, Honoria. But do you think that Sybilla will be able to accept my hand once she has committed herself to becoming my mistress?"

"Leave that to me. While you are absent, I shall start talking of your need of a countess, and my desire that George should not become the tenth earl. I shall discuss with Lady Evelyn all the eligible young ladies that are out or expected to come out and suggest how fine an alliance between the Hartingtons and the Swaffhams would be. She will be ready to acquiesce to anything, once I have done."

"Very well, I shall contrive to speak to her privately today, but I shall be gone by the time she rises tomorrow."

Honoria nodded approvingly and left the terrace, well content with her work there. She went upstairs and found that Sybilla had calmed down, washed her face, and was doing her best to sit impassively looking over the plans for the watercourse, checking them for errors and flaws.

"Do you think they are ready for presentation, Honoria?"

"I do. There are two sketches I would like to improve on, but those do not require your assistance. Why do you not go for a ride or practice that sonata by Scarlatti in readiness for this evening's entertainment?"

Listlessly, Sybilla took herself off to the music room. She dreaded a second encounter with Ampthill, but she could not, she knew, closet herself in her room all day; the chances of bumping into him again were slight, for he had too much to keep him occupied around the estate. This did not stop her from looking up every time she heard a bump or a creak as she was practising, so that the effectiveness of the time she spent at the piano was distinctly limited. She had intended to play the Scarlatti that evening, but perhaps a more familiar piece would be safer.

Eventually, the clock chimed one o'clock and she gave up on the music, heading for the dining room and lunch, where the company of others would defend her against the earl. Honoria was there, looking carefree and waxing enthusiastic about her plans for the watercourse, while Lady Evelyn attempted to draw the somewhat distracted Sybilla into revealing a little more about the surprise the sisters had prepared for their host. Ampthill appeared infuriatingly impassive, his manners as polite as ever, his demeanor calm and unruffled. It seemed impossible to believe that this was the man who had so overset her earlier.

After lunch, Sybilla could not bear to be confined in the house any longer. She sent a message down to the stables to ready Norah and went up to change into her riding habit. It was a lovely afternoon, Norah was skittish and the groom was mounted on an equally lively gelding. Sybilla suggested riding from the stable yard up the woodland path and onto the ridge of hills to the south of the Park. There, she knew, there would be ample opportunity for a fine gallop which would perhaps rid her of the persistent sense of awkwardness that dogged her.

The brisk trot through the woods warmed up both Sybilla and her mount so that when they broke through onto the open ground leading up to the ridgeway, it was a matter of seconds for Norah to ease into a canter. The beech and oak trees gave way to bracken and gorse bushes alight with their garish yellow blossom, and the wind rushed past as Sybilla urged her horse on as though the hounds of hell were following them. Just then, she noticed a rider heading towards them equally precipitately from the other end of the ridgeway. She gathered in the reins, gradually imposing control on Norah, but the groom was less secure on his mount and hurtled past her, unable to control the gelding's pace with equal dexterity. Sybilla watched in horror as the two riders seemed set on a collision course, but then realized the approaching horseman was in firm control of his mount. A mount uncannily like Blaze, the earl's impressive stallion.

It was Ampthill.

"Sybilla! I should have known today was too fine a day for you to remain indoors. Will you allow me to accompany you?"

There was no way she could see of denying him her company without sounding unconscionably rude. "If you have business elsewhere, please do not stand on ceremony. I am accompanied by a groom."

"One who does not yet have the knack of that gelding, I see."

The groom, having finally exerted some mastery over the young chestnut, had turned his horse and was returning to Sybilla. Ampthill dismissed him, declaring he would provide Miss Smethwick with an escort. The groom nodded his acquiescence before clapping his heels to the chestnut's sides and bouncing off.

"I have had time to reflect on what passed between us in the library this morning," said Ampthill. Sybilla's eyes widened. She had not expected him to speak so freely. She ducked her head, avoiding his gaze, fiddling at her stirrup in a vain attempt to disguise her confusion.

"You must know, Sybilla, that I love you. I had imagined that you understood that, but as I considered the words I spoke this morning, I realize that perhaps my most heartfelt passion might have been misunderstood. I said nothing of the gentler emotions." He paused, and Sybilla watched him, still unable to speak.

"For me, there can be no other. In you I have found the one woman with whom I wish to spend the rest of my life, as every passing day of the last weeks since you came to Swaffham has shown me. But you have made clear that you must be your own mistress, so I bow to your terms. I would prefer to have you as my wife, to show the world that I honor you and treasure you before all other women, but since you do not wish to marry, so be it. If, after you have visited Spain, you can see clear to make Swaffham Park your home, I think we might go on very happily together. I can but hope that, in time, you will come to love me as I love you."

Sybilla was stunned. He had declared her will as his, the battle was over. The fight was done, she was the victor. But it did not taste so sweet as she had expected. Ampthill's smile was tentative, his caress delicate as he reached out to touch her cheek with his gloved hand.

"I do not believe I have ever silenced you so thoroughly. I shall have to declare myself more often. Come, let us make our way to the village."

Naturally, Sybilla's mind raced as the horses cantered forward. She did not see how Augustus could make her his mistress under his own roof, either before or after her return from Spain. Skulking about corridors at dead of night would not serve, and he could scarcely take her publicly to his bed under the noses of his mother and her sister. She must speak to him on the subject before leaving for Spain, and yet, to do so seemed indelicate and forward.

By the time she reached the stables, Sybilla's state of confusion was greater than ever. Augustus helped her down from the saddle, losing no opportunity of holding her tight by the waist and running his hands up to her shoulders, a touch which seemed to electrify the skin beneath the somber cloth and left Sybilla dazed and longing for more of his touch.

"Go in and change, Miss Smethwick. We shall meet again at dinner."

Meekly, she followed his instructions, still somewhat stunned by his capitulation to her demands. He claimed he loved her. Yet that statement had produced simply further confusion and anxiety in her. She had not thought to name the emotion which surged through her in his presence and indeed, she acknowledged, in his absence, too. Perhaps she did love him. He seemed to dominate her thoughts, her waking moments, for good or ill. His very glance seemed to set her on fire in a way that she had certainly never before experienced, and yet she had not led a cloistered life. True enough, no man had ever taken such liberties with her person, but she had never before felt inclined to allow any man close enough to do so. Only Augustus.

Under normal circumstances, Sybilla would have gone straight to Honoria and laid out her troubles before her sister. But now, reticence overcame her. She was the one who had stipulated an arrangement which would undoubtedly arouse lively censure, one which for all her brave words this morning, would be felt by all her family. Yet she could hardly back down and demand that Augustus renew his offer of marriage. The coil in which she found herself became more entangled over dinner, when the earl suggested a new arrangement of rooms once the journey to Spain was completed. He proposed that Sybilla's current bedroom should become George's while the lad's current bedroom was knocked together with the present temporary schoolroom on the other side. Miss Sybilla might then go into the Blue Room, a commodious chamber most often used by Lindsay. It was across the corridor and down the wing, considerably closer to Ampthill's own quarters, a fact which did not escape either Sybilla or her sister, who smiled serenely at the notion.

After dinner, the company repaired to the music room, where Sybilla was prevailed on to play. The earl came over, ostensibly to help her choose some music. They stood by the piano, looking over scores, when he said in a low undertone, "I hope you do not think my contrivance too unwieldy and obvious. Whilst I long to make you mine, I hesitate to do so in such a way as would cause our families any pain."

Sybilla looked up at him, yearning and fear mingling in her heart. He was putting her brave words to the test and she must not fail. "You are very thoughtful."

"I am very eager. If only I did not have to leave early on the morrow, I would come to you this very night."

"You must go away?"

"Yes, I have some business which cannot be delayed. I will be away for a day or two, no longer." Ampthill hesitated, then decided to commit himself fully. "If all can be ordered to my satisfaction, you may have an additional escort for your trip to Spain."

"You wish to accompany us?" The thought had not occurred to Sybilla. Now that it had, it seemed only to complicate matters further.

"There is a possibility that I will be able to do so. Honoria and I have spoken of it. I would take great comfort in seeing Harry's last resting place. I was not so enterprising as you in planning an excursion to Badajoz, but I know that it would ease the loss to see the scenes of his final months. The added attraction of spending additional time in your company must also weigh with me."

"Your company on the journey would be much appreciated."

"By you, as well as by Honoria and George, I hope. Now, have you decided between the Haydn or the Scarlatti?"

"Whichever you care for, my lord."

"Surely to you I am Augustus? I care for neither as much as I care for the pretty fingers which will play it." He raised her fingers to his lips and so swiftly she thought she had imagined it, drew her forefinger into his mouth before restoring her hands to her and placing the score in them. She hoped that her swift intake of breath was not audible and that no one would notice the hungry look of passion in Ampthill's eyes as he turned away from her.

The next morning, as he had said, he departed before she was down to breakfast, leaving no indication of his whereabouts. The day dragged, and was slowed further by Honoria's cheerful demeanor, for she seemed scarcely to notice that Ampthill had departed on the very day she was due to present her ideas for the watercourse, instead keeping Lady Evelyn company and talking endlessly, or so it seemed to Sybilla, about the need for the earl to marry and get an heir. Then, just as Sybilla was preparing for dinner, in came Honoria, fretting and anxious lest George be left heir to the earldom of Swaffham, prey to the most ridiculous scenarios in which Ampthill would meet an untimely death, including his decision to ride home in the dark and falling off a precipice. Much as she would have liked to dismiss these fears, Sybilla found herself instead infected by them, and did begin to wonder what would happen if she should find herself rich with Ampthill's issue, but unmarried. And then she began to fear that he would meet with an accident before he could return to Swaffham and she would have no chance to find herself even an unmarried mother.

The next day seemed also to pass at a wearisomely slow rate, despite the gathering excitement felt by George over their increasingly imminent departure for Portsmouth and the Bay of Biscay. Sybilla greeted with relief the chance to retire early. But she was not tired when the maid finally left her, hair brushed, night attire carefully arranged, and the candelabra alight. She took a book and sat in the wing chair beside the unlit fireplace, listening to the muffled chime of the clocks around the house striking the quarter hour, the half hour, the hour, leafing through the pages of a novel with only limited attention. The heroine was a very silly young woman and the hero scarcely any more sensible, for it was a Gothic tale of lost nephews and wicked uncles, in which common sense and plausibility were sacrificed to sinister deeds and eerie atmospheres. A soft knock came at her door. Thinking it was Honoria, she said, "Come in."

It was Ampthill, wearing an embroidered waistcoat over his shirt and still sporting riding britches and boots. He carried a candle which he placed on a side table by the door. Then he came over and gathered Sybilla into his arms and kissed her hungrily. Finally, they moved apart.

"How I have been longing to do that!" He grimaced as he looked down at his clothes. "Excuse me please for visiting you so precipitately, but I have missed you dearly while I have been away, and I knew I could not rest until I had seen you. Do you forgive me?"

"Of course." She stroked the side of his face, then moved to the window seat, inviting him to join her there. "Where have you been? Do you know yet whether you can accompany us?"

"That depends on you, my dear."

Sybilla was filled with confusion. "How so?"

"Sybilla, I have been thinking about the arrangement we have come to. I fear that to make you my acknowledged mistress will cause our family nothing but pain. Either we should be harried into marriage by our relatives, or we shall be pilloried in the fashionable journals. Our quiet life here will be made impossible. If we do not conceal our liaison, we must ourselves go into hiding, and then what will become of all our projects?"

"I too have been thinking about this. Honoria is most reluctant to see George remain your heir. To her mind, an earldom is no recompense for the loss of one's independence. And what if I should . . ." Her voice trailed off.

"If you found yourself with child, our lives would become still more complicated."

"So. We must give up all idea of an intimate connection." Sybilla stood up and moved away from the window seat.

"Must we?" Ampthill followed her and took her hands. "What if I told you I still have hopes of marrying you? If I confess that my urgent business was a visit to the bishop to secure for us a special license?"

"You still wish to marry me?"

"Sybilla, it is my dearest wish to marry you. With every passing day, my love for you increases in strength. I can imagine loving no other woman." The earl drew back and reached into the inner pocket of his waistcoat. He pulled out a slim document and handed it to Sybilla. "Here is the license. If you cannot endure the thought of marriage, you may destroy it. But if you can contemplate the possibility, return this to me tomorrow and we can be married before leaving for Spain."

"You are leaving me the choice?" She turned over the document in her hands.

"It is the only way. I know my mind. Now you must show me that you know yours."

She sat down and unfolded the license. She read it carefully and folded it up again. She looked up at him and then stood and handed the license back to him. "I do love you. I have fought against it because it seemed ridiculous. Presumptuous. But I do love you."

"As I love you. You were not the only one to resist this call." He took her face between his hands. "Will you not do me the honor of accepting my hand in marriage? It would make me the happiest man in all the Empire."

"Well, in the interests of science, I must accept, although I am not familiar with any accurate means of measuring happiness."

"I should be happy to provide you with the space and equipment to experiment." The earl bent his head and, all barriers between them fallen, he and his scientifically-minded love gave themselves over to passion and each other.

# ABOUT THE AUTHOR

Madeleine Conway lives with her family in England. Her next Zebra Regency romance, *The Reluctant Husband,* will be published in February, 2004.

For further information and news of forthcoming books, check her website: www.madeleineconway.com.

## Historical Romance from
# *Jo Ann Ferguson*

__Christmas Bride        0-8217-6760-7      $4.99US/$6.99CAN

__His Lady Midnight       0-8217-6863-8      $4.99US/$6.99CAN

__A Guardian's Angel      0-8217-7174-4      $4.99US/$6.99CAN

__His Unexpected Bride     0-8217-7175-2      $4.99US/$6.99CAN

__A Sister's Quest        0-8217-6788-7      $5.50US/$7.50CAN

__Moonlight on Water      0-8217-7310-0      $5.99US/$7.99CAN